Shirley Jackson award-winner Kaaron Warren published her first short story in 1993 and has had fiction in print every year since. She was recently given the Peter McNamara Lifetime Achievement Award and was Guest of Honour at World Fantasy 2018, Stokercon 2019 and Geysercon 2019. She has also been Guest of Honour at Conflux in Canberra and Genrecon in Brisbane.

She has published five multi-award winning novels (*Slights, Walking the Tree, Mistification, The Grief Hole* and *Tide of Stone*) and seven short story collections, including the multi-award winning *Through Splintered Walls*. Her most recent short story collection is *A Primer to Kaaron Warren* from Dark Moon Books. Her most recent novella, *Into Bones Like Oil* (Meerkat Press), was shortlisted for a Shirley Jackson Award and the Bram Stoker Award, winning the Aurealis Award. Her stories have appeared in both Ellen Datlow's and Paula Guran's *Year's Best* anthologies.

Kaaron was a Fellow at the Museum for Australian Democracy, where she researched prime ministers, artists and serial killers. In 2018 she was Established Artist in Residence at Katharine Susannah Prichard House in Western Australia. She's taught workshops in haunted asylums, old morgues and second hand clothing shops and she's mentored several writers through a number of programs.

Her most recent books include the re-release of her acclaimed novel, *Slights*, (IFWG Australia) *Tool Tales*, a chapbook in collaboration with Ellen Datlow (also IFWG), and *Capturing Ghosts*, a writing advice chapbook from Brain Jar Press.

T0118848

Kaaron Warren titles
published by IFWG Publishing

The Grief Hole (2016)
The Gate Theory (2017 - short fiction collection)
Slights (2021)
Tool Tales (2021 - with Ellen Datlow; chapbook of microfiction/photos)
Mistification (2021)
Walking the Tree (2022)
Morace's Story (2022 - chapbook/juvenile fiction)
Tide of Stone (2023)

TIDE OF STONE

BY
KAARON WARREN

Tide of Stone

All Rights Reserved

ISBN-13: 978-1-922856-32-6

Copyright ©2023 Kaaron Warren

First Published 2018; this edition 2023

Printed in Garamond and Grantmouth Standard font types

IFWG Publishing International
Gold Coast

www.ifwgpublishing.com

To my parents, for teaching me to think outside the ordinary.

The Time-Ball Tower of Tempuston houses the worst criminals in history.

Given the option of the death penalty or eternal life, they chose eternal life.

They have a long time to regret that choice.

PHILLIPA MUSKETT: THE TIME BALL TOWER KEEPER'S REPORT 2014

Did you ever have that dream where all your teeth fall out? They say it's preparation for when you die, so it won't seem like such a shock.

There's something very gentle about death. Not dying itself, but afterwards, when things are calm and empty, when the body is still.

Perfect photographic subjects.

I'd miss some, in my year on the Time Ball Tower, on the island, but no matter. Out there, I'd have plenty else to photograph, especially the ancient, immortal prisoners and the tower itself, one hundred and fifty-seven years old, mildewed in places, broken in others.

I'd have the ocean, the sky, the town itself, all from an almost secretive standpoint, a *you've forgotten I'm here* place.

Plenty to keep me occupied.

Still, I made an effort in my last few weeks on dry land to get as many portraits as I could. Just in case.

It was a busy time, filled with farewells, celebrations, gifts, goodbyes. I've started my report early, wanting to record all the things before I forget them. Out there, things will be different.

We keepers are treated well. I'd miss Tempuston; I loved the town, although I hated it, too. None of us ever really left, no matter how far we went. People tried, mainly women in their early twenties. Sometimes they succeeded, if success can be measured by the fact they never came home again. Some never even called, so severed were the ties.

Iwas fortunate to capture Mr. Madden, a couple of days before his death.

I got up after noon that day as I often did. I liked having the house to myself and ate cheese straight out of the fridge and drank leftover cold coffee. My mother would say warm it up, but I liked it cold. It was bitterer, and I felt the caffeine work in a blood-stripping instant. I'd need it; I had a shift to work in the dementia ward.

I didn't mind the job. You had to stay cheery and acting cheery really did cheer you up sometimes. And I quite liked the new start you got with the patients every time you saw them. Even if you let them down, or they snapped at you over something, next time they're all, "Oh, you pretty young thing!"

And you could tell them anything. Confess all, get it off your chest, and they wouldn't remember. They thought you were vibrant because you were upright, and they focused on you intently when they were capable of focus at all.

I didn't mind the uniform, either. Crisp, clean, mint green, I wore mine shorter than most. I liked the way my legs looked in it: smooth and brown, even with the awful white flat shoes we had to wear.

And it's quiet, mostly. None of them have the voice to be loud anymore.

I signed in just before one. They were finishing their lunch, old jaws working at soft food, old fingers clutching napkins. Old heads nodding.

None of them knew the time, but still, at 1:05 everyone held their breath. Not a soul in the town did otherwise. No matter where you were, you listened for the Time Ball to drop, and then the day could continue.

All of us did it. Once a day, every day, at 1:05. It was part of us. Even away from Tempuston, we did it.

The Ball dropped.

"I'm heading out to the Tower in a couple of weeks," I told Mr. Madden as I settled him and photographed him. "What year were you there?"

His eyes cleared for a moment.

"1942. Being out there'll change your life. You think us lot are bad. Wait'll you see them."

"I don't think you're bad. You lot are fun. But I've always wondered what the face of pure evil looked like."

"No different than anyone else to look at if you don't know the truth about them. You know who's over there? Hidden? You'll have to look."

"Who?"

"Oh, a terrible lot. Hitler. Mussolini. Francisco Lopez. They didn't die at all; they're over there waiting for you. Don't go looking for them, though. If you find them…"

He nodded sagely, but his vision shifted slightly, and I wondered if he was hiding something. Or if he was simply forgetting.

"Anyone else?" I asked.

But he was gone, his mouth flapping, pointing at dust motes.

As kids, we told stories about this. The worst monsters of all time live in the basement over there. You don't go too far down, or you'll be eaten alive. We used to say the Grade Five teacher slept out there. She was terrifying. Spittle flew when she spoke, and she hated every child she ever taught.

She left, mid-year. Had enough of the awful children, people said.

I cleaned up and walked down to Burnett Barton's room. He hated when I came smelling of the rest of the ward. It made him envious, wishing for the company of even a dementia ward. But no one wanted him out there. He was better off way at the end of the hall, alone, where people could forget he existed except when they needed him. Sometimes they came seeking advice; sometimes they used him as a wailing wall, a confessional, font of knowledge. His slow, drawn-out speech meant not many had the patience to sit and listen to him finish a sentence, let alone a whole series of them, but still they came. He was so old, the first of our Preserved, and the idea that he wouldn't die, that he couldn't, imbued him with a sense of wisdom he may or may not have deserved.

The room was bright and glary with sunlight. He lay on top of his bedclothes, dressed in soft tracksuit pants and a long-sleeved shirt whose cuffs reached his fingertips. I was the only one who bought him new clothes. I found them in the children's section, usually. He was once a big man, but decades had shrunk him. His eyes were yellow, his hair pale strands. His fingernails grew quickly, and I was the only one who could bear to cut them. His ears leaked green earwax, so we kept them stopped up with cotton wool. He was mostly deaf, anyway.

Burnett had a long thin neck. It didn't look like a swan's though. It looked like a petrified piece of rubber piping.

I tried to drape a sheet over his legs, but he breathed out, *ehhh*, and I knew he wanted me to stop fidgeting.

Burnett Barton did not like bedclothes. The weight hurt him, he said, although the doctors were sure he could feel nothing.

Truth is all that matters, but of course one person's truth may differ from another's.

3

Nurses were supposed to take care of the medical stuff. But it was mostly me. They all made it clear I was just an aide, but they left a lot of the Burnett work to me. I did a lot more, too, above and beyond. I'd been visiting him since I was a kid, because who he was, what he was, fascinated me.

"Do you want to do some work today, Burnett?" I asked. I lifted my notepad. "We could get some words down on your book, if you're in a nostalgic mood." I reached out to hold his hand. Stroke his arm. I'd be in the Time Ball Tower soon, if things went as planned, and it was good to acclimatize to touching bodies like his. His skin was dry, flaccid, and it hung off his bones as if he carried no flesh at all. I squeezed tighter and felt no veins, no muscle, no tone at all.

"Here," I said. I put a pencil under his fingers (one of his favorites, sharpened to a dangerous point). Sometimes it helped to inspire him.

I poured a glass of water for myself. With a dash of vodka. If it worked for Dad, it worked for me and forget about lessons learnt or whatever. I pulled out my camera and snapped some shots of Burnett from different angles. I had photos going back fifteen years and one day I'd collate them all, looking for changes.

As he spoke, I tidied his bed, placed his hands on his chest, ate some chocolate and gazed at the spider webs in the corner of the room.

I dusted the clocks that ticked on every surface.

"Read—to—me."

He hadn't spoken for days, so his voice was scratchy and slower than ever.

"How about this one?" I held up an early volume, the one that laid out the history of his old village. I'd helped him with it, typing it up, printing it out. I'd done it a number of times, because he kept changing his mind.

In one version, something helped him climb out of the sunken church.

A giant tree, he says sometimes. At others, he talks of a crucifix, bending in the middle to make it easier to climb out. In some versions, he helped children. Saved a dozen lives, carrying them all like a strongman at the circus. But that lie made him cry because it was so far from the truth. Burnett did this often. Confused the story of his town. Burnt? Drowned? Who knew?

"God—guided—us—through—the—collapse—of—the—earth."

"I thought it was a flood."

"The—flood—led—to—the—ground—turning—into—a—sinkhole.—You've—seen—that?—It—happens—all—the—time."

Yet one side of his face, across both shoulders, both palms and his right arm were all badly scarred from burning. He'd muttered once, "From—when—my—village—died—in—a—fire."

I hadn't asked again. I was young, that first time, and still believed I could ask any question and have it answered.

He said, "All—we—have—is—our—story—telling.—All—that's—left—to—us—is—our—voices." He said this often.

The ward shuffled and snored. Many of the residents were up and wandering, but there were no staff to be seen, except my friend Renata, who was going into Mr. Madden's room. She loves the nightshift. I love it, too. The quiet. You're mostly left alone. And the patients are quite sweet when they're asleep. I imagined this was a favorite time for patients who stayed awake, too. Moments of freedom.

I figured I'd talk to Renata later. We could grab a coffee and some fruit salad, catch up on the gossip. Bitch about our mothers.

Renata was born a day after me and we were close as kids, before we realized how far apart our families sat politically. We still hung out a bit, partly because we both worked on the dementia ward, partly because of all we shared.

Night had fallen, and the glow of stars gave a depth to Burnett's room that it didn't have during the day. The windows were high in the wall, eaved, so they barely let in the sunlight.

Burnett sat in the near-dark. It was never completely dark in his room. He had no curtains, and his eyes reflected moonlight. "Are you awake?" I said.

"Read—the—tortoise—story—to—me.

He always wanted this one from his own work of history.

1810CE

In this village, there were people who could turn into tortoises. Tortoises are slow moving. Slow growing. Slow thinking. You could say this of the people of Little Cormoran.

Only one tortoise man lived by 1810. His name is no longer remembered. He would transform himself to get out of school or duties on the farm or at work. As a tortoise, he'd walk so slowly through the village that by the time he got to his destination the work was done. A lazy man and thick-skinned, he didn't care what people said or thought about him.

But he carried a heaviness in his chest that he complained about, boring the other villagers, making them lose any sympathy they may have had for him.

He never married. He never saw a doctor, even when the growth on his chest became obvious to all, pressing out in an unpleasant bulge.

He was four hundred years old when he was murdered. A disgruntled employer, perhaps? They'd slashed his throat. Cut his wrists. Opened his chest. Made him bleed from many places. He crawled around and around the village, dragging himself along in his tortoise form.

"My stone," he said. "My heart."

It took five days for him to die. At last, he crawled in among the seven stones, and they could not get him out for the longest of times."

Burnett had a small tortoise in a terrarium on a shelf above his head. I was tempted to set it free; it barely had room to move and I hated looking at it. I'd asked him about it, why he kept it when he couldn't see it, couldn't touch it, and it was surely unhappy. "I know he's there, even though I can't see him. He belongs to me completely. That is the way to prove love."

"He's not as old as the man in your story, is he?" I said. "What do you mean when you say, 'My stone. My heart.' What's that about?"

Burnett closed his eyes. "Every—old—tortoise—has—one." He clutched at his heart.

"Are you okay?"

"Stone—sits—heavy—some—days."

"What stone?"

His tongue protruded, and I dropped some water on it.

"Stone?" he said.

"The stone you just mentioned."

"I—knew—your—grandmother—when—she—was—a—young—girl," Burnett Barton said. "She—reminded—me—of—Harriet."

Harriet was my great-great-great-great-great-grandmother.

"Such—a—beauty.—A—darling," he said. "I—adored—her,—and—I—proved—it."

I didn't want to ask him how he proved it. I didn't want to think about my parents having sex, let alone something as old as he was.

"Ehhh," he said again. He pointed at his bedside table, but I wasn't touching that. He had disgusting things in there.

"Which thing?"

"Ehh," he said, pointing. "Harriet—gave—me—that.—Undying—love."

It was a supermarket scented candle, not more than five years old. There was no way Harriet, who'd disappeared a hundred and forty-something years ago, could have given it to him. His desire to believe their love was eternal overrode any sensible thought.

"Every—man—should—be—loved—like—that," he said, lifting a finger to point at his heart.

There were opaque drops in the corners of his eyes and I recognized them as tears. He wasn't capable of real tears, so it was like watching a memory of crying. As if he imagined doing it so powerfully that it almost happened. Maybe his heart wasn't made of stone, after all.

If I let the droplets sit there for an hour or so, they'd be solid enough for me to collect.

His lip curled slightly over his toothless gums and I wondered what he was thinking.

I said, "Did you actually marry Harriet? On paper or…in the biblical sense?"

His lip curled further. "A—gentleman—never—tells."

Regardless of how he worded it, I didn't think Harriet had liked him much.

I placed the candle on his chest and lifted his hand to rest on it. He tilted his head slightly and sniffed the candle. It was cypress, woody and spicy, but the scent was faint.

I snapped another quick shot of him. One of my projects was capturing emotion; here was nostalgia, a heartache for something that never really was.

I took a sip of water.

He coughed in irritation.

"What did she think of you?" I asked.

"I—slipped—into—her—good—books—by—displaying—good—deeds."

"And concealing the bad ones?"

"I—did—none."

I was unconvinced by this.

"She—never—forgave—me—for—the—tower.—She—used—to—say,—'Still—and—all,—we—should—not—have—done—what—we—did.—God—will—decide—what—will—become—of—us.'—Ironic—given—her—abandonment—of—us.

"She—used—to—chitter—chitter,—like—an—insect.—Such—an—annoying—sound.—Did—I—ever—miss—hearing—that?—I—did—not.—All—the—ladies—are—gone.—Only—me.—Eternal.—But—she—is—mine—forever—nonetheless."

"Does the treatment hurt? Is it really that painful?" I had asked Burnett this many times. It was always on my mind.

"I—don't—remember.—Yes.—Your—body—separates—from—itself—or—so—it—feels."

On his bedside table was a small framed quote. He waved his arm (tried to wave his arm) at it.

I give them eternal life, and they will never perish, and no one will snatch them out of my hand. John 10:28

"You know they're talking about Heaven, right? Not life on Earth?"

But his eyes were closed. His notes said, *There is a prescription for long life. Sleep. Salt. Breathe well.*

"Is that it?" I asked him every time I could. We all knew there was more to it than that.

His eyelids slid open and closed. He nodded.

I wasn't sure that was true, but even his lies helped me prepare for a year on the rocks.

"No—one—should—outlive—as—many—as—I—have.—I'll—out-live—you,—too," he said to me. Was he boasting, or envious?

I set alight some incense. The smell of him was subtle, but after a while it became overpowering. I hummed to take my mind off it, and he closed his eyes, waved his fingers slowly, meaning, be quiet.

"I'm going to the Club tomorrow."

He'd been telling me for years about the place.

"You—are?"

"I am. I'm going in as keeper in a month."

He was almost animated.

"Good.—Proud."

He said it as if he was my father.

"I'm not sure I can last a year," I said.

"A—year—is—right.—Any—less—means—too—much—change—in—the—Tower.—Any—more—and—there—can—be—damage—done—to—you."

I thought he was exaggerating. I'd never known a keeper to come back worse off, even those who didn't fill the year, or who were there a little longer.

"Bye,—superstar," Burnett said. "Take—every—advantage—you—can.—You—will—be—famous."

I left him. He wasn't being sarcastic. Stupid to let that make me feel good, but it did.

I want that. I want exactly that. To be a different person. Stronger, smarter, actually brilliant.

I'd always wanted to be a great, a star, known, and somehow the Time Ball Tower helped people succeed. I knew it would help me to become famous, at least. Burnett had been telling me that all my life.

I'll be famous for always having a camera, if nothing else.

I had most of the staff and patients photographed. Only a few to go.

I usually slept well, but with the Time Ball Tower looming over me, the year I would spend there, each night I struggled to calm my brain enough to drift into that space. Not sleeping worried me. I had a clean bill of health, physically and mentally, and didn't want to lose it. Worrying about not sleeping made me sleep badly.

"Why don't you take a nap?" my mother said most afternoons, and she showed me articles about sleep deprivation, hallucinations and degradation. She slept a very particular ten hours a night because she was as scared of oversleeping and missing something as much as she was of not getting enough sleep.

Tempuston was a sleepy town in every sense of the word. I knew no one who slept less than ten hours.

I lay in bed, mind racing. I knew that people would be still up partying in town. I was tempted to join them, but instead got up and sat on my small balcony, looking out over the water.

In the distance, the Time Ball Tower stood, a long shadow on this moonlit night. I waved and laughed at myself for thinking the preserved prisoners out there could see me. That they could somehow look out, see me on my balcony and be thinking that I was going to be great, the best Time Ball Tower keeper they'd ever had.

Stupid thoughts.

The yellow flag was raised, as it should be. It meant bravery, sacrifice and strength. Yellow was my color. That flag would stay raised until I changed it, if I ever did.

I picked up my camera and clicked some shots, trying to capture the shadows that shifted and fell below.

I wanted to be alert, bright, for my visit to the Club. I wasn't sure what to expect, but knew I'd be under scrutiny. It wasn't just that I was a woman. All new keepers were looked at this way.

The sun was coming up, but I felt not in the least sleepy. I called Renata, got her to drop in on her way home from the hospital. She seemed elated, for someone who'd done a night shift. She said, "What are you up to today? Wanna do something? I was thinking of driving down the coast for a surf."

"I'm going to the Club tonight. I'm too nervous to do much of anything but panic."

"Yeah? Tell those fuckers I'm waiting for them. They'll be old before long and I'll be here." Her family hated the keepers. If we were lovers, Renata and I would be like Romeo and Juliet.

What caused the difference? That goes way back. While my family are keepers for generations, her family has been fighting against the tower and the process of mortification for almost as long. They're fighting for the wrong side, though. They have more reason to hate than most of us do. More reason than many to wish criminals into the tower.

Renata's grandmother was known as the Curse Bringer. The Witch.

Renata's grandmother had been out to the Time Ball Tower, although not as a keeper. The curse of that unofficial visit caused the school to burn down and all sorts of other terrible happenings. Every little thing was blamed on her. She came back pregnant (or it happened soon after, no one knows) and she tried to abort, and it failed, and the baby is Renata's mum. Her mum's got one withered arm and is deaf in one ear. But she's living a life. Sort of. She's got Renata; they've got each other. No one knows who Renata's father is.

So yeah, they could have a lot of hate against the prisoners, but they're against the tower and all it stands for, and me, dead set on being a keeper since I was about seven. That could have made me and Renata mortal enemies, but it never bothered us.

"Why do you defend the prisoners? Men like them destroyed your life, and your mother's," I asked Renata's mum once. I was a teenager then and you know how mothers are desperate for teenagers to talk to them.

"God has shown me that all life is precious. Even those lives out there. Some are meant to live, and some are meant to die, but we all die in the end."

One of her ancestors was out there. But it still didn't make sense.

I went for a swim. You can feel so beautifully alone, under the water.

The water was so salty, my eyes stung. As it dried, I felt my skin tighten. I could sell beauty treatments like this. Salt water swims for good muscle and skin tone. I'd take the before and after photos myself.

I didn't bother to dry off for the walk home; I'd be dry in minutes, anyway.

The Ball dropped.

We all paused, as ever, even the people with places to go, like work or school or college.

I hadn't told anyone yet that I'd flunked my course at Technical College. It seemed such a ridiculous failure. A ridiculous endeavor to begin with. I'd hated it there. So much noise, and too many people with too many places to go.

I was looking forward to the Time Ball Tower and its finite space.

I jogged home, tiredness starting to hit. Showered. Ate some leftover pizza. Then fell asleep on the couch, one of those beautiful instant sleeps where no thoughts nag at you.

I woke up when the weather changed, and the air was damp. I showered again, then agonized for an hour over what to wear to the Club. I asked Mum, locked in her room.

"Maybe you shouldn't go," she said.

If Dad was home he'd say, "You always look beautiful," when he hasn't looked at me in years. Unless we're talking about sex; he's obsessed with giving us a "normal attitude." He failed medical school so can't even be a gyno, but he's a sex therapist and he doesn't want any of us ending up screwed up. He reckons, "So long as you're making your own decisions, anything is acceptable."

L ong skirt, old lady blouse?
  Short cute dress with cleavage?
  Jeans and a funny T-shirt?
  I borrowed a Chanel rip-off suit from Mum. She hadn't worn it in years.

T he Club stood like a box on the outskirts of town. The size of a small house, it had no windows. People thought that was for privacy, but Burnett told me it was because none of them wanted to look at the Time Ball Tower. The buildings around it were all like mirrors, and the Club reflected back, all wall, in them. There used to be workers homes in the streets surrounding the Club, but they all collapsed. Shoddy work? Shows how they valued the working class.

I walked up the three steps that led to the front door, feigning nonchalance. All my life I'd known of this place. My friends and I had imagined wonderful things inside. fairy floss machines and a bowling alley. A swimming pool. An elevator that moved around the outside of the building, invisible to the naked eye. Sex shows, the boys had said when they were teenagers. Live sex shows and all the keepers reading and naked and waiting. The image made us laugh. Burnett told me very little beyond, "You will love it. It's a very special place," although he'd only been inside once or twice. My father always came back from the Club blind drunk. Drinks were cheap, and someone drove him home. My mother didn't go. "It's nice inside, but there are too many mirrors on the way there."

Mum called anything that she could see her reflection in "mirror." This included windows, still water, shiny metal. She hates mirrors. Hates the sight of herself. The photos I took of her are the only ones in existence. The fact she let me take them is a sign of...love? Pride? Or exhaustion. She says she can't bear to look back at herself, because she'll never be that person again.

I was supposed to be at the Club at 7pm, but I got there early, so waited around the corner until five past.

I knocked because there was no doorknob. Over the door was a sign saying, "Never Forget."

Tyson Keeney, 1992, the local projectionist, answered the door. Rarely seen in the daylight, he stood, blinking, his nose twitching.

"Phillipa Muskett! Welcome to the Club."

He looked over my shoulder sharply, and I turned, expecting to see somebody there. No one. Nothing.

Suddenly nervous, I wished I'd brought a friend. Not Renata. She hated everything to do with the Time Ball Tower. I lifted my camera, glad to have that.

"Come in! Have a look around. We've got lots to show you." He squeezed his eyes shut and turned his shoulder, as if blocking something he didn't want to see.

It felt momentous, walking inside. A goal achieved.

It was dark. The carpet was burgundy and very soft. The walls were burgundy velvet, the hall furniture dark wood. And so quiet. Muffled. I said loudly, "Nice place," to find out if my words echoed.

No need to sign in. I liked that.

He pushed open a large wooden door and led me into the bar. Lit by a dozen or more bankers' lights, it had an odd green glow.

There was little to indicate this club was connected with the Time Ball Tower or the water that surrounded it. It wasn't a seaside club or a sailor's club. No sea pictures, no anchors, no ship wheels, no netting with fake fish. No Time Ball Tower models. It was more like a sports club. Photos of footballers, cricketers, tennis players. Some were labeled with keeper names, others seemed to have been cut from sporting magazines.

The walls were lined with solid, full bookcases. "Does anyone read all those?"

"Yeah, sure. Crime and punishment, most of them, as you'd expect. We've got the world's biggest collection on penal systems."

"Really?"

"Dunno. Check the Guinness Book of World Records. We've got a bunch of those, too."

There were portraits of many of the keepers. Some women: my mother and grandmother included. My mother's eyes looked bluer, and clear. Her face unlined.

I recognized most; many of them no longer lived in town, but I knew them from the news and from magazines. They were designers, writers, financiers, CEOS. There was an honor roll of the famous.

There was one of William Bunting, 1932. I knew this keeper. He'd become a successful politician. Used the experience in the tower (learning patience, he said) as fuel for the future. His kids were lawyers, politicians, talkers. Two of them had been keepers. They are that kind of family. He was one of those people kept away from, though. One of the men my mother warned me about.

There was one of the keeper of 1921, Ambrose McCarty. This man had died within five weeks of returning from the Time Ball Tower.

Under his portrait was a newspaper article. It was almost pornographic in its delight. *Man's Rectum Pierced in Freak Accident,* it said.

Seriously. This poor guy. Fucking in an open top car and a god damn branch flies up his arse.

How can you not laugh at that?

There was the keeper from 1872, Tristram Barton (somehow related to me, I think), with his massive dark beard. On a table under his portrait sat a small collection of items. A wedding ring, a silver plate, a bowl.

"What are those?"

"Just some symbolic things. Meaning lost for us, but they meant a lot to him."

And on another wall, pictures of the prisoners, on sentencing.

"That's the one they call Wee Willie Winkie. You'll meet him in there. He's even worse off than Burnett. Should see him." The portrait showed a handsome young man, hair tousled. His face was badly bruised, his eyes not looking at the artist but sideways, as if seeking escape. "He's not so pretty now."

My father wore the same aftershave every day of his life and I could smell it here, as if it were being pumped through the vents. Dad used it to cover the stink of booze, which oozed out of his pores day and night.

There were ten or twelve people in the room. I knew them all on sight or in person.

We walked past Leo Adler, 1972, a tall man, hunched over the bar, whiskey in his hand, more drinks lined up as if he couldn't bear to wait. He spoke to no one but the keepers, and even then he was selective.

"Tell him anything; he won't whisper a word," Tyson Keeney said.

"He's like the wailing wall. Come on. It's dinner."

Tyson Keeney had been dying of cancer for years. Most people thought he didn't really have it.

We walked down a short hallway lined with more photos to a solid oak door.

The music was so bland there might as well have been silence. I thought they might play Peter Mosse, keeper 2011. He's amazing, especially his Long Life Mix. The prisoners breathing. Whining. And that incredible trumpet. It's a huge seller, his most successful work. Phillipa was already thinking of ways she could capture something similar. The menu in the Club was pretty plain, he warned me. "Our members aren't big on spicy food."

"Remember, fellas? What it was like back then? When we could eat anything we wanted?"

"That's all right, I usually take my own chili." I held up a small jar.

"Might be the last spicy food you want," 1981, Louis La Rocca said.

I knew I'd always love spicy food. No way that would change.

The food was simple, and fresh, and they all seemed to enjoy it. A bright green spinach soup that tasted almost sweet. A mild curry chicken. An Asian-style salad, full of herbs grown, they told me, in planters in the courtyard. Huge bowls of steamed vegetables also provided, and for dessert, platters of fruit. It wasn't "plain" at all.

"We all come back craving fresh fruit and vegetables. That never goes," Louis La Rocca said. "You'll want them forever." An old man, keeper 1940, Kim Adler winced. Was he Leo's father? They didn't look at each other. Kim gave "the face." I called it "old people's whinge face." They pig out, drink so much booze they fall over, then complain about digestion as if they haven't brought it on themselves. Seriously, how bad could it be?

During the meal, a number of them burped, and tapped at their chests. It made me laugh, and I had to comment. "My mother does the same thing." She was in the Tower in 1973. Dad in 1970.

"Heartburn. Most of us have it. It's how you know who's been out there. Odd, isn't it? Could be the crap we end up eating out there."

"And the painkillers eating the stomach lining."

"Why painkillers?"

"Headaches. For some reason. Air pressure or something. Might avoid it if you're lucky."

I asked about the prisoners, wanting some warning of what, of who, to expect.

"The evil man's heart is like stone," Dale de Feo, 1974, said. I wondered why the others turned silent, and why he shrugged and turned away, red in the face.

"He's drunk. Rambling," another man said. My dad wasn't the only one, then, who coped like this. I wasn't going to let the tower, the isolation, get me that way.

"You know who should be out there?" Kate Hoff, 2010, said.

"The heinous, the unrepentant, the undeniably guilty," four or five of them said together, and that set off a long discussion about the latest crimes, the latest evil.

"There's plenty of space out there. We should be cramming more in," Michael Todd, 2005, said.

"We could stack 'em in boxes, fit hundreds that way. Little peep holes they can see out of. Maybe we poke a candle in there." Luke Harcourt, 1998, smiled as he spoke.

"Who's the worst one out there?" I asked.

They exchanged glances.

Louis La Rocca said, "That'll be for you to decide. Some things we can't tell you and it's best to go in not knowing."

"I've heard that Hitler is there, and Hess and all sorts."

"Conspiracy theories, that's all." Michael said it, but they all agreed. "You'll go through many moments of doubt. A year is a long time for a young person, but it's over so soon," Michael said. "Even if you never work again, you'll be able to get by on the money you've earned if you invest it sensibly. Of course, we're all far too ambitious to simply want to "get by.""

"So, no regrets? No wishing you didn't go out there?"

David Costello, 1988, the boatman who'd row me over shook his head. "Never. Best thing I ever did."

They murmured agreement.

I hoped that wouldn't be true. If I did the best thing I'd ever do at this age, it meant an unfulfilling life ahead.

"The only thing you'll ever regret is if you listen to those mongrels. They're unrepentant liars. Manipulators," Louis La Rocca said. "We might call them Preserved, but most of them are anything but."

"They go through the phases, every time, don't they? Claiming inno-cence, then admitting guilt, then begging for mercy, then they get furious, deny guilt again. Or say they've paid for it. Whine whine whine whine whine whine," Costello said.

They all got into this, whining, "I'm innocent. I didn't do it."

It struck me how annoying these voices would be. Listening to them day after day, no other conversations. And I wondered if that was part of it for my parents. They tried to escape the voices but couldn't, so took to booze and fear of the outdoors instead.

"You have to stand firm through all of it." David Costello held up a fist; solidarity, I guessed.

Louis La Rocca whispered, "The boatman will try to come in with you. Don't let him. It's a curse if you do, and even he knows it. And what's the point? He thinks they'll remember him as the best ever keeper, even though we've all told him they don't even remember him at all."

I took photos of them all. Some of them posed; others preferred to be candid. I'd be away a year; who knew what could happen in that time? I'd asked my photography teacher to take the funeral photos while I was away. He'd be happy to do it. What else did he have to do?

Jerry Butler, 1990, gave me a thumbs up as he left.

"Say hello to Mrs. Palmer and her five daughters, Jerry," someone said, wriggling their fingers.

Men exchanged glances and a couple of them imitated wanking. It was a bit pathetic, really. Boys at high school made this masturbating joke; I couldn't believe men still did it.

There were after dinner mints with coffee, and then Kate Hoff took me into the office and pulled out my file. "Now, we've got twenty grand to go in once your arse hits the boat seat. Then forty grand each solid month you're out there, with pay docked five thousand a day each day you're not out there. Fair enough? Then, there's a bonus of fifty thousand at the end if you've never left the tower. Sum total five hundred and fifty thousand, interest-earning, for the easiest job ever devised. Considering. You won't have to worry about a degree or anything else."

They knew everything about me, it seemed, including my failure to complete even a year of Tech. If I'd gotten into the course I wanted, it might have been different. How do you stay motivated when you're doing something you hate?

"You can talk to Kenny Campbell, 2001, about your investments. Or he'll be in touch. He's a genius with funds. He'll also help you sort your will. You have to have one of those."

I was going to leave it all to Renata. The money I'd earn, all my stuff. All of it. She needed it the most.

Kate led me to a two-drawer filing cabinet, covered with stickers and fridge magnets: *Albert's Car Works* and *Sunny Queensland*, and a large black cat and many more. I saw a tapestry that read, *Cut Nice.*

"What does that mean?"

"You're observant. Most people wouldn't notice that. It's one of those things you'll find out once you're over there. Another one of our little secrets." She pulled out a handful of files.

She tapped her finger on the one labeled Burnett Barton: The Time Ball Tower Keeper's Report 1868.

The folder was blood red, thick. Inside, handwritten notes. Ornate, hard to read. It was a photocopy, though.

"The originals are in the tower."

"This is pretty cool." It was cool. I knew how old Burnett was, of course, and I'd seen his history. But this was different. The history was sanitized, written after the fact, as a much older man. This was when he was, what? Only about sixty? And living what I was about to live.

I couldn't wait to read it.

"Yep. We're lucky to have this stuff. It's like a bible." She rapped the filing cabinet. "It's all in there. Nothing can really prepare you, but this does help. You can take them away to read, but don't let anyone else near them. Not even a look at the cover."

"Have you got a lock box or something?"

"Best not. People will think they're valuable and want to take a look in." She tapped her skull. "Up here for thinking, in there for drinking. Speaking of which, must be about that time."

She showed me to a chair. "John Barton, 1873, barely left that chair, for decades. Someone would carry him there in the morning, carry him away in the evening."

I'd ask Burnett more about John Barton, Harriet's son, I thought.

"It's a lot to absorb. So much to take in."

"You're only just beginning. And I should talk to you about something. While you're here. This is going to sound strange, but I figured you'd rather hear it from me than one of the men."

I was sure whatever it was, I didn't want to hear it from anyone at all.

"They can be easily stimulated, and that makes them difficult. Women keepers in particular. Smell of a woman. You'll need to take a good supply of highly scented douches."

"No way!"

"Seriously. You do not want your scent to reach them. Lemon scent is good. Some women use ordinary bleach, but I think it smells a bit like... you know."

"Are you trying to terrify me?"

"I just want to be really clear. You can never be in a state of sexual desire around them. They can use it against you. They'll find anything to manipulate you. The men take magazines out there to take the pressure off. There's a pile left behind, but I think take your own if you want them."

"You mean you want me to masturbate a lot?"

"Yep. You can be prescribed with a drug that lessens sexual desire if you want, but the long-term effects aren't so good. Now," she said, as if that was done with, "these are the most honest pieces of writing you'll ever read, probably. We put our hearts, our guts, our feelings into them. Only keepers ever read them. People like you, about to go. And sometimes us old farts will read back, or read the new reports, just to get that feeling again. Some of them are about as long-winded as you can get. But who are we to say what people can write? It's important to get it down, get the thoughts and impressions down.

I didn't tell her I already knew about the reports, that'd I'd started mine a month ago. Something occurred to me, though. "So, any of them can read it? My parents were both keepers. And my brother Cameron. What if they read mine?"

"They'll read as keepers, not as your family. I think they'll probably choose not to read at all, though. There are some things you don't need to know."

"But I'll be reading theirs. And my grandmother's."

"And you'll have to read as a keeper, not as a daughter or granddaughter or sister." With that, she led me back to the bar. The others were all settled into conversation, all of them looking up at me, inviting me to join their circles. I wanted some time to process, though, so I got a big glass of wine from the bar (Dad always said they had an excellent cellar), curled up in an armchair in the corner of the bar, soft leather worn smooth from decades of use. Good bright light over my shoulder.

On the cover, a handwritten, carefully-wrought message: *It calls to the best of us.*

Susan Mosse, 1982, came in with a plate of tiny crispy toasted cheese for me. Some gherkin. Some pieces of dark chocolate. And another drink. Coffee with, I realized on sipping, whisky in it.

"Take your time," she said. "The place stays open twenty-four hours. Most of us will head off in a while, though."

I wondered how long I was supposed to stay. I was tired, and the air was thick. I wanted to be outside.

I made my quiet farewells then I headed home.

???

Mum was in a state; almost incoherent. Dad's sisters had organized a big party for my grandmother, Frances. Mum needed to do nothing, and she pretended to be offended by that.

"Don't worry, Mum. We'll let them do all the work. We'll just have a good time."

Mum was sure it would kill her.

"I'll drive. You can lie down in the back with your head covered the whole way. It'll be fine," I said.

"I can drive. I can drive myself."

"We'll do that, then," I said, knowing there was no way she'd get in the driver's seat.

The next day, on entering the ward, I heard a thin, constant wail. All of them made noise; that was standard. But this was higher, more distressed than usual.

"We thought we'd leave him to you," one of the nurses said. "We're behind the eight ball today. Poor old Mr. Madden died last night. The residents know it. Doesn't matter if we try to keep it secret. They're like dogs, sniffing it out."

I went to Burnett. Somebody had dressed him in a Wiggles T-shirt and it was so bizarre I laughed.

The noise was coming from him. He'd been shifted sideways. "He dragged me," Burnett told me.

One of his brittle, dry fingers had snapped off.

"Ouch!" I said, wincing.

"No—pain," he said. "Loss.—Loss."

I sewed the finger back on and hoped that would do.

"Are you sick apart from that?"

He shook his head. There was a register of his illnesses, sporadically kept up-to-date. Chicken pox, measles, rubella—he caught and was scarred by all of it. It wasn't as noticeable now that his skin was so old.

I saw he hadn't touched the beer I'd set beside him. I stretched, took one for myself from his fridge, and settled back into the armchair, which now rested in direct sunlight. The cushions sagged, and the arms were greasy from the touch of many visitors, all of them hoping for solutions or salvations from the wise old man. It was positioned so that visitors didn't have to look at Burnett directly, and that suited most people.

"I went to the Club. They gave me all the reports. Yours is first!" I thought this might give him a moment of joy.

"You'll—understand…soon."

He began to shake. It was a revolting thing to watch.

"What's wrong?"

He squeezed his eyes as tightly as he could manage. "Thought—I—saw—someone."

"A ghost?"

He said he didn't believe in them, but I was pretty sure he did.

To comfort him, I picked up a ball of purple glass, set inside with small red bubbles. Such a beautiful piece, and old.

"Mary—Louisa—Barton—gave—me—that," he said. His voice weak now, almost inaudible. Thinking of times past made him sad.

I had loved this piece forever.

"Take—it.—Reminds—me—of—my—beautiful—Harriet.—My—love."

"When I have my own place," I said. I imagined the glass would be lost in moves. Taken by flatmates if I ever moved to the city. "It's safer here."

I carefully replaced it.

"Did the town love Harriet? Apart from those who thought she was too loud, of course. I'm surprised more effort wasn't made to find her when she disappeared."

He said, "Ran—away.—Anything—in—the—news?" He only meant one thing by that. He was waiting for the day when his forgotten village was re-discovered, hoping to hear news of "Precious watchmaking tools found" or whatever.

He had this fantasy of Little Cormoran rising from the ashes.

There was none of that in the paper. I read to him for a while, then he sighed. Sometimes I think my voice moved too fast for him.

"Show—photos—of—town."

I reached over and turned on his bedside lamp. His eyes watered, even though the wattage was low.

On the wall were his beautifully-framed copies of drawings by Sir Joseph Banks. One was an original, with the rest long since sold and the money invested.

Living a long time made you a rich man, he would say.

He'd received them as a farewell gift from a man he greatly admired, William Barton. I loved the original. I'd already penciled my name on the back for when and if he decided to disperse his things. He also had a drawing he'd done himself, of the cameo William's wife Louisa had given to Harriet. I loved that more than anything else.

They weren't all by Banks, though. One was signed "Eugene."

"Who was Eugene again?" I said. He loved to talk about the past.

"My—adopted—son.—A—very—special—man."

The Ball dropped.

There was a tap at the door, and I opened it to reveal a group of people waiting to talk to Burnett.

Some of them held parcels and boxes. They'd show him the contents, items they considered of great importance and worthy of secrecy, much of it dull.

An elderly woman said, "Ask him if I should go today or tomorrow. He'll know."

I whispered to Burnett.

"He says tomorrow. He says today you should stay home and bake and freeze what you bake for later."

Burnett's fingers twitched, although not his newly-repaired one. Even that small movement caused his bones to crackle.

He liked me to sit and watch over him. People stole from him.

Or took liberties.

The last of the visitors left, so I laid Burnett down and settled him with a podcast playing (History of the World, variations). I needed to do some work out on the ward, otherwise they'd stop me coming at all. If I actually had a nursing qualification, maybe not. They never let me forget I was just a nurse's aide.

Renata was on shift and said, "Help me move the bodies around."

"You really shouldn't call them that," I said. "'Specially not with Mr. Madden passing away."

"They're all as good as dead. Seriously. Look at them. You know I'm right."

I was the only one who knew about her. Knew the truth. She didn't want me to tell anyone else. She didn't want to be stopped.

She hadn't done many. Three, to my knowledge. Mr. Madden was the fourth. I figured, with my stint as keeper coming up, that if I let her do her thing, she'd let me do my thing, and it would all even out.

I helped her shift them about, moving them like random pieces in a game I didn't understand. I stopped to photograph each one; I might not get the chance again.

"You're in denial, Phillipa, telling me not to call them the bodies. Look at you. Why are you taking photos if you don't think they'll all be dead soon?"

"I'm going for a year. And I'm not saying they're not all close to death," I whispered. "Just that at least you could *pretend* in front of them."

"Death is nothing to fear. It's the great beyond. The next big thing," she said, but she was particularly kind to the rest of them.

I was helping to sort out the lunches (mushy, extra-mushy, sludge) when there was a call from hospital. My mother had run into a brick wall and they needed permission to operate because Dad was incapacitated.

I tidied up, got changed and drove to the hospital.

She'd smashed into the wall on purpose. That was clear. She was making a point. "You see I can't cope. I can't go out," about her mother's ninetieth birthday. "This is why I don't leave home. This."

I waited at the hospital for two hours until she was allowed to go home. Dad was blind drunk somewhere.

They wheeled Mum out. I almost cried at how tiny and vulnerable she looked, hunched over, withdrawn. I had her favorite scarf which I wrapped around her shoulders and over her head, making a colorful cave for her. She kept her eyes closed until we got home, then opened them wide to absorb the comfort of the familiar.

"Thank you, Phillipa. Beautiful girl," she said.

I made us a cup of tea.

"Can you tell Grandma? That I can't go because of my accident?"

I nodded. It wouldn't achieve anything to force her.

I was hoping to catch my father in a sober mood, but I'd missed the moment. My mother had joined him in a booze up. Her leg was in a cast, her face covered with bruises. She seemed to be happy about that. At least when they drank together, he was less depressed. Less likely to have a go at me. But the more he drinks the angrier he gets at himself, so no one wins.

He was sitting in his chair, bottle of brandy beside him. He had a very small glass in his hand. Some days he said he drank that way because it felt like less. Some days he said it felt like more.

I said, "I was thinking we should all skip Grandma's party. I've only got a couple more weekends and I'd kinda like to hang out here with my friends."

Dad started shoving things into a bag.

"What are you doing?" Mum said. "Leaving me?" That cracked them both up.

"I'm going to Mum's for the party," Dad said. "Phillipa, you're coming with?"

Mum clutched at my arm.

"Nah," I said. "I don't mind staying home. I'll keep Mum company."

We all knew it should be him staying home, me going to Perth for the party. But I didn't mind, really. The idea of the long drive, and all those hours having to talk to people?

Ugh.

The Ball dropped.

It was a nice week. I called in sick to work, and just hung out at home. Did a bit of shopping. Took a lot of photos. Watched bad TV with Mum.

Ghost stories, things like that.

Mum said, "I was possessed while I was in the tower. A spirit entered me, four spirits, and they sat waiting there until you four were born." She bent her ears forward to show where they hid. "You are those spirits. That's why you're so drawn to the place."

"Doesn't that make you scared of us?"

"Ay?"

I said again.

She looked at me then, studying me seriously.

But she didn't tell me otherwise.

I felt musty, as if the dust of years covered me, so I went for a swim, carefully, amongst the rocks. I tread water for a while on the shadow side of the old pier. I liked it there. Such silence and privacy. People liked the sunny side.

On the way home, I checked out all the buildings named for keepers, built with money donated by the keepers. As Burnett said, live long enough, anyone can become rich. You just have to be patient. And money buys recognition like street names. Park names.

Dad came home with a scarf my Grandma had sent for me. He said, "She made me take it out to the tower, too. Disgusting thing, really!"

Last time I saw her was when I spent a week in Perth, maybe six months ago. Grandma lived in an apartment looking over the harbor.

My grandmother is amazing. Wild, adventurous, brave, a successful children's author with a whole shelf of delightful books about children who became what they wanted to be, not who they were born, in all the variations.

"I wrote the first one in the Time Ball Tower," she said as we stood by the bookcase. "You're going to be transformed out there, if you're willing."

"I am," I said. "I want to be famous."

She didn't laugh. I loved her for that.

"Never be afraid to follow your dream. Too much of life is wasted." It was good advice and she'd been giving it to me since I was fourteen.

She wasn't grandmotherly. Loving, incredibly generous, kind. But she wasn't a grandmother. She seemed tired, vagueing out in the middle of sentences sometimes. My dad's sisters discussed locking her up all the time; I knew she'd die if they put her in a nursing home.

"You'll be marvelous in the Time Ball Tower," Grandma said. "But do, do make sure you have something to keep you active out there. Don't let boredom eat away at you."

She was dressed in a loose-fitting suit, with a dark cravat tied around her neck. I never knew what she would wear. She wasn't like lots of old ladies, who wear the same thing every day as if they've finally identified the perfect outfit and no longer want to think about it.

A large picture window with a view of the water dominated the room, but on an antique sideboard sat a series of beautifully-framed photos. Phillipa liked the one of herself, caught at the moment of highest arc on a playground swing, her hair streaming back, her eyes squeezed tight. There was a large, colorized photo of Phillipa's great grandparents, her grandmother's parents, Rossiter and Ruby. Ruby sat, tiny and doll-like, while Rossiter stood over her, one hand on her shoulder, the other clutching a book.

"Poor man. He kept up a good façade, pretending he wasn't illiterate." Her grandmother tutted.

"He never learned to read?"

"Never really needed to. It was only people's expectations. Their judgment. But he was a wonderful storyteller. I've always been good at pretending and this is where my gift came from. The ability to pretend to be someone else."

Sitting beside this picture was a portrait of Harriet, strong and certain. "An inspiration. A woman who eventually escaped her chains and ran free. Somewhere. I love to think of her living out her life, barefoot, untethered." Grandma sighed at that, as if she didn't really believe it possible. There was a wonderful picture of Grandma, standing with one foot in the boat, pointing out at the tower. I had a copy of this one myself, because I loved how keen she looked to get out there. It made some sense of my own enthusiasm.

"I beat out a lot of young men for the privilege of going to the Time Ball Tower," Grandma said." There were some who wanted to use the stint at the Time Ball Tower as an excuse not to go to war. Weak and pathetic and cowardly. I did more good out there than I could have working for the war effort. We're keeping society safe, Phillipa. Don't ever forget the importance of what you're doing."

The other nurses hated going into Burnett's room and were grateful I took the brunt. But I found him easy to deal with. He had so few bodily fluids. Some of my other patients could be stomach-turning. Burnett literally had cobwebs. It was true. No one had been near him in the week I'd been away.

I fixed his bedclothes. Placed a vitamin pill on his tongue.

"Club?" he asked. He'd forgotten to ask me last time.

"Bizarre. Fascinating seeing pictures of the prisoners as they were."

Burnett said, "They—are—lucky.—Known—for—what—they—were.—When—they—were—real—people.—No—one—alive—knew—me—as—a—young—man." He blinked.

"What sort of young man were you?"

It was minutes before he answered, as if he was adding up all the words in his head before speaking. I was one of the few who could cope with this. I had endless patience.

"I—was—a—little—shit," he said.

I laughed.

Renata came in, bringing a small dose of antibiotics. "Strep on the ward again."

"Kill—me.—Kill—me.—Kill—me." She was the one who'd do it, he'd said to me.

"Maybe one day," she said. "How, though? Three days without air? Three months without water? Three years without food? That takes a lot of dedication on my part."

"Kill—me.—Kill—me—before—you—go."

"I can't do that," I said, voice cheery and bright, mimicking the nurses I sometimes despised. I'm not that kind of nurse, that fake stuff. Even these old patients can see right through it.

"Give—me—blessed—relief.—Release—me."

"You should do it," Renata said.

I knew that if I ever did decide to proceed, he wouldn't have the courage to die.

"No—one—will—come—in—the—whole—time—you're—gone."

"Renata will. And she might even take pity on you, who knows?"

It was a thought that concerned me. Would she do it? Given her background, her beliefs?

She wouldn't do it. He was too important to the town, our cautionary tale. *This is what happens, this is why we don't want to go against God's will.*

I asked her not to. I told her I wanted to be the one, if it was going to happen.

"You know it should be me. And it should happen out there, too."

If she'd been smarter, she would have figured out a way to be keeper. She could kill the lot of them, every last prisoner out there, and no one would know for months.

"Anyway, time for the *Burnett On Display Show,*" Renata said.

Burnett tried to sit up as a group of young men were ushered in. Wanting to pretend to be a real man, for a few minutes at least.

The group were caught partying at the old school. They left a mess of bottles, vomit and food wrappings. That's as wild as it got in Tempuston.

The burned-out, unrepaired primary school served as a perfect place for the teenagers to gather. This was probably deliberate on the part of the adults, keeping the kids contained while giving them the impression of freedom.

You could still see the scorch marks on the walls, and there was a plaque with the names of the children who died around the base of the oak tree in the courtyard. The whole town believed that the school burned down. Renata's grandmother had gone out to the Tower uninvited and brought a curse down on us. And of course, the keeper had been killed. That was her fault, too, everyone believed. She'd gone out there on her own and back all full of change and vim and whatnot. Wanting to fix things. All she fixed was dead kids in a burned school, people thought. They blamed her, and her daughter, and her granddaughter.

Renata learned to be thick-skinned about it. Any sign of emotion and kids go for the jugular.

This bit of our history was part of our cautionary tales, our *do as you're told* warnings, our ghost tales. Telling stories to scare each other off.

I had loved these classes in school. We'd go on an excursion to the museum, one of the oldest buildings in town, and we'd set up in a circle. The lessons were called Local History, but it was just an excuse to show terrible photographs and talk about atrocities. They spoke of lives ended too soon (victims) and of killers taking the easy way out (a quick death).

It was a standard part of our schooling and it surprised those who made it to university to realize that others learned none of it.

Good and evil seems clear when you're a kid. Wrong and right. The lines are not blurred. No gray areas.

From the age of five or so we knew what the prisoners had done. Hanging out in the burned school we'd take it in turns, whispering stories. Like the one about the man who drove into the lake with his three sons and left them to drown while he climbed out and had a cigarette. When the rescuers came, he complained that most of his cigarettes were wet and was almost drowned on the spot by those men they were so furious with him. They say that those boys haunt the lake, but not everyone sees them. If you see one of those boys, it means your dad hates your guts and wishes you'd never been born.

Then the Ball dropped, and Burnett froze as he always did.

Time passing.

Listen.

The teenagers were ushered out and the two of us were alone again. I watched him for a while, his fingers moving slowly in a small ray of sunshine. The broken one had worked its way loose again, so I tried to attach it. I should have broken it off while the kids were in the room; that would have scared them straight.

I made him as comfortable as I could. "I'm heading out in a couple of days. We'll need to say goodbye today."

He'd be here when I got back. No doubt. The other residents? Unlikely. No one lasted long in here.

"Please," he said.

"Don't ask me to kill you again."

"Be—careful.—Look—after—yourself.—Think—of—the—future.—Don't—be—too—curious.—Don't—think—you—need—to—explore—everything.—Don't—go—far—down."

His kindness almost made me cry. "I'll see you," I said.

I left him.

I did the rounds, saying goodbye to the patients, but yeah. None of them were really capable of goodbyes because they didn't understand the concept of departure. Departure means the future; it means I am here and then not. All they understand is the present.

I put my head in to say goodbye to the head nurse. I thought I was just being polite, that I'd put my leave form in and there'd been no problem. She's a Tempuston girl, she knows that people have a year off and come back to their jobs.

But she said there'd been complaints from the nurses (not from the residents; no way they'd come from the residents) and that I should be thinking of other options on my return.

I laughed.

I knew what I'd be like when I came back. I'd be far too good for this place. I did feel sorry for the residents, though. And I'd have to figure out what to do about Burnett.

I had a quickie with my friend Max, 2013. We'd done it before plenty of times and I knew it came without attachments. "Wait for me?" I said, then laughed at his horrified face. "Kidding! You'll be married by the time I get back."

"Let's talk when you get back. We'll have a lot to talk about. I wish I'd had someone waiting for me."

We snoozed until the Time Ball dropped, then stretched and got out of bed.

He stood naked by the window but stepped back when the protestors on the street jeered him.

"Ignore them. Let's have one more for the road."

He wasn't usually good at ignoring things, but he managed.

We hung out for a while, hoping the protestors in the street below would disperse. No such luck.

"Awful women," Max said. "They seriously have no idea. Do they really think they're going to change anything?"

"At least we notice them; if they behaved like quiet, well-bred women we wouldn't even hear them, let alone listen."

"I wish they wouldn't film everything we do."

Max had a touch of paranoia.

I'd learned to ignore them, as most did, but this was more intrusive than usual.

The protesters are rarely men. Never have been. There were maybe eight of them today, although do you count children? Because there were two or three of those, snotty-nosed, bored, dirty, being indoctrinated. Renata wasn't there, but her mother was.

Protester numbers swelled as a keeper prepared to leave; this had always been the case. Some died, others took their place. There were always one or two; never more than ten, even at these times, when they stepped it up a notch.

They'd been violent in the past. They stopped (delayed) one keeper from leaving by attacking him and breaking his leg. It made the keepers more determined and brought calls for the protesters to be sent out there themselves.

Naked, I waved to Renata's mum from my window, flashing the pro- testers clustered below.

Nothing deterred them, though. They probably liked looking up at me. Probably fantasized about being locked in a women's prison, and all the perving they could do there.

I showered and dressed, wanting a swim.

They tried to stop me. Renata's mum asked about my mother, because everyone knew about the accident of course, but we were interrupted by a rolling gaggle of drunk women, on their way home from. Or to. It was hard to tell. One of them fell over, head first, into the bushes, but none of the others noticed.

I pulled her out, tugging roughly at her. Too roughly, probably, but it annoyed me that she was incapacitated.

So much of our town was like this.

It was one of the reasons I left. Tried to leave.

The tower never left me. I'd dream about it, hallucinate it when I was away. It calls to the best of us, they say.

"You'll never get a husband if you go in there," one protestor said. "They'll smell it on you." Her comment made me laugh, because look where she was, sat there in the middle of the road with her wild hair, her desperate face. It was only the street sweepers who cared.

"You know this is barbaric. Against God," Renata's mum said, as if this was a new argument. "Burnett Barton begs for death, day after day." Clearly, Renata had passed this on. "It's not human."

"Shut it Down. Let them Die," they chanted at me. It's familiar. I've heard it all my life.

I used to think Renata and I would be friends forever. But you can't get over this kind of fundamental difference when you're adults.

"Fucken bitch," they said as I pushed through them.

"What sort of woman are you?" and quite seriously, one of the children spat at me.

"This is not the way to argue your point," I told them.

"How, then? How the hell else?" They moved closer to me, and I pulled back.

"Is human life worth this?" they said.

"The people out there are evil. They deserve it."

"You fucking bitch," one said again.

"You weak, pathetic, man-loving fuckwit." This is honestly how they spoke. "Think about what you're doing. We'll be waiting for you, you'll be destroyed by this and we'll look after your pathetic simpering body until you die." Renata's mum did nothing. A woman who'd known me all my life, lets them abuse me like that.

The one thing Renata's mum had learned over the years was that if you looked crazy, no one listened to you. So, she kept her silver hair in a neat bob. She wore the country women's outfit of chambray shirt and comfortable pants, or linen pastel dresses (although those were a pain to launder) or paisley dresses in the new no-iron style.

Even so, most people avoided her. Some of the teens went through a rebellious stage and would sit with her, listening to her arguments, hearing her version of history and Renata always supported her.

Her argument: "How do we know they are all not innocent?"

Even though we had all the records.

"Even if they are guilty, surely they've paid for their crimes? And who are we to decide who should be there? Give them unto God to decide." She was all about fate because she was a failed abortion. But you know? A doctor out there in the tower performed late abortions without the mother's permission. And that's just the beginning of what he did. He filmed it. Babies dying out of the womb...

He's never coming home.

He's never going to die.

Renata's mum had it tough growing up, with a palsied arm, and one foot shorter than the other. The patience of kids is limited with the imperfect. "Our ancestors have done enough, paid the full price. Should I be paying too for a crime long since paid for?"

"No one wants you to pay."

"But I am, with my ancestor there. Don't you see that his suffering is mine?" she said.

Another woman said quietly, "You're an evil bitch, and you're a traitor to your sex," as if women were somehow held to a different level of moral behavior.

The Ball dropped.

I walked away.

I swam further than I'd planned to, but the water was perfect: salty and cold. I swam so far out I could only see the tops of the cypress trees that dominated our town square. I treaded water a quarter of the way to the Time Ball Tower, thinking that if it wasn't for the rocks, I could swim all the way. My arms ached, though, and my legs, so I started slowly for shore.

They were partying around a fire, some friends, some out of towners, and I joined them for a while, drinking the cheap brandy mix they had in a large jug. The protesters never walked on sand (they hated the sight of the Time Ball Tower) so I felt unassailed.

I took some photographs of the Time Ball Tower, wanting to catch it from every angle, at every time of the day.

I'd first been inspired to take photos at about nine, when a newspaper photographer came to the town, interested in Burnett. We had it every year, media coming out on a slow news day for Burnett's birthday.

I had watched the news photographer closely. She'd walked with her head tilted slightly, as if assessing the scene from an angle would give it new clarity. I loved the way she leapt about with full confidence, seemingly unaware of anything but her subject.

I liked the way she didn't have to talk to people. She focused on her work. That would be good.

You could hide behind your camera.

"People don't see you," the photographer said. "All they see is the camera and they imagine how the photo will look as you take it. You might as well be invisible."

I loved the idea of being invisible. Not having to react or show feelings. Able to take time to decide how to respond. From then on, I carried a camera everywhere.

I started taking a series of photos of my mother when I was fifteen. My way of fighting back, of proving something. My worth, perhaps, or my existence, even. They were awful, dead-faced snaps. My mother in the bathroom. Looking out a window. Touching a book. The way I did it, she was part of her surroundings. Objectified. I really liked the way they turned out, but others were surprised by them.

I photographed my mother surrounded by flowers, by the good smells. She'd never forgotten the smell of the Time Ball Tower, was always trying to smother it. She only ever wanted perfume for a present. She wore a lot of it. The good kind, not the cheap. She said, "Good perfume has the ability to chase away the bad smells. Cheap perfume absorbs and magnifies it."

She should have had help a long time ago. It was probably spousal abuse that my father did nothing—*she'll be right*—and at the same time hated her for her behavior.

The photos were truthful but cruel. I showed my oldest brother, who laughed.

"Fuck, those are nasty. Are you going to show Mum and Dad?"

"Do you think?"

In the end, I showed my father. "Nice," he said without really looking at them. "Workmanlike. Not a work of genius."

"I want to be a genius."

"Want want want. You can't be what you're not."

I knew I should do something with it all, but I didn't know what. When I came back from the Time Ball Tower, I'd be smarter. Wiser. I'd be able to figure it out.

I had that dream. Of my teeth falling out.

My mother watched me a lot, a grateful look about her.

"We should throw you a farewell party. That's what people do."

"It's okay, Mum." That would be her idea of Hell.

"No! Let's do it. It'll be fun."

Dad got way into it, writing up guest lists, deciding on cocktails. I let it happen. Why not?

Renata came over early to help set up. No one else would. Mum was "preparing" in her room. Dad was out buying the booze, which meant drinking at the pub until the last possible minute. My brothers would show up later. We didn't talk much, although Renata made lots of jokes for me, making me laugh, "filling me up," she said, as if I could draw on that stuff when I was out there. She gave me a wooden puzzle to give to her ancestor.

"To keep him occupied."

"Why do you even care?"

"I don't know. Habit, I guess." Some families did cling to it.

Renata and I had a quick pasta meal. She toasted, "Here's to getting rich on the suffering of others."

"Bitch!" I said. It did annoy me. I never gave her a hard time about the residents and how she treated them.

"We'd never lock up an innocent person for money," I said.

"It depends on how much, doncha reckon?"

"No, I don't."

She spilled pasta sauce on my camera and I wiped it off.

The food tasted bland, so I added extra salt and a bit of chili.

"You eat too much salt."

The house filled with people. My brothers, their wives, girlfriends, kids, friends. The noise of it. I felt myself shrinking. Disappearing.

Home was always full. "I'm looking forward to peace and quiet over there," I said. I had to say it again; no one heard me.

"It's not actually silent," my brother Cameron said. "Be ready for that. Some days they are as rowdy as a pack of crows. And if a new one comes in, he'll be like a puppy dog compared to the rest of them. Yap yap." He did a weird spin on his heel, tongue out, panting.

"Is that meant to be a dog?"

"Meant to be? It is a dog. You have no imagination."

Cameron and Damian had been to the tower, Cameron in 2006, Damian in 2012. Nolan had not. I wondered if he would ever regret it. He sat in front of a computer, gaming. We looked a lot alike, but we had nothing in common.

Damian and Nolan were shits, Cameron was not. All had left town. My mother was happier when they weren't close by.

You know she thinks we're all ghosts," I told Cameron. He gave a kind of mouth shrug, maybe meaning, "what can we do?" Then he said, "When you come out, let's talk." He'd spent a lot of time with Burnett, too, before he moved away. We often visited together.

Max was there, sexy as ever, wearing a tight T-shirt, jeans, his hair mussed up. He smelled good, like fresh air, and I wanted to snuggle him and more.

My photography teacher wanted to talk, though. He was the opposite of Max: baggy pants, faded old checked shirt, hair neat.

He talked about the solitude and how wondrous that would be. "You really must enjoy this. What you will see out there will astound you. The patterns. The shapes. What lies beneath when you are no longer distracted by the outside world. You will come back bursting at the seams with ideas."

I didn't like the image of "bursting with ideas." It made me think of a body with the orifices sewn up and bloated with gases. I'd never seen such a thing, but Burnett described it for me, to try to scare me. "This is what happens when you die. Why do you think I want to keep this body alive?"

I asked my photography teacher about his own time there and how it inspired him, because I knew he had achieved very little of what he had hoped to achieve. He was one of the few failures of a keeper. That was a bonus for me. It meant he'd stayed in Tempuston. Without his encouragement, I would not be who I was. What I was.

My teacher said, "Don't wish the time away out there. The isolation will make you great. Take the time to explore your work, really explore it. You'll be a much greater artist for it. It's like what's in a whirlpool."

We were all in our backyard. Animals kinda everywhere. Rabbits in hutches. Three cats. Four dogs. And of course all the markers; all the dead ones I couldn't just bury and forget.

I couldn't resist a stray. My mother calls them the straifs. Waifs and strays.

"You'll look after the animals while I'm gone, won't you, Mum?"

She ignored me completely. In the end, I knew I'd have to find homes for them all, but I played with the fantasy that she'd help me out. She was scared of animals, though, which made things hard.

"At least if they die, bury them properly."

"You don't want me to freeze them for you?" my dad said. "I need an excuse to buy one of those big arse freezers. I'll put a sign on it. Phillipa's Straifs, DO NOT EAT."

I wished I could take the animals with me. Dad was off his face. A happy drunk. He made everyone laugh; he really was funny. He did mimicry and told long, involved, hilarious stories. I tried to match him drink for drink but no way. I felt numb, tongue-tied, and he was dancing on tables. My brother Nolan (the one who had never been a keeper, so he really couldn't afford it) gave me a really good bottle of scotch and told me to drink it all myself.

The whole thing depressed me. Dad being an idiot (he was so morose and quiet when not drunk), Mum in her room, Max pretty well having sex in the corner with some woman, Renata gone; she didn't say why.

The only thing that cheered me was the music: Peter Mosse's Time Ball Tower Mix. I loved it.

I wished he was at the party. He was in Vienna, performing in something or other. I loved his music and I would have liked the chance to tell him. I would when I came out. He'd be interested, then. When I was one of them.

Nate Deeming, 2009, said, "I'll miss you when you're gone."

I was tongue-tied. He was an actor, charming, sexy, intelligent. He never used to be. He used to be a pimply guy, no confidence. Now he was a star. Superstar. Girlfriends all over the place, but I don't think he ever forgot I was always nice to him when he was ugly.

He was the most handsome man I'd ever seen.

I wondered if he'd still be around when I came out. He wasn't much older than me. He winked at me.

"There's one thing out there...you'll need to look for it. You'll know it when you find it. If you don't, no biggie. No big deal." He seemed smooth and flat and ordinary and I wasn't sure that's what I wanted. But still. He did for the night.

I spent the last night alone. My parents were...somewhere. Mum was in the house, I guessed, but quiet as a mouse. I gazed at the Time Ball Tower. Ate fresh vegies until I felt bloated.

And I read the Time Ball Tower Keepers' reports.

I read all of them.

There was so much. So much to understand.

It would make sense when I was out there.

BURNETT BARTON: THE TIME BALL TOWER KEEPER'S REPORT 1868

The ball itself is a thing of wonder.

Made of copper, it glows like the most glorious sunset. I cannot find the seams, no matter how hard I look, how carefully my fingers run its surface. It spans the length of my arms twice over; if I had a companion here, we could touch fingertips only just. It feels warm to the touch, most days, even when the sun has not shone.

As if there is something within; some hidden power source.

I know there is not.

I am the keeper of history. The sole survivor of Little Cormoran. The creator of Tempuston and the Time Ball Tower.

I set my words down here, as shall all who follow me. All who come to this small rocky island, this Time Ball Tower, and watch over the prisoners here. All those who sacrifice.

I am proud to say I built this beautiful thing.

It stands tall, solid, white, centered on this rocky island.

We do this so that there is a record.

So that the truth is not lost.

1150 BCE

The giants Cormoran and Cormelian had a falling out, and in the mêlée, seven people were killed. The giants didn't notice until one young girl, known for her beautiful singing voice, hit a note high enough to get their attention. She pointed at the poor dead villagers. Instantly contrite,

Cormoran left his village, saying he wouldn't return until he had saved seven lives. In further penance, he rolled seven great boulders before him everywhere he went, so every night he fell asleep exhausted and aching with effort.

Along the way, he did save seven lives. The last was near the very field where Little Cormoran was settled. He heard crying and, leaving his stones in a pile, he walked until he found the source. It was a tiny boy, his leg bent and broken, his head cut wide open.

The child was terrified of the giant, of course, but he would bleed to death if left alone.

Cormoran was too big to tend to him, so he picked the child up and, taking two hundred and ninety giant steps, carried him in one calloused palm to a village where the hearth fires burned, and they could be expected to understand healing.

He watched and waited as the boy grew healthy and strong. They never did discover where the boy came from. Once he was well, Cormoran felt lonely and redeemed and he traveled home again, leaving his stones behind him.

1300CE

Before the founding fathers settled Little Cormoran, they were nomads, gathering knowledge, learning about the perfect existence by seeing many flawed, shallow, short lives.

As their numbers grew, they began to seek permanence. So, when they found the wide green field, a pile of seven big boulders, moss-covered and grey and stacked carefully one upon another at its center, they knew they were home. This place represented permanence and reliability.

Little Cormoran, village of the long-lived, was established.

1820CE

In 1820, Milton Carlisle came to the village. No one ever asked why he left his old one, but he was scarred head-to-toe, and he caused quite a stir. The young women, apparently unpleased with the men of the village, went all out to capture his eye. He was almost a giant himself, docile and plodding.

He focused only on work, building the church, carrying dozens of stones where other men could only manage six.

My father and I hated the man. All brawn, no history, he offended everything we believed in. So, when his name came up as the man next to be preserved, we had to act.

"We must stand against him. One of *us* must be preserved to carry forward the true story of our village," my father said, although both of us knew he would be the one.

1821CE

P reservation was a dying practice in the village; too many had gone wrong. One or two people per generation were selected, that was all. We knew it was against God; it was unnatural and sacrilegious. We could reconcile it if we only preserved a certain few. My father wanted to be the one. He would not cede his place to Milton Carlisle.

He visited Edna, the oldest living woman.

Because she spat bile and venom at anyone who approached her, she was kept locked away. Edna was famous for her vicious stories. Gossip of the nastiest nature. She'd say, "I was there," as if that made it true.

My father said, "I need more time on the planet. One life is not enough for me to achieve all I'm meant to achieve. History is told by the survivor. And the longer I live, the more I'll have to tell."

My father was a great historian, with as much fascination for the future as for the past. He believed we lived the history of our descendants. History is carried through the ages in the mouths of the people. We can be living history books.

We visited many ancient places together, places I will never forget. Like the Shetland island of Jailshot, where we saw stone houses from the eighth century BCE and an iron broch tower from the first century CE.

Edna said to my father, "God made our bodies destructible for a reason. We all need to grow old and be ready to cross over into His arms. This is what God wants." Edna spoke so slowly, sometimes you forgot where the sentence began.

"And yet here you are, alive after centuries. Do you feel Godless? Abandoned?"

"I am an abomination. If any of these villagers had the courage, they'd gut me and let me die in the sun."

She spoke so slowly, my father wanted to throttle her.

"You are no abomination. You are magnificent, a Great Mistress of Time."

There was a creak as she lifted her shoulders.

Edna had no real physical needs. She was one hundred and twenty then, it was thought, and whoever had preserved her had done a good and careful job. Sometimes she would suck on a sweet, and sometimes she craved meat, diced to the size of rice grains. Sometimes she needed to be shifted, because her slow blood pooled beneath the skin if the pressure wasn't released.

"I'm the one to be saved. Not that great dumb lump of a man."

At last, she agreed. She had him stay at her house and no one knows what payment she exacted.

My mother stayed at home to manage all the children, although half were of adult age by then. The older two were moved away already and children of their own.

I tried to sneak a look in at my father but could see nothing. And all I heard was low moaning.

When it was done, my father's lips tasted of salt, so no one would kiss him. He couldn't eat with his fingers, not even a piece of bread, because of the salt that seeped out through his pores.

It didn't work with him, for all that. It didn't stick.

He had a short, fat neck, and that was surely the reason. Because the old, old people all had long, thin necks like tortoises. I didn't point this out to my father, though. The man hated to notice his flaws. Especially because my mother's neck was long and beautiful like a swan's.

My father didn't ever return home. He lay dying, turning to sludge, bitter and furious that he wouldn't get to see the future after all, or to keep the past fresh.

"Don't you let that man Milton Carlisle survive you," he said to me. "Don't let him be the carrier of our history." Over and over, he had me repeat names and dates, impressions. Always the combination of those things. He wanted me to know the dates, because those are the things that people trust. And names, because those are the things that people remember. I was Burnett Smith, then. Not a name to be remembered. It was not even my actual family name; my grandfather was a horse thief who escaped prosecution and changed his name to Smith, a profession he had never carried.

"You learn to tell a story, Burnett," my father said. "Make it come to life with your descriptions. Then live to tell the tale. Live a very long time. This is the only way to stay out of Hell. Out of the eternal fires."

"I'll remember," I said.

I spent a lot of time with my father at Edna's house, escaping the noise of my own home, and avoiding work when I could, because my master clockmaker employer did not understand how well I could work if I was allowed to. I listened to stories and came to care for Edna deeply. I came to care for her helper, too. Young Harriet, who was bright and cheeky. Clever and hard working. She could even make Edna smile.

Harriet's face glowed.

"So young," Edna said.

1822CE

My father dried into a husk, shrank into a ball like the mollusks we found without their shells on the shore sometimes. It took six months for him to die. A year? Who can remember? He began to leak, leaving sludge where he lay.

My father said, "You marry that good strong girl Harriet and have a dozen babies, each of them brighter than the last. She's no catch, but she'll see you through."

"She's too young, Father."

"You can wait."

I agreed, but I knew I would not marry Harriet.

She was a child.

1823CE

When Grace came to Little Cormoran, it was love at first sight. Fate.

She was not, at first, agreeable to my thoughts of our future together.

I was patient, though. She was young. She would come to love me. I was apprenticed to the chief watchmaker; I had a bright future.

I did not count on Milton Carlisle, however, who also fell in love.

"I'll marry the man who rolls those rocks," Grace said, pointing at Cormoran's pile of seven, thinking it impossible. But a big man could move them if he was full of beer and bravado, and we say that our troubles started just over five hundred years after our village was settled when Milton Carlisle moved those rocks and God's wrath fell upon us.

Some say the stones he rolled acted like a dam stopper, and that he unleashed the water on us. Some say it was the curse of the tortoise man, because there he was, skeleton-old and crumbling, inside the rocks where he'd rested for five hundred years.

Some may blame Grace, because she asked him to roll the stones. I did not blame her. She never expected Milton would do it. She had no interest in him. Grace preferred more intellectual companions.

And yet Milton Carlisle asked her to marry him, and everyone waited for her to say yes.

1926CE

Edna called for me. Her room was filled with clocks from ceiling to floor, an inheritance from her father, one of the great watchmakers in a town famous for its watchmaking.

She said, "There are changes afoot. I see it. I see the flames and more heat than you could ever imagine."

She thought herself a seer. Most paid no attention to her, because she hadn't been right beyond the obvious in all the times she'd made predictions. But I'd proven myself a listener in all those sad, dead days.

"How can we stop it?"

"There is no way. These things are set in motion."

"There's always a way. Dream again, Edna. I'll stay with you."

I did, holding her cold hand as she slept.

"We must," she said. "We can't. I can't make another. Not after your father."

"My father chose that." It had been two years since my father died from the failed preservation.

"We do need another. Someone grand, beautiful and worthy."

"Grace," I said. She was the most beautiful creature who ever lived. "Grace would fare well," I said. "I'd rub her with lanolin every day, keep her smooth."

Edna looked at me through lidded eyes. "No one ever loved me that way."

"I will care for you both," I said. "If we preserve her, as is, she will keep our verbal history alive. She will tell your story. Your bravery. Your beauty as a young girl."

Edna had been a handsome young lady, with a good solid chest, a tiny waist. Lips thin and beautiful.

Now, she looked like a child, her appearance matching her intelligence. Her breasts were gone, and all her hair had fallen out.

"She will tell of the way you were misunderstood, mistreated."

Thus, I convinced Edna to proceed.

This time it was a success.

Grace breathed slowly, deeply.

I said, "Marry me," but Milton Carlisle's evil influence was too strong. "No," she said.

I used all in my power, but nothing would change her poisoned mind. "I love Milton."

The Banns would be posted in church on the Sunday (even though Grace, still suffering under her preservation, would not be there.) We were all in church, as we ever were on Sundays.

I remember little of the vicar's sermon; he was not a riveting speaker. Milton Carlisle gave a reading, as if all blessings were upon him. Perhaps the congregation were asleep and dreaming. I certainly was. Dreaming, perhaps, of a different ending, where I had rolled the rocks instead. I awoke to find the church rocking. Or so it seemed. And a great noise came from outside; something I'd never heard.

"It's a wall of water!" the baker's wife screamed, running back into the church. I never could ask where she'd been, why she'd been outside.

There were only tiny windows in the church. We raced to the door and saw a wall of water, twice the height of the steeple and rising.

We barricaded the door, pushing the pews up against it where we could, and we huddled together, praying.

"Milton Carlisle did it!" people called out. "He moved the rocks! It's an act of God."

The church was washed off its foundations. If the builders hadn't died, I would have tracked them down and punished them for their incompetence. Tied them to a stake by the beach and allowed them to slowly drown as the tide came in.

The church collapsed into the ground, sank like other villages before it, leaving the congregation to scrabble for purchase, trying to keep their heads above the gushing water that so quickly filled the church.

The priest was silent; killed in an instant. The mayor was silent; always a weak man, he couldn't lead even now. The school teacher was silent; crushed. Milton Carlisle? For a big man his lungs were small. He drowned with the rest of them. The baker's wife too, with dough from the day's bread still under her fingernails.

I was the only one left to lead, but I was sunk so far down it took three days to climb out.

I climbed over dead friends, to my great shame. I didn't carry a single one out of that pit. My terror of falling deeper and deeper into the pit of hell, had me climb, climb, climb. My mother was lost to me, although I called and called. Some nights still I lie awake wondering how long it took for her to die. One month? Two?

I didn't bury the bodies that floated up. I didn't have the strength for that. God forgive me, I burned them.

I heard scrabbling noises. I thought it was rats, that there were so many of them the ground seemed to move, wave-like.

Then I heard a tiny call for help.

I dug through the rubble, moving rocks and bricks, wary of glass and other sharp objects.

There, I found Phillip, a fourteen-year-old, who was expected to do well in the world. The boy was bloodied, torn, mute. We went to my home, through the silent, silent streets, and we found bread hard but not moldy, and some apples still crisp to the bite. I cleaned Phillip's face, gave him dry clothes, comforted him.

When he was settled, we went to see if the floodwaters had reached Edna. Bedridden, as always, she never came to church.

She was drier, if that was possible. Not hungry. Never hungry.

"You were right," I said. "We have drowned. We could not stop it."

She tried to shed tears for our lost town. I hadn't seen her so frustrated before; all she wanted to do was cry, and she couldn't.

"We are the only survivors," I said.

"No. There are more. I dreamed that, Burnett," she said. "Your true loves across the ages. Your destiny. There is me," she said. "And there is Grace. And there is my girl, Harriet. She is safe." If Edna was capable of searching for survivors, she would have.

Grace was resting in her home, unaware. She was always unaware; it was one of her graces. I lifted her up and held her close to my chest. She smelled faintly of sour dough, but I didn't mind at all. I could not believe my fortune. Me and Grace! Alive! I carried her to Edna.

"You go hunting," she told Phillip and me, and we walked through the village until we found two final survivors: Harriet and her five-year-old brother Eugene.

They were in the back of the bakery. They had gorged themselves on lumps of sugar.

"Did you steal this sugar?" Phillip asked.

Harriet was outraged. "We did not! We left coins behind!" She always did have strong morals. Never did wrong, that one.

What did Edna and Grace talk about together while I was searching for Harriet? Such a long talk.

We rested at Edna's house for a day or two, but I knew by my nose that we couldn't stay much longer. In my heart, I understood the town was no longer safe. I could feel the house rocking and soon it would all sink, that is, if it wasn't destroyed by marauders.

"Salvage what you can from the rubble," I said. Grace was too weak to gather much. Harriet gathered broken pieces of china, saying, "I'll make a mosaic. We learned how to do it at school," and I didn't have the heart to stop her. I collected my own watchmaking tools and those of the others as well. As many as I could carry.

We collected jewels and jewelry, knowing it was better with us than with thieves and scavengers.

There were many tears, saying goodbye to Edna. "This is how it has to be. There is no choice," she said. We left her in the greatest comfort we could give her and began our long walk

We barely spoke. We noticed things like the birds singing, and a wolf footprint in the dust. We knew we would not set foot in our town again. We looked back now and then to seek the smoke rising as strangers moved through our beloved streets, setting fire to all they didn't want. Did we seek revenge on those who burned the village down, destroyed it in their search for salvage? No. Seeking revenge is a sure way to shorten life.

How did we come to choose Australia as our final destination? I read the shipping news, and the soonest to depart was *The Frederick*, bound for

Perth. It transported mostly workers for the Australian Agriculture Company, and that seemed to confirm the choice. No convicts would be on board.

Harriet didn't agree with the decision. "You are taking us to an island full of thieves and murderers." She didn't think we belonged amongst them, or not herself, at least. Even at twelve years old, she was the harshest judge of character I ever met. She was already fiercely independent, and I had no concerns about her welfare. Perhaps, in time, she would grow to love me.

1827CE

The Frederick

We traveled to Portsmouth, buying new clothes: hats and veils for the ladies and good shoes for the boys and for myself.

My beloved Grace was feeble and more bad-tempered than previously. She was slow and would prefer to be in bed. But she managed. Marvelous woman. Her smile never left her face. In theory, she would outlive all of us.

She looked old beyond her sixteen years, at least thirty, and we decided to present her as my widowed sister, the children hers. I still loved her, but my hope for a marital future had passed.

Phillip and I signed up as crew members. Phillip, a tall, broad boy who could easily pass for twenty, would do the heavy lifting. I'd never been any stronger than God made me and was glad to have Phillip along to carry the load. Harriet and Grace were the ladies, and Eugene would play on the decks and keep us all entertained with his antics. He was a lively boy, innocent and without guile. Harriet kept him in place, as she did with all of us, to the extent that if she did not approve of a companion, she would draw us away, hissing that this person was not worthy of conversation.

So very determined.

We were in the crew's quarters. We made many new friends there, men of all types, all hired on for the Australian Agriculture Company. The company itself sounded like a pot of gold in a land of opportunity. So, I said to the overseer, "Will they hire me once we land? I'm not cut out to be a sailor. I like dirt, not water."

"I can see that in your grimy face," the overseer said. He was one of those types who think only those born like him were worthwhile. Nobody higher, nobody lower, nobody older, nobody younger. I played the chameleon and became what the man wanted to see, and before long had work lined up in Perth.

Grace stayed mostly in her cabin over the long and tedious journey. Her proudest possession was a jar with a mysterious substance in it, which was intriguing to all. The roll of the ship made walking difficult for her, so she mostly kept indoors. I tried to keep her company. Tried to make her happy, at least momentarily.

When she did step out, she wore veils and made some kind of magic with her face.

A preserved person can watch a spider build a web for five hours. They can listen to the grass rustle and hear stories of the past and future, conversations and praise.

For them, time passes differently.

Harriet roamed the upper decks. I asked her to keep away from the men; she was well of age, and lively enough to gain their attention and I wanted none of them near her.

Fortunately, she came to the attention of a gentleman and his young wife: William Barton and Mary Louisa. Charming, charming pair. If we'd known such blood in Little Cormoran, it would stand to this day. Pure quality.

Mary Louisa Barton was kind and only eighteen. The couple had been married days before departure, and she was now far from family and friends, so she was keen for a young companion.

I felt that Harriet deserved such company and could learn from this gracious lady. I had words with her about privacy, though. "You mustn't discuss Grace and how long we expect her to live. This would lead to considerations of madness, or criminality, and as such they may no longer be interested in our company."

That I could not bear.

The men below deck teased me mercilessly for my friendship with "upstairs." They said, "Anything for a good job!" but they didn't really mind. They knew they'd be looked after if ever it came to that. I was known as a man of courage, conviction, honesty and strength.

We disembarked in Fremantle; our new friends did not. "Come and find us for work," William Barton said, "If you ever come to New South Wales." They were traveling on, another long journey.

Mary Louisa gave a very special item to Harriet; a most unusual cameo. A top-hatted man holding his head forward, lighting a pipe.

And for me, a glass ball. Purple, with red bubbles., with William Barton himself giving me a magnificent etching by Joseph Banks.

A generous man indeed.

1839CE

Time passed. We found work in Perth and some companions, but we were never truly settled. Harriet was a wonder; always had been. Looking after Grace and Eugene while also going out to work for long hours. Eugene was feeble-minded, we discovered. Harriet did what she could for him, but he could not complete his schooling. Could never sit still. They had him working on the docks, because he could manage that, so long as someone told him what to do.

I was not a weak man but did find physical work unpleasant; fortunately, there is always the need for paper work.

It was a man who'd once traveled through Little Cormoran (although he did not remember its name) who told us of a place we might explore. "I know you were all good at clocks," he said, and I barely contained my fists at the flippancy. "You know there's a place way up North, with a half-built Time Ball Tower? Strikes me might be the place for you. For a bunch of clockmakers."

I had long discussions with my collected family from Little Cormoran. While I allowed them a voice, the decision was mine in the end and it was never in doubt. I wanted them with me.

We were a village.

Harriet was keen to go. She was not happy in Perth. "They have the morals of alley cats," she said.

We considered leaving Grace behind but how to explain her condition? Who to leave her with? She was still functioning quite well. She'd been acting as if she were ordinary: eating, sleeping, doing the things ordinary people did. So, while she had started to feel a stiffness in her bones, she was not yet a husk. She tapped at her chest often, as if willing her heart to continue.

Harriet would hear nothing of leaving her behind and the boys would not allow it, either. They relied on Grace for words of wisdom they didn't ask of me. I tried to impress upon the boys that I was of a similar age as Grace and therefore she was no wiser than I, but still they went to her.

Harriet took on most of Grace's care. She wouldn't have it otherwise. Phillip helped as much as he could, but we all sensed the rebellion in him. He wanted his own life but had no idea of how to make one. This imbued a sense of anger and frustration in him, so we never knew when he might lash out. He was a strong young man and his propensity to violence had protected us on a number of occasions, but at the same time I had concerns about his stability and his level of loyalty to the family. I was never certain he would not turn his anger upon us.

It was a very long journey. Along the way, Harriet collected beautiful stones and pebbles to make art. She had a magic eye for such things. She became fascinated with the stories of flickering lights, seen in the outback, although we never saw them ourselves.

I feared the idea of the dryness; how would it affect my Grace? We were told stories of people dying in the desert, of thirst, of exposure. We planned well. I hired a number of natives as guides, and I found myself enjoying their language, their stories, their humor.

This set me apart from many of the other men, but I considered myself set apart anyway.

On the journey, we re-invented ourselves, changing our family name to Barton because we admired that family so much. William was a man of great power, with a great future. Mary Louisa was beautiful and intelligent and so very kind.

I hoped this would draw us together, and it did.

Too much so.

I was proven right as ever and always before. Phillip was antagonistic from the start, wanting the power to lead the group but lacking the intelligence and the resources. I outdid him in all arenas except for one; Harriet adored him.

To what extent, we did not realize until we were ten months into our travel.

We should have known he would press himself on Harriet.

It was Grace who broke the news. She was breathless with excitement, although she breathed very slowly, of course.

"I'm not sure how far along but I think she should stop and rest until the baby is born," Grace said. She said that she envied them. That she'd never loved anyone such. Nor had she been so loved. Did she notice the hurt she inflicted? Surely it was not deliberate, her forgetting how much I had adored her when we were young? I felt momentary fury at Milton Carlisle, who had caused such destruction for the sake of her love. And yet she'd forgotten Milton's love as well.

I confronted Harriet and Phillip and there was a terrible scene. Phillip refused responsibility and ran away. We do sometimes wonder if he made it somewhere safely, but I have grave doubts. He was not the most resourceful of men.

Of course, it was all my fault according to the ladies. Eugene missed Phillip terribly, and seemed to blame me also.

I grew used to the idea of a baby. Harriet carried the first-born citizen in our new town!

It was many day's travel (many days when Harriet wept) before we reached our destination. Even then, we weren't sure we had arrived. There was one single road traveling in to what appeared to be the town center, but there were so few buildings, and it was dusty, with a sense of lifelessness about it. But there, out on the marvelous rocks that made me think of Little Cormoran, was the half-built Time Ball Tower. It stood, blocky, tall, reaching for the sky. It was a message; here, time is yours to manage.

I felt a sense of homecoming on seeing the tower.

The town of Wilson was almost dead. You could say it had never really been alive.

"You're the first visitors in many months," the shopkeeper said to us. Her shop was almost empty. "We haven't had a delivery in six weeks," she said. "I only stay open because I've got nothing else to do. I'll sell you any produce I've got." She lifted some potatoes. "These are good, from a local man. His wife knits, if you need anything like that. She does a lovely baby blanket." She said this with a side glance at Harriet. Harriet was full of glow as she ever was.

Harriet blushed, held her stomach. When the men stepped away, she whispered, "I am with child!" It was a relief for her to tell someone real. Much as she loved Grace, Grace barely existed.

"Oh, darlin'! We'll get you to see Mary. She's lovely with the babies. She's delivered every last one in this town! No doctor will come near us and some of us think that's a good thing!"

Thus, it was Harriet who eased our welcome. People seemed desperate for company (even company as odd as ours) and a pregnant lady made everybody happy. Everybody! The population was thirty-two. You could call it a ghost town.

We were welcomed with afternoon teas and a civic function, held in the home of the town's founder, Martin Wilson. He no longer lived there, so they used it as their hall, their school, their church. It was a wonderful building. So full of precious things. A storage house of memory which would one day become a museum.

There were abandoned houses, built by Wilson for his workers. We took two for ourselves, well back from the water. We moved into the small upper bedrooms and nobody commented. Eugene undertook much of the maintenance of the house and proved to be extremely good at it. We felt proud that he could manage it and certainly it helped our welcome in the town.

I learned much about the man who established this town. Wilson had been a wealthy cattle owner, who, in a philanthropic frenzy, commissioned the building of the Time Ball Tower. Building had halted when the man and his family left abruptly. Rumor had it that he murdered his wife and perhaps the children as well, but no bodies were ever found. His wife was desperately unhappy here, it was said, and she was bitter about what she had lost. Who can say, now?

For me, the tower was like a beacon. It brought to mind the Iron Age Broch Tower, I'd seen on Jailshot so long ago, on a visit with my dear father.

Harriet cleaned all the windows of our two houses. She took down the old curtains and stood gazing out at the Time Ball Tower.

"Is that someone in the window?" Harriet said. "Is there anyone out there?"

"Some say it's haunted," the local policeman told us. He's the one she'd marry before long. He was the kind of man who could accept a bastard child as long as he had plenty more of his own. "By a killer. He murdered a young mother and her tiny baby, small as yours will be. Seduced her with soap, they say, fresh wrapped, smelling like roses. He escaped capture by swimming out to the Time Ball Tower. No one was game to follow. He must have felt very pleased with himself until the weather came over. It would have taken him weeks to die. No water or food. Even if he caught water from the storm, soon it wouldn't be fit to drink. Made many of us happy, I can tell you. Looking out there, thinking of his suffering. Some say he's still there."

"Some would say he deserved such a punishment. Child killer like that," Harriet said. "They should shut him up in a boab tree."

We had seen this done, on our journeys. Criminals imprisoned overnight in the large, round, hollow trees.

Shortly afterwards, Harriet gave birth to a healthy baby girl. Such a beautiful angel! And she looked like Harriet, with barely a glimmer of Phillip. I wondered how Harriet felt, looking at her child. If she was reminded of the man who deserted her so easily. Sometimes I cursed Phillip for leaving us; we needed him.

And yet Harriet called the girl Phillipa. Harriet proved very fertile, producing Tristram, William, Lawrence, Neville and Lorna over the next years. She did her bit to preserve Little Cormoran.

1845CE

I called a town meeting. Others have said I was like a religious leader when I was young, charismatic and brilliant. People followed me when I led. I didn't see myself that way, but still; we do have this town, and the Time Ball Tower, don't we? That I built myself, that I asked people to build with me.

The people sat with cups of tea and biscuits made by Harriet. I sat amongst them, because I wanted to converse, not to lecture.

"This is a good place to live," I began. "The best I've found. And yet there is a sense of the unfinished and I believe that is why we are fading."

I told them stories, weaving magic, then I unveiled a large drawing by Eugene, of the imagined, completed Time Ball Tower.

"Look on this. With the Time Ball Tower, we will be in control of the minutes, the hours, the days."

I talked about commerce, shipping and prosperity.

They cheered.

Such a moment. That room full of people, listening to me. We would build the Time Ball Tower. We would become a timely place to live.

We would become Tempuston. I did consider calling the town Tempustide, because Time and Tide Wait for No Man, but I think that was beyond the learning of most of the townspeople.

1850CE

As the Time Ball Tower grew, so did the rest of town. School was the most important thing, I had them understand. The Time Ball Tower for lives and routine; school for the future. We built a courthouse, where we sat to discuss the town's future. At the entrance, Harriet planted seeds that came from the cypress tree by Michelangelo's grave. She was always an admirer of that brilliant man. I myself know nothing of the artist, or indeed any art at all.

Perhaps that is the origin of her disdain towards poor me.

1857CE

The Time Ball Tower was completed in 1857. When the Ball dropped for the first time, there was great celebration.

The town loved our Time Ball Tower, liked the way it watched over us, providing us with a sense of place. It changed the very nature of the town. The ball dropping every day at five past one managed the passage of time; relentless, dripping on.

At first, young people traipsed out there to camp away from adults for a night or two. The school took a group out, expecting lessons to be learnt and great bonds to be made.

But the place was so unpleasant, so cold, and dark, the smell of the ocean rich and dank, that none lasted beyond a night. Some dreamed of a troll watching over them, drool dripping onto their blankets. Some found they couldn't swallow properly, that the air was so thick it was hard to breathe, or that their limbs stiffened. Others spoke of the ghost out there, a dark malevolence, the murderer starved to death.

Still others spoke of the smell of roses where no roses existed.

Harriet's daughter Lorna was one of the last to go out. She came back with nightmares that would never leave her, and she would never marry.

She blamed the tower for that. She said, "That place is only good for criminals of the worst kind."

Of the worst kind.

The seeds were sown.

Harriet heard a victim's mother saying, "Death is too good for him. Stealing my son and my family's future like that."

She began to collect evil as others collected sea shells.

When she had enough, she approached me with the idea of using the tower as a jail. Her husband, the local policemen, saw this as the greatest development in crime control since transportation.

1865CE

Harriet said, "We could fill a dozen Time Ball Towers."

"With whom?" Grace said. "Ordinary men? Or those preserved?"

Harriet had long been against preservation.

Grace said, "Why should I suffer more, when they most certainly should as well? And imagine confinement on top of this."

Harriet thought it was against God, but she would only whisper this opinion, not wanting to offend Grace.

Grace was not offended. She thought we should ensure the sun rose time and time again on these criminals. That they deserved blood guilt for eternity.

Grace's skin was flaking off, leaving another layer, red and sore. The town was scared of her; children sang songs about her and told ghost stories. Stories involving the Time Ball Tower, and how at night time she flew out there, leaving flakes of skin behind, and if you look out at midnight and see a face in the window, you'll die from the outside in until all that's left is a shriveled heart.

Because the sentence against an evil deed is not executed speedily, the heart of the children of man is fully set to do evil. Ecclesiastes 8:11

Grace took this to mean that the sentence or the punishment should be executed very, very slowly. She said, "If this doesn't give us license to perform the preservations, I don't know what does."

Eugene had no opinion either way; he barely understood what we were talking about.

With her husband a firm supporter, Harriet was finally persuaded that we should preserve the worst of the prisoners.

Between us all, we convinced the townspeople to assist.

People listened to Harriet. She made them feel younger, just to be around her. Time stopped with her.

1868CE

Three years later, we sent out our first long lifer. This was a man about whom nobody argued. "Consign him," they said without disagreement.

He called himself a drifter, but what he was was a thief and a killer. He called himself Wee Willie Winkie, and he'd told tired parents he could settle the children. We sleep well in this town, but it takes some time to train the children. He said he could teach them how to sleep, and he was a handsome man, his eyes bright blue, his hands large, his moustache neat under his nose. The women took to him as they did to anything new.

Harriet had three grandchildren, the newest only just born. She still had care of Grace, whom I rarely visited.

Wee Willie Winkie did run through the town.

Strangling our babies.

Why we trusted him is a mystery. We should have known; we should have seen the evil.

The babies slept and slept and slept until we saw what he'd done.

He didn't get far. The young men of the town were fast on the horses. They caught him and made him run behind them back to town, so his shoes were worn to the soles and it looked as if his flesh would drop off him.

Prison was too good for him. Death was too good for him. We didn't want him to find relief. We wanted him to suffer for eternity. There were many in government and business who supported us; we'd be paid well for our work.

"But Hell is suffering, isn't it? Eternal suffering," the local priest said. He was the last to be convinced.

"We wouldn't see him there. And if there is no Hell? And if he repents before he dies? He will not receive that suffering." Grace was determined.

"You have a choice," the judge told Wee Willie Winkie. "You can be put to death. Hung, here as we stand. In our own way. We hang you gently. No neck break, no quick death. Then we save you, give you ten minutes to recover, then hang you again. The man who endured this the longest lasted twenty-two hours. The shortest fifteen. Or we can give you something few men have had. Eternal life. But you'll spend it out there."

He pointed at the Time Ball Tower.

"I'll take the Time Ball Tower any day," Wee Willie Winkie said. His fingers flexing, strong, marked. There were tiny scratches on his wrists from those tiny, tiny fingernails.

Harriet and two other women led him away. We would not see the treatment; none but a few can know.

I was the first keeper. An honor I hold dear to this day.

1869CE

Before I left to attend the prisoner on the island, Harriet called for me. She said, "Grace wants to see us both. She has a request."

Grace was so light, so dry, if the room was darkened I would not have seen her.

"I'm tired," she said. "I feel as if I have seen my destiny, in that we will preserve evil men in the Time Ball Tower. I have passed my knowledge to Harriet." They exchanged glances here and I didn't understand why. I didn't like it when people exchanged glances and I was left out of it.

Grace took a breath every ten minutes. We didn't feed her anymore. She seemed quite peaceful, and certainly accepting.

Grace said, "I want you do to this thing, if you ever loved me. If you ever cared about me. You will need it if you are to keep watch over the prisoners over in the Time Ball Tower. We can't trust anyone else to do it."

Harriet poured something into a glass from a large jar. Even from where I stood, across the bed, it smelled bitter. It was a pale-yellow color, clear liquid below, with floating gobbets of what looked like clear, solidified fat. She passed the glass to me; I did not want to take it. The very look of it made me shudder.

"Please," Grace said. It took her a minute to say the word.

I loved them both so much. I wished to never lose them. That's how much I adored them.

"Please, drink it. For all that was Little Cormoran, all that is Tempuston, all we were and all we are now. For all you have created." Harriet said these words and I found it hard to say no to her. She had been with me from the beginning, supported me, helped this town to grow. Her children and grandchildren made it what it was; they were good people.

The first sip made me gag. The taste was of bile; bitter, irredeemable. The texture was liquid and solid, the gobbets of fat melting slightly on my tongue.

"Drink it all," Harriet said.

"What is it for?" A belated question which will give you to understand how much I adored these two women.

"For the future," she said. "To give you the ultimate power and strength to take us into the future. Drink it like a glass of milk. You drink yours, and I'll drink mine, and we'll be together."

I drank it all.

I would never, ever, be able to eat or drink anything again without that texture, that flavor in my mouth. Even now, the thought would bring bile, if I still produced such.

I slept for three days solid, woke hungry and thirsty. I could eat hard biscuits; they dissolved slowly and seemed to digest well. And beer. I loved beer. I thought it filled my blood with fire. I liked fire.

I felt okay at first, on the inside, but my body dried out, and it creaked at times. The noise upset people; they stared at me as I moved. Became impatient with my slowness.

I lost very little as far as power; truly they listened to me more. I'd threaten to tell their great-great-grandchildren some home truths, "I'll let them know about the sort of person you are," I said and that would keep them honest.

The worst thing was knowing my ladies had done this to me deliberately. I considered insisting Harriet join me, as she had promised, but I did not, in all honesty, want to spend eternity with her.

And no matter what else, I did not wish this suffering on her.

I told Harriet, "I would not have done this to you. Better you should let me die."

I wasn't sure that was an option for me, now. Grace, meanwhile, Grace was tired and wanted to go. I asked how this would be managed, but Harriet didn't answer for me.

I did consider speeding things along for her, as I had Edna, but I didn't want to go through that again.

Harriet brought three of her grandchildren to visit me and their voices were high-pitched and hurt my ears. She had this horrible habit of chittering away, clicking her tongue, disapproving.

I could not wait for the isolation of the tower.

No, the worst thing of all was that Grace was gone. She was gone, when I would have kept her forever, kept her safe and near to me.

She was passed beyond.

I rowed myself to the Time Ball Tower, where I stayed for a few short months when I had planned to stay forever. Too short. My time was cut short because they needed me on dry land. They sent three men to replace me; Jackson Sheward being the best of them.

Three men, I often said. Three for one.

And still they couldn't manage.

Burnett Barton

Jackson Sheward: The Time Ball Tower Keeper's Report 1869

There is rhythm in our town. The great tick-tock. On dry land the tower looms over us from the island, and we are always of the tick-tock. We are aware of each day passing, the ball dropping, each day.

We are good men. We three. And yet two have gone, refusing to return after shore leave, leaving me here, amongst the filth and the evil and the sound of that ball dropping, dropping, dropping.

They talk of a dark hole of obsession and sadness.

I am stalwart.

Jackson Sheward

Tristram Barton: The Time Ball Tower Keeper's Report 1872

These precious criminals. Lucky creatures, to live forever. Oh, the things they'll see. All thanks to our sacrifices.

Jackson Sheward finished his year damaged. Changed forever. Suffering from Soldier's Heart, you might say.

This will not happen to me.

My mother Harriet begged me not to go, but I said to her, where would we be? If you hadn't traveled from England and from Perth, been brave?

She is much loved in our town.

She was much loved. She's gone, and Burnett Barton is back. People tell me this makes sense; God's Will, but I do not see it this way.

She'll be sadly missed. But her sacrifice will not be wasted.

Tristram Barton

John Barton: The Time Ball Tower Keeper's Report 1873

Ah, time. How we live by it, adore it, abhor it. My brother Tristram was a most decisive man. A man willing to make sacrifices for the greater good and sacrifice he did, out there on the rocks.

Time has passed since then. I hear the tower calling, as many of us do. Some say to my very face that I am saved by going out there; that I would be a criminal without it, because I have no wife or child. I have no true friends. I have no mother left, and my father is a man lost in his thoughts.

They do not know; all my life this has been my ideal. If our mother had not left us (gone where? We do not know), Lawrence, the brother-in-between, would not have stayed home, insisting on watching for her.

So, I am here.

Fateful, perhaps.

We landed on the rocks at five to one, and we sat in our small vessel until the ball dropped. The water rose, I imagined, but the boatman told me no.

I knew what we would find; my poor dead brother. I did not know his circumstance and it was shocking to my very heart and core. I will not forget it; not ever.

There he was, at the base of the stairs.

His neck clearly broken.

His body black with decay.

Oh, my dear dead boy.

The boatman took him away, and I began my work.

I would have stayed forever, if the gout hadn't got me.

I kept my agony quiet, refused shore leave more than once, and by the time I owned up to it, my legs had to be amputated and that was it. I was back on dry land and there I'd stay.

No one could say I did not do my duty. And I think I spent the time worthily.

One oddity; I thought I saw my other brother. Not the ghost of the dead one but Lawrence, the one living, who stayed at home to watch for our mother.

He would not come, surely?

That would not be right.

John Barton

Horace Ross: The Time Ball Tower Keeper's Report 1874

I'm seeing things. It must be the dust.

Horace Ross

Allan Brennan: The Time Ball Tower Keeper's Report 1875

I see my wife and children on the shore.
Waving.
They are with another man, I think.
Are they with another man?

Allan Brennan

Charles Butler: The Time Ball Tower Keeper's Report 1876

Such a year I've had. No man could ever have the learning I have had.

Charles Butler

Nate Staunton: The Time Ball Tower Keeper's Report 1877

All should question what we do. Few will doubt that this suffering is deserved.

I have read their files. There is no doubt of their guilt. Wee Willie Winkie is pure evil. Beside him sits Robert Freidel, who murdered children and sent vials of their blood to their parents.

The prisoners whine to me, "We are innocent! We are wrongly accused!" They speak so slowly that sometimes the meaning is almost lost, but the whining tone is familiar. I can easily ignore their entreaties; I have children at home who whine and whine without relent and my hearing is selective.

They'll say, "Your children need you," or say I've hurt them, try to make me believe I've killed my own children. Beware their weasel words.

They question my routine, trying to undermine me. "You haven't done such and such yet. Out of order! Out of order!"

But I knew very well what I had and had not done. They could not send me spare that easily.

I have fifteen evil sacks of poison blood in my care. Uneducated swill. They deserve their punishment.

I moved amongst the prisoners, replacing candle wicks with these new ones. We were not obliged to provide them with evening light, but there could be a time when I am delayed, and I would not want to walk amongst them in the dark.

"We are starved," one creaked. I understood who he was. Wee Willie Winkie, the famous killer. He's been here eight years. He's thirty-six and he looks ninety. He looks like our very own Burnett Barton. Wee Willie Winkie was twenty-eight when they did him, not long preserved so the work must have been hard, at the beginning, just to contain him.

I tossed candle stumps to them. "Lighthouse keepers eat those if they're hungry enough. That will do you, too."

I sunk my teeth gently into one, just to know; there was an unpleasant give and a taste redolent of the Sunday roast on Wednesday.

"We're so hungry," the man I call the Councilor cried at me. Their voices are like the creak of a gate, almost identical to the gate of my childhood home, and so hearing it raises my spirit because it meant Father was home, or some other kind of visitor. I do not remember a time when that gate brought unpleasantness, but then I have been a lucky man with little to test me.

Irritable group of blaggards they are.

I lit the oil lamps, pondering as I sometimes did, the nature of preserving men such as these rather than one like Edward Heming, a great performer in bringing the oil lamp to prominence. I take a look at the suffering and understand that no man can continue to be an appraised member of society under such circumstances.

It took them a week, but they sucked the fat off those candles, leaving the wick behind.

I slept a lot. We do sleep a lot, in our town.

When they say sleepy town, it's different in Tempuston. We sleep for our lives. We know the benefits; we know how much longer you'll live if you sleep well every night. At the Club (many thanks to John Barton for setting that up for us), we nap quite happily, company or no.

If you see ghosts out and about, ignore them. Some would say they are the hauntings of the men who died building this Time Ball Tower, sixteen in all, though you could say thirty-five if you included the influenza the others came down with.

I say these ghosts are only the evil of those men made manifest and best ignored.

I spent my time talking of the outside world, letting them know all they'd missed. All the things I'd done, the things I'd seen. My children and their voices whining or otherwise, and the soft touch of my wife's hair.

I could bring them to tears with a few words. This is worth remembering. I did not intend to be cruel, and it didn't strike me until I was home again and my wife castigated me for this.

I said, "While the action may have been cruel, my intention was not. Does that still make me cruel?"

The way I tell it is the way it is, because history is written, and re-written, by the survivor.

Nate Staunton

Sam Stewart: The Time Ball Tower Keeper's Report 1878

Nate Staunton is a man of vivid imaginations. I might call him Dickens, I think. I will call him WhattheDickens.

That's what I'll call him.

Sam Stewart

William Webster: The Time Ball Tower Keeper's Report 1879

It's better than being at war. But these things. These things. They'd make a newborn baby feel the guilt.

William Webster

Alexander Manning: The Time Ball Tower Keeper's Report 1880

I spend my time staring into the prisoners' eyes. Work has been done to show that images can be captured in the retina. More usually it is the eyes of the dead examined by researchers but perhaps?

Imagine that.

If all your bad deeds. All your evil. Would be captured in your very vision itself.

Alexander Manning

Percy McCarty: The Time Ball Tower Keeper's Report 1881

On one thing we agree; there is evil elsewhere in the world. The very President of the United States, murdered at a railway station. Assassination is not new, but it does not make it any less shocking.

Nor does it make these prisoners any less deserving.

Percy McCarty

Stephen Moore: The Time Ball Tower Keeper's Report 1882

I like to call them The Bones. I have twenty-five men in my care; twenty-five bones, if you like. Each one worse than the last, and I can only imagine what suffering they wreaked on dry land. This one is a cannibal. He still talks of it. That one committed acts so abhorrent I wish my ears were deafened. I would give up hearing for life, to not hear him speak.

But. But. Can we keep them long enough for repentance? If they live long enough, they may be in a position to ask the Lord God for forgiveness, and we will have saved twenty-five souls from the devil. Perhaps the angel Gabriel will take them from us. Who can say?

We can do no more than that, as Burnett says.

Skin and bones, most of them. Slow as mockery and twice as vicious.

I carried *Bleak House, Dombey and Son, The Old Curiosity Shop. Sketches by Boz*, as well. Burnett Barton ensured I was well supplied.

Grief never mended no broken bones. That's Charles Dickens, in *Sketches by Boz*.

And bones never mended no grief, either.

I came here full of grief.

Distance will help, they told me, when they recruited me for the job on the mainland. Shanghaied, more like. As if I can stand separate from what lies within.

I am haunted by memory of my lost tiny one. The sight of the children seeking mussels on the shore fills me with bitter regret.

With my binoculars I can see them, boys with shorts or pants rolled up, tiny girls with skirts tucked up in bloomers. The older girls on the shore, watching, I think, with nostalgia for this lost freedom. How we steal from ourselves small choices. How constrained we are, how tight are our nooses.

I am weak. A coward, for all my war record. My daughter thrust out into the world with a great roar, but that was the most we ever heard from her, as if she used up all she had in that moment. We had five gentle years together, although the pain of our daughter in pain…and the knowledge that she would not reach maturity, she wouldn't live life's full gifts… As she lay dying, her mother begged for Preservation, to keep her alive. But how could I do such a thing? She will blame me into the afterlife as I will myself.

Why did I travel to Perth for business that week? Why did I go? Because the doctor assured me she was no nearer to the end than she was last week or would be next week. My wife insisted we needed the money, to buy comforts to ease our daughter's pain and sorrow. I was so pleased she was speaking to me, I would have agreed to almost anything.

Five days I was away from my beautiful girls. I bought gifts galore because away from them I think of them even more. Other men mocked me for my devotions. I pity such fellows.

On my return, I dearly anticipated my daughter on her chair in our front garden where she sat each and every day, with her mother or friends who came by with treats and stories to cheer her. She wasn't there and at first I was pleased, thinking she was out with friends, enjoying herself. That somehow she had recovered her youth and strength.

That was not the case.

My wife's handwriting was a beautiful thing to behold and a source of great pride to her. The letter she left for me (I found it first, before I found them) was in that beautiful hand. Yet uglier words were never written.

"I cannot bear her pain anymore. I will not take the laudanum I gave to her, though. I don't deserve that easy release.

"We are both in God's Hands."

I do hope so. My daughter, of course. But my wife committed two mortal sins and is therefore probably elsewhere.

I blame my distress for the mistake I made in the Tower. If I had my chance again, I would tell my charges, these remnants of human decency, nothing of meaning. Take this from me; tell them nothing they can use against you. I was lonely, desperately so, and they drew out of me my terrible story of loss.

One night, I heard the voice of my daughter, calling, "Father, Father don't let her do it, please Father, I want to live," her sweet voice asking me for treats, *open the windows*, she asked for air and for food, but only when I had crawled on my hands and knees towards the voice, too distraught to walk, my tears so salty and numerous the cracked skin on my cheeks gave me pain, did I realize it was the prisoners, the bones, calling out so cruelly to me.

"He believes in ghosts, the innocent!"

I made the further error of defending Dickens, dead these twelve years, saying, "He speaks the truth. He knows how to express the pain of a lost child because he'd lost both child and sibling as I had."

They took that advantage. They drew it out of me like leeches.

I call them The Bones.

Nobody should come here to forget sorrow, but somehow, at night, every night, I dream that history is rewritten. That my wife and daughter wait for me at home and that it was all a terrible dream.

This is reality.

I said as much to Lawrence Barton, who came to relieve me for a while, although perhaps he was not supposed to, having never been a keeper. He spent time in solitude, down in the basement where I choose not to go. Cleaning up, he said. Such a good man.

There always needs to be a cleaner.

Much as I have loved my time here, I can't wait to see my wife and daughter.

Stephen Moore

J.C. Harcourt: The Time Ball Tower Keeper's Report 1883

I wish Lawrence Barton would visit me, too. These prisoners are not enough company. All they have to talk about is their terrible crimes, and all I have to tell them is more crimes and more.

"Did you hear about William Gouldstone?" I ask them, "One of your lot. Wouldn't be surprised if he ends up here. Killed all five of his kiddies, drowning and hammering, every last one, and said he was a good man for the doing."

Do you know they all shifted over, as if making room for William Gouldstone? A good man would not assent like this lot did.

J. C. Harcourt

Freddie Heath: The Time Ball Tower Keeper's Report 1884

The one we call the Mayor because it makes him cry to think of what he lost. This man systematically murdered every member of his isolated village one, by one, by one, by one, before transporting himself to Australia.

He tells me, every day, of the death of another. He has not forgotten a single one.

Freddie Heath

Thomas Bunting: The Time Ball Tower Keeper's Report 1885

The executioner still has family ashore. You can hear them singing on a clear night. They still believe he killed correctly under the auspices of law.

His thumbs. Long, and thick, twice the size of mine at least. So strong they can stop a pulse.

He has done this.

He could stop the pulse of a sweet young teacher, or perhaps a shop girl gone missing.

I have stopped him now. He will not use those thumbs again. The crack as they broke is one of the sweetest sounds I have ever heard.

Thomas Bunting

George Parsons: The Time Ball Tower Keeper's Report 1886

Bunting did a bit of damage all right.
I don't blame him, though.
Don't blame him at all.

George Parsons

Ned James: The Time Ball Tower Keeper's Report 1887

My grandfather built this place. He always was a solid man. Died when I was nine but had already made an impression. He'd take me out in the brightest part of the day and have me look out.

"See that?" he'd say. "That's our troll. While we look after him, he looks after us. But let the tower fall and he will need to be reckoned with."

I get out here to find it's all illusion. A stain.

Doesn't mean I don't keep the place maintained, though.

Ned James

Jack Barnes: The Time Ball Tower Keeper's Report 1888

You'd think they'd be used it by now. You'd think I'd be used to it. My small house, right on the shore, rowdy as all get out, so you know I'm used to the noise. But I hear chitterings and unimaginable things. These prisoners do all they can to disconcert me. Making me hear things in the night.

Jack Barnes

John Sheward: The Time Ball Tower Keeper's Report 1889

It is a pleasant thing to be fêted, and something I could get used to. Mostly, it's the victim's families, who thank us, who give us gifts, who give us many favors. They would love to see the suffering up close, but good enough are the stories we can tell on return.

Should they be keepers? It seems not.

Even the best people are capable of revenge.

John Sheward

David Hennessy: The Time Ball Tower Keeper's Report 1890

Such big boots to fill and here my feet the size of a twelve-year-old's. Is that any reason to take on this job? To make myself seem larger than I am? My great-grandmother Harriet would have wanted this, had she been here.

It's as good a reason as any other.

We stood, the boatman and I, on the shore. I had boxes and packages galore; *did others have such a load?* I asked. I never want to do out of the ordinary.

Every man is different, he told me. He was a quiet one on most days, but today he seemed loquacious, as if trying to fill me with words as sustenance.

He rowed out with his back to the Time Ball Tower, leaving me with the vision ever approaching.

"What is that? All up the side, tall as a giant, full of color? It looks like a stain, as if someone has thrown a rotten bowl of meat and fruit against the wall."

I could make out no features.

"That is a troll. Painted by the builder who believed in such things." He shook his head at me as if surprised by my ignorance. Yet I have kept myself away all my life, deliberately, wanting this experience fresh.

He did not turn around to look, and as we neared I understood the reason. Such malevolence! Such anger and bitterness painted into the features!

"What did the painter hope to scare away with this?" I asked, but the boatman did not respond.

Each man is different indeed. Many do not feel the need to make a good report. Others cannot do so because of circumstances, such John Sheward, whose life ended in tragedy. The boatman set out with him on a clear, bright morning. Yet somehow they capsized, too far out for rescue.

The shattered boat washed to shore by the tide, but their bodies were never found.

Some children claimed they saw a troll reach out and grab the boat, tipping the men out, then plucking them out of the water to eat.

Long scratch marks down the side of the row boat lent power to their story, and that's why you'll hear it well into the future, I'm sure. All we have of Sheward's report are the notes he left behind in the tower.

Some keepers make you feel small with gloriousness of their reports. You feel as if you couldn't match their words.

Stephen Moore, 1882, now, was a social reformer. Came back from the Tower determined to do good works, and did, until his ticker gave out. He established a food kitchen in the streets of Sydney, ensuring that no child who came to his door went unfed. Old Eugene Barton was his greatest helper until the end. There is much to read between the lines in Moore's report. He talks of his dreams and how he imagined the deaths of his wife and child. There is barely concealed anger in this, and of course terrible grief, and guilt as well. He felt as if he caused their deaths by his absence and he loses touch with the truth. He knows they are dead, but he doesn't at the same time. They all re-write history to suit themselves. History should be set in stone, as is, done is done. Beware the nature of the tower; the real may seem un-real before long.

There were plenty of cleaning rags in the Time Ball Tower. All had a touch of grease to them, a sense of filth I have not seen, even on the streets of Sydney, even in the poorhouses. Using sand as an abrasive, I tried to remove the troll from the side, but there was nothing I could do. Instead, I outlined it in charcoal, thinking at least to define its edges. Perhaps we can contain it this way.

As for the men; if we consider them less than human, then we will find our lives far easier. If we tell them nothing of ourselves, they will have nothing to use against us.

They are capable of so little and yet still, one managed to smother another, fill his mouth with sawdust, hold his nose.

I blame myself. I could not bear to be near them so left them alone for days at a time.

I recommend solitary confinement for all, ongoing.

David Hennessy

Carl Potts: The Time Ball Tower Keeper's Report 1891

"The Mayor" tells me I should find a wife. He tells me we have ladies here, all I need to do is sniff them out.

I like a quiet one. I like one who has the sense to know who has the sense.

Too many of the ladies in our town take after the ladies who founded the town, those ladies like Harriet Barton who were so big for their boots you'd think they were giants.

Then there are the ladies who pack the baskets, who send the provisioning once a month. Sweet treats. Oranges. Little notes from them, and dried flowers, and all the best produce.

Such kindness makes a man weep.

Carl Potts

Robert Deeming: The Time Ball Tower Keeper's Report 1892

I couldn't spend a year without clocks! I bought two dozen with me and I've placed them with the prisoners.

They beg me daily to stop the ticking and I say, I can stop the ticking, but I cannot stop time.

I take great satisfaction in that.

Robert Deeming

Alfred Merton: The Time Ball Tower Keeper's Report 1893

The Executioner convinced me to make a list. He says he'll get to them, one by one if I set him free. He'll do it as a favor to me; a reward.

He is well past any real violence, but his intent remains. Is it wrong of me to enjoy our discussions?

Alfred Merton

Stephen Cooke: The Time Ball Tower Keeper's Report 1894

Move them around so they don't become too familiar. Shift them into each other's spaces and puddles.

Stephen Cooke

Willie Muskett: The Time Ball Tower Keeper's Report 1895

The creak of the door as I rose early one morning alerted me to the possibility there was another in the tower. Not likely, of course, but women have been known to venture out and I admit I would be delighted to simply touch the soft skin of a woman's inner arm.

I did venture downstairs to investigate, but all I saw was a small disturbance in the dust, and all I heard was the soft slap of oars on water. By the time I climbed the stairs to look out, I could see nothing at all.

Willie Muskett

Michael Dyer: The Time Ball Tower Keeper's Report 1896

A new prisoner. This one says he is Franciso Lopez, a man described as "a monster without parallel. A man whose name will live in infamy."

Of course, he is nothing of the sort, all gossip aside. He is a man who killed many, most certainly. But he has no name.

He has no place in history.

Michael Dyer

MILES BARTON: THE TIME BALL TOWER KEEPER'S REPORT 1897

There is a woman they call a witch, but this inappropriately lessens her evil. Calling a woman a "witch" takes away her power, I believe.

My ancestor Harriet was called a witch sometimes. She had sharp opinions. After she ran away, her husband was angry, wouldn't hear a good word about her. Being the chief policeman, he carried a fair bit of weight in the town, and he could make true whatever he wanted.

Miles Barton

Thomas Penfold: The Time Ball Tower Keeper's Report 1898

Some days the tower feels far colder than it should. I shiver in my bed although I have eight blankets piled heavy.

These are the days, I think, when the troll is stretching, reaching around the tower to touch his own fingertips.

Thomas Penfold

Phillip Ross: The Time Ball Tower Keeper's Report 1899

Tick tock tock tick tick tock and the ball drops and the ball drops and the ball drops. Such beauty in the time pieces.

Phillip Ross

Logan Brennan: The Time Ball Tower Keeper's Report 1900

You can know an evil man by the hardness of his heart. A man who has no kindness, no joy in him.

Logan Brennan

Ben Butler: The Time Ball Tower Keeper's Report 1901

I took delivery of a new prisoner, one Anne Elizabeth Graham. Baby Farmer. Forty-two tiny bodies found buried in her backyard, eighteen near-dead babies inside her house. The descriptions in the popular press of their conditions would make a grown man cry.

She arrived preserved, but still full of spit and vigor. A diet of pure tallow and some time in the box will soon settle her, as will leg irons and as many indignities as I can lay upon her.

My only regret is the entertainment the other prisoners take from her punishment. I turn their faces away, or I carry her to another part of the Time Ball Tower, but that does not help. Still better it is for her fall to be witnessed. Her suffering compounded, I hope, by the shame she must feel on them watching.

They'd kill her if I gave them the chance. We've got them all so isolated, though. Only together rarely.

Ben Butler

Roland Staunton: The Time Ball Tower Keeper's Report 1902

It was quiet on shore as I departed. So many of the families have gone, moved away. Families of the prisoners, with the connection lost, little to tie them anymore except tradition. They stay for many years and then they go.

In one of my monthly deliveries of fresh food, I found notes folded into tiny shapes, addressed to the prisoners.

I took great pleasure in throwing them out onto the rocks. Why should these foul bags of bones receive notes from home when I do not?

Roland Staunton

Walter Harcourt: The Time Ball Tower Keeper's Report 1903

The chief of police saw me off personally. That is quite something, isn't it? They are the men with power.

This is what I will have when I return.

Walter Harcourt

Monk Heath: The Time Ball Tower Keeper's Report 1904

A short visit to the Keepers' Club. Marvelous! Absolutely marvelous. Worth a year out here just for membership, in my opinion. Such good people there, such support. A place to call home away from home.

Monk Heath

John Bunting: The Time Ball Tower Keeper's Report 1905

The others talk of tick tock, I talk of click click. There is a certain vision a photographer has that others do not. A certain understanding of timing, of exposure, an acceptance of these things.

A photographer must understand the nature of cruelty. A photographer must be cold, or the subject can be lost.

John Bunting

Joshua Parsons: The Time Ball Tower Keeper's Report 1906

"Who's there?" the prisoners call out, "who is it, who is there?"
They are trying to cause a disturbance and I won't be listening to them.

Joshua Parsons

Marshall James: The Time Ball Tower Keeper's Report 1907

The Black Widow married men still in their teens and murdered them. For blood? She never said. She says that this place was built on blood, that my granddaddy sacrificed actual human babies to ensure it keeps standing.

She also says I'm more handsome than any of her other husbands, more charming, cleverer.

It is lonely here, I'll say that.

And she is more than willing.

I will not love her, though. That would not be right.

Marshall James

Ray Bailes: The Time Ball Tower Keeper's Report 1908

These things barely have a pulse. A heart. They are barely alive, barely human. Like stone. They fascinate me with their slow blinking eyes, their begging, pathetic words. They are close to insanity from solitude and they are irrational. I decided to move them back together; they are more manageable that way.

I hung one of them upside down through the window. A traveling sales-man, took his own daughter with and sold her as they went along. Picked up another, sold her. Didn't care what happened to each of them. Laughed about how many "daughters" he'd had. I could not bring myself to make him suffer minute for minute what his victims suffered. Even after just twelve hours, his head was suffused with an awful pus that seemed to squeeze out of his ears and drip onto the rocks. His moans became so disturbing that I relented and pulled him in. He was blind as a bat anyway.

Others who follow should attempt longer periods of observation.

Also, the woman. There are certain investigations underway with her and again I encourage all who follow to proceed with such.

So many decisions to make every day. And some of them larger than others.

Ray Bailes

Oscar Sheward: The Time Ball Tower Keeper's Report 1909

Many of the prisoners had no family, of course. They slaughtered the lot of them.

Oscar Sheward

Aiden Hennessy: The Time Ball Tower Keeper's Report 1910

The traveling salesman asks me if I'll ever have a child. He says, "You'll never be loved like a child loves you. You can't even imagine the beauty of unconditional love."

I think of his daughters, all those poor young girls. Some of them never found.

I'm kind to him, though, and I talk to him, because, one by one, he tells me where he sold them, and sometimes to whom.

At least the girls can be saved.

Aiden Hennessy

Morrison Webster: The Time Ball Tower Keeper's Report 1911

From the work of Aiden Hennessy, three girls were found and saved. This is something to remember. Not that these prisoners can be redeemed; that will never happen. But that, perhaps, they can give us information. They can help us to help the victims or understand evil.

Prisoner Thirteen has no right hand. He says he lost it in the Congo, a victim of the truly horrendous Leopold II, who insisted on seeing right hands to account for bullets. Of course, Prisoner Thirteen said, in order to save on bullets, or to steal bullets, the soldiers would cut off the hands of people they hadn't murdered.

He thinks we don't know. That he was one of the soldiers, responsible for many deaths. That he cut off his own right hand to try to prove his innocence.

Morrison Webster

Rufus James: The Time Ball Tower Keeper's Report 1912

When my grandfather, Michael James, built this Time Ball Tower, he expected that it would make our family famous. That there would be a family tradition of engineers, and that we would be known throughout the world. Like Christopher Wren or Robert Adam. He told me much about the place and its nooks and crannies.

I would not have liked to see the prisoners when they were first preserved. They would have been more solid, then. Louder. They would have looked more like men and less like husks. They're not a happy bunch. They were given the choice, life imprisonment or eternal life. They chose eternal life. But were they shown the results? Did they see our own Burnett Barton? Did they talk to a man who's been given the treatment, see what he thought of it?

Yet husks they are, and husks they remain.

And yet. Inside.

Inside, they carry a heart of stone.

SUMMARY OF CONDITIONS: I found the prisoners to be well nourished and of sound mind. Prisoners bathed successfully. Prisoners appeared distressed on waking and have trouble sleeping. Prisoners experienced dry skin, chronic pain and halitosis.

All normal for this report.

Rufus James

Hitchens Manning: The Time Ball Tower Keeper's Report 1913

They used to get gifts from women, too. Crazy bitches who fell in love with them. They'd send proposals of marriage and other stuff. Underwear. Nude photos. Shit like that. These days, the prisoners are too far from human. No one falls in love with them now.

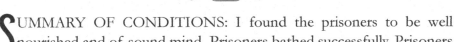

SUMMARY OF CONDITIONS: I found the prisoners to be well nourished and of sound mind. Prisoners bathed successfully. Prisoners appeared distressed on waking and have trouble sleeping. Prisoners experienced dry skin, chronic pain and halitosis.

All normal for this report.

Hitchens Manning

Spencer Harcourt: The Time Ball Tower Keeper's Report 1914

It's a beautiful thing and I shall not question it: the appearance of the whisky bottle on my kitchen table.

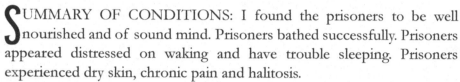

SUMMARY OF CONDITIONS: I found the prisoners to be well nourished and of sound mind. Prisoners bathed successfully. Prisoners appeared distressed on waking and have trouble sleeping. Prisoners experienced dry skin, chronic pain and halitosis.

All normal for this report.

Spencer Harcourt

Porter Heath: The Time Ball Tower Keeper's Report 1915

There are those who fight and die for the greater good. But who is to say what that greater good is?

Better to be here, keeping these prisoners confined. Than there.

SUMMARY OF CONDITIONS: I found the prisoners to be well nourished and of sound mind. Prisoners bathed successfully. Prisoners appeared distressed on waking and have trouble sleeping. Prisoners experienced dry skin, chronic pain and halitosis.

All normal for this report.

Porter Heath

Warren Bailes: The Time Ball Tower Keeper's Report 1916

I could vaguely see the charcoal outline of the troll but didn't get to it myself. Superstition never helped a soul. Why should I follow a tradition that only helps me to be cold and wet with all that outdoor work?

Mr. James, the builder, thought the troll would act like a gargoyle to scare off the evil spirits. It began as an error, a flaw in the building that stretched from the ground up, and from afar it became clear this was a menacing mistake. I remember how the painting disturbed him; he couldn't imagine he had such horror within him. I say the tower is a giant: great and powerful.

My brother was here in 1908, but he has spoken little about his time. His report shows how stretched he was. With war work looming over us, I worry about him more than most others. He has a delicate soul, more than any woman I have known. I cannot even imagine how he survived out here, and sometimes I think perhaps he didn't. That these men, over the decades, these women, have developed a method of taking one's body. Filling themselves into the corners of it and animating it that way, with very little of the original inhabitant left. Certainly we all return more bad-tempered than when we arrived.

It's the noises, for me. Things that can't be explained.

SUMMARY OF CONDITIONS: I found the prisoners to be well nourished and of sound mind. Prisoners bathed successfully. Prisoners appeared distressed on waking and have trouble sleeping. Prisoners

experienced dry skin, chronic pain and halitosis.
All normal for this report.

Warren Bailes

Rossiter Styles: The Time Ball Tower Keeper's Report 1917

Here I am at last, at last. Waited so long, and all I've seen, and all I've loved, all the world I've known.

I should have come at eighteen, but if I had, would I have met my lovely Ruby Bailes? She would have been a tiny child then and I perhaps would have given her a toy, a ball and a chuck on the chin.

The cruel, the envious, will say I am far from the best man. That I only got in because all the good men are at war.

Ruby's brothers are all gone to war. I do feel the weight of guilt upon me. I am so grateful to be here, to love my Ruby.

But then she knows it is up to her to carry on. I dream of our babies sweet in their cot and I glimpse the future. Generations of us, just as Burnett wishes.

There were plenty of us, all right. My cousins numbered twenty-eight, many of them with children. There was no sign of my family dying out.

Yes, I was twenty-seven, well beyond the years of usual keeperdom. But you could say I was young at heart. Never to know the suffering of war, because the Lord saw fit to make me unsuited for all that. But I kept at them and at them.

And thus, I met my lovely Ruby.

Tiny, tiny thing, so small she had to wear weights in her shoes to stop her floating away, people said.

Ruby was home from school for the holidays and felt the isolation more intensely than ever. She hated her home, hated her responsibilities, hated the shadow of the Time Ball Tower hanging over the whole town. Her father had talked to her about the possibility of going in herself, taking the place of the brothers gone to war, and she had stood screaming for a full ten minutes before she could settle.

I had admired her young girl's spirit for some time. Never in a romantic way because of her age. I'm not like that. I knew I wouldn't stand by and have her forced into the Time Ball Tower. Not when I so very much wanted to go myself.

"We prefer to keep it in the family," I was told.

"I fully intend to become family when the time is right," I responded.

Ruby never told me how she felt at that moment, but I hope she understood how deep and respectful my admiration was.

Ruby called me a very dear man for stepping forward. "So many of our men are lost, and they were going to make me go into the Time Ball Tower," she said, her head on my shoulder.

What will I be like when I return? Her brothers were different. Stronger, I think, prouder, more powerful, and judging by the lady attention they received, more attractive, too.

None of it saved them, did it? All lost in that war.

We've never seen a keeper come back unchanged. I don't want to change. I want to stay me.

The prisoners found out about my lack of a war record and my shame in such.

I tried to go to war. I am no coward. The recruiters took me on against their better judgment, pure desperation, but I slipped and fell on boarding the crew ship, breaking my arm and collarbone and a bang on the head needing monitoring.

Didn't the medics hate me for wasting their time! Fix me up only to send me back home.

Pure fortune. That fall meant I could take the place of my dear beauty Ruby on the Time Ball Tower.

The prisoners found out I didn't fight in the war and tried to use this against me. They love to find weakness.

They didn't know how much I'd endured. How much cruelty. All they could do was not enough.

As far from human as they are, they still have power. And yet they are weakened by loneliness, by stillness and boredom, and by the silence they live with.

Tell them stories. Play 1001 nights, draw it out, draw them in, make them want to see you and hear you, and then they will not try to destroy you.

Frightening them with ghost stories keeps them quiet for a while, but it also seems to make them restless at night.

First thing I did when I got to shore was go to Ruby.

It was nearly her sixteenth birthday. She had been begging my father to let her go away to university, to learn something. She knew I would understand. I knew she wanted to live a life, not eke out an existence.

"You do look handsome, far more handsome than I'd remembered," she said, nervous as a fawn. I made silly jokes, lots of funny little animal jokes.

What do you call a sad bird?

A bluebird!

What's small and cuddly and bright purple?

A koala holding his breath!

What happens when a cat eats a lemon?

It becomes a sour puss!

Why are elephants wrinkled?

Have you ever tried to iron one?

Why do elephants never forget?

Because nobody ever tells them anything.

She was doing well in school. The headmistress recommended she attend Sydney University to study medicine. But what to do? She couldn't be a doctor and a wife and mother all, could she?

I clarified things for her. I said, "Women can affect the world around them. But only in close proximity. If they try to go beyond that, they waste their talents. It is in the home, the village, that women can make a difference. Do you want to make a difference? Do you want to bring children into this world who could help to make it a better place, or do you want to be a "professional," loved by no one? Admired, perhaps. But I have seen that world. And there is no respect for women there."

I said we should marry. Have our children early. Then we would travel to a place where she could study and become a doctor, too. I would support her. So we married.

The only dissenting voice was one Henry Penfold, a foolish fellow who thought that Ruby was his.

Of course, I promised such things. The lies men tell! Look at poor Harriet and the dreadful Phillip. How poorly he used her, to hear Burnett tell.

My beautiful Ruby, baby growing inside her! People say she is so tiny, her stomach will tip her forwards! How do you carry the weight, they ask her, as if her baby was a burden.

"She's stronger than she looks," Ruby's mother told all those busybodies. Her mother often did not notice much, so sunk she was in grief for her sons, and how could we judge her for that? She looks at Ruby sometimes, as if surprised she is still alive.

They put so much onus on this child of mine we are expecting. It comes from such a line; from the woman Harriet, who the ladies idolize. I hope I will be a good father. And if Ruby does not become a doctor herself (and in all honesty she will not), at least we will name our child for one.

SUMMARY OF CONDITIONS: I found the prisoners to be well nourished and of sound mind. Prisoners bathed successfully. Prisoners appeared distressed on waking and have trouble sleeping. Prisoners

experienced dry skin, chronic pain and halitosis.

All normal for this report.

Rossiter Styles

HENRY PENFOLD: THE TIME BALL TOWER KEEPER'S REPORT 1918

He never wrote it. Rossiter. Can't read, can't write. Had his lady write it down. If ever there was one too good for another, it was them, for all his striding about town, handing out instructions.

He didn't write it. As ever, he let someone else do the hard work. And it killed her. We all blame him for Ruby's death.

"Weak as shit," the Executioner told me. "Weakest piece of shit we've had out here."

I told them they could have had Ruby. I said,

"You've never seen a woman with a brighter glow than that lovely creature. Anyone who met her adored her. And that…that…"

"…shit," the Executioner said.

"That shit was the one who married her. By some miracle he did the job required. Can you imagine how beautiful her baby would have been?"

"Tell us how babies are made," the Baby Farmer said. "Go on."

And I did, to take my mind off Ruby and how she didn't live to see the new year or hear her newborn daughter cry. How we had to watch that fool, that Rossiter, present his girl as if he'd created her alone.

He called her Frances, after Dorothy Frances Gray, the first female dentist. His one and only child.

At least at the Tower I could cry. Because I loved her too and I would have kept her alive.

SUMMARY OF CONDITIONS: I found the prisoners to be well nourished and of sound mind. Prisoners bathed successfully. Prisoners appeared distressed on waking and have trouble sleeping. Prisoners

experienced dry skin, chronic pain and halitosis.
All normal for this report.

Henry Penfold

Walter Bunting: The Time Ball Tower Keeper's Report 1919

Pencil knife fork rolled up paper stick stone fingernail clipping toenail clipping no bacon rind for fear of stench wool straps seagull feather egg shell cigarette butt match stick dried tea leaves china doll arm washed up at shore piece of shoe suitcase handle fishing net fishing line tin can label hair ribbon with strap watch fittings rusted nail pennies. Baby-farming bitch deserves this and more.

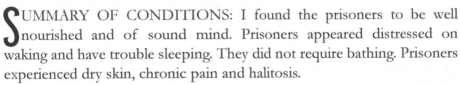

SUMMARY OF CONDITIONS: I found the prisoners to be well nourished and of sound mind. Prisoners appeared distressed on waking and have trouble sleeping. They did not require bathing. Prisoners experienced dry skin, chronic pain and halitosis.

All normal for this report.

Walter Bunting

Marshall Moore: The Time Ball Tower Keeper's Report 1920

They ask all the time, *what's the time?* And me with my Swiss precision watch, made by my own hands, and another in my pocket made by the hands of my father. I say to them, "Tick Tock Time. Time for you to be quiet and think yourselves lucky. Think about where you were born! You could have been born in the Philippines when Jacob H. Smith was about. That man issued an order that anyone over ten should be killed. That could have been any one of you given different circumstances."

I tell them that and they whine as I should have known they would. "You see? We are not so bad!"

SUMMARY OF CONDITIONS: I found the prisoners to be well nourished and of sound mind. Prisoners bathed successfully. Prisoners appeared distressed on waking and have trouble sleeping. Prisoners experienced dry skin, chronic pain and halitosis.

All normal for this report.

Marshall Moore

Ambrose McCarty: The Time Ball Tower Keeper's Report 1921

This week I took in a visitor. They told me not to, but she was so nice. Older woman and all that. Twenty-three, she is. Nice and smooth as any woman you ever saw. She brought with her boxes and boxes of figs and dates and other delicious items. Pure bribery!

I thought she was coming for me, but she told me she wanted to see her grandfather. She said he was innocent. That he was a good man. She lived with this fairy-tale fantasy. Tell them the truth, I say. Children need the truth, young women need the truth as much as we do. I told her it.

That her granddad killed her aunt and many more. There was plenty of evidence. Then I took her to stand near him. We watched for a while, her sobbing quietly at the look of him and who would blame her? She recovered herself and greeted him as if he looked like a real man.

"Look at you," he said. Even if he didn't know who she was he was happy to have someone to talk to.

She said to him, "Granddad, did you do it? Did you kill Auntie Missy?"

He took a great snarl at her. No love there at all. Broke my heart to see her recoil.

They whisper, "I'm innocent." They all whisper it.

They are trapped. But not in a jail. In their own desiccated bodies.

Oh, she was lovely. We fell in love. We married out there. We had the priest sanctify it and, my word, it was consummated.

When she left, I was tempted by the red flag. Just to be with her.

SUMMARY OF CONDITIONS: I found the prisoners to be well nourished and of sound mind. Prisoners appeared distressed on waking and have trouble sleeping. They did not require bathing. Prisoners experienced dry skin, chronic pain and halitosis.

All normal for this report.

Ambrose McCarty

Percy Hennessy: The Time Ball Tower Keeper's Report 1922

One of them has turned to sludge.

It happens.

I didn't want to clean up but who else would?

In the end, you have to decide for yourself what sort of person you are. Who you want to be.

I'm not cleaning it up.

The prisoners tell me there is a cleaner; that person can deal with it.

SUMMARY OF CONDITIONS: I found the prisoners to be well nourished and of sound mind. Prisoners did not require bathing. Prisoners appeared distressed on waking and have trouble sleeping. Prisoners experienced dry skin, chronic pain and halitosis.

All normal for this report.

Percy Hennessy

ERNEST POTTS: THE TIME BALL TOWER KEEPER'S REPORT 1923

How casually Ambrose McCarty talks about his visitor, caring little for the consequences. She has become known as the Curse Bringer for all that occurred after.

I hope he enjoyed himself because that was his last chance, too.

He died in a freak accident. Fateful, I say.

Scars from wounds inflicted. Vicious bastards, every one of them. And insane. Crazier now than they ever were. We shouldn't have had them in solitary for as long as we did. Mistakes, mistakes, mistakes, and I'm the fucker bears the brunt.

Sometimes I feel as if I'm not alone. As if there is someone here. It's the scent of lemon, lemon-scented cleaner, or something.

I know I'm alone apart from these bastards.

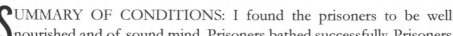

SUMMARY OF CONDITIONS: I found the prisoners to be well nourished and of sound mind. Prisoners bathed successfully. Prisoners appeared distressed on waking and have trouble sleeping. Prisoners experienced dry skin, chronic pain and halitosis.

All normal for this report.

Ernest Potts

Phillip Deeming: The Time Ball Tower Keeper's Report 1924

I will not read the files.

Phillip Deeming

Gerard Cook: The Time Ball Tower Keeper's Report 1925

Sad story, that Philip Deeming. One of those bleeding hearts, slipped through the cracks. The prisoners ripped his throat out. Wonder if they ever knew he might have set them free?

The evil hearts of men. These things we must do. Is my heart now stone as well?

We've had an arrival. Young man. Won't be young for long. Calls himself Grayson Alexander.

I've taken to calling him Lothario. He must have been a lady-killer once upon a time. Even as a teenager.

SUMMARY OF CONDITIONS: I found the prisoners to be well nourished and of sound mind. Prisoners bathed successfully. Prisoners appeared distressed on waking and have trouble sleeping. Prisoners experienced dry skin, chronic pain and halitosis.

All normal for this report.

Gerard Cook

Donald Muskett: The Time Ball Tower Keeper's Report 1926

The witch, the Curse Bringer, stands screaming on the shore, like a banshee or something else altogether. "You're nothing!" she's screaming at me as if I haven't heard this every day of my life.

Maybe I am nothing.

But I will be something, when I return.

SUMMARY OF CONDITIONS: I found the prisoners to be well nourished and of sound mind. Prisoners bathed successfully. Prisoners appeared distressed on waking and have trouble sleeping. Prisoners experienced dry skin, chronic pain and halitosis.

All normal for this report.

Donald Muskett

Carl Dyer: The Time Ball Tower Keeper's Report 1927

There's a woman in town who thinks she'll marry one of them. Quite truly, she thinks it's a match made in Heaven. We've shown her photographs of them, but she thinks we're lying. She thinks they're sitting over there preparing themselves for one great love.

It's Grayson Alexander she's most keen on. She's read his letters; what a charmer. What a charming evil twist of a man. I'm not decided yet if I'll read her letter to him. She's not much of a speller.

SUMMARY OF CONDITIONS: I found the prisoners to be well nourished and of sound mind. Prisoners bathed successfully. Prisoners appeared distressed on waking and have trouble sleeping. Prisoners experienced dry skin, chronic pain and halitosis.

All normal for this report.

Carl Dyer

Ronald McKeown: The Time Ball Tower Keeper's Report 1928

I'm taking over a lot of photographs. Ones my father got in the war when he was in France. Ooh, they're lovely. Lovely lovely lovely not a living woman alive can be as lovely.

I'll reward them with a look if they are good and quiet.

———◦═⟨∞⟩═◦———

SUMMARY OF CONDITIONS: I found the prisoners to be well nourished and of sound mind. Prisoners bathed successfully. Prisoners appeared distressed on waking and have trouble sleeping. Prisoners experienced dry skin, chronic pain and halitosis.

All normal for this report.

Ronald McKeown

Edward Carroll: The Time Ball Tower Keeper's Report 1929

He was a nasty one, that McKeown. The filth he left behind, although it was all swept up into one big pile, which is odd that he'd go that far and no further.

What did he do to the women here? Even the Black Widow pulls back from me as if she's terrified and there's no evidence of her being scared of a thing before.

"Cleaner," she's saying, but you wouldn't call McKeown clean, not even with it all swept into a pile.

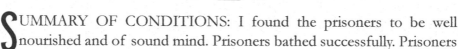

SUMMARY OF CONDITIONS: I found the prisoners to be well nourished and of sound mind. Prisoners bathed successfully. Prisoners appeared distressed on waking and have trouble sleeping. Prisoners experienced dry skin, chronic pain and halitosis.

All normal for this report.

Edward Carroll

Peter Rouse: The Time Ball Tower Keeper's Report 1930

The troll looks benign up close. From the shore he terrified me, but I see now he is nothing but an outline, a shadow.

I'll be happy to be without news for a while. It's too much sometimes. The Fox, as he called himself, he kidnapped a little girl, took the ransom, then gave her back in a blanket.

Strangled.

Her limbs cut off.

The troll seems very benign.

SUMMARY OF CONDITIONS: I found the prisoners to be well nourished and of sound mind. Prisoners bathed successfully. Prisoners appeared distressed on waking and have trouble sleeping. Prisoners experienced dry skin, chronic pain and halitosis.

All normal for this report.

Peter Rouse

Oscar Webster: The Time Ball Tower Keeper's Report 1931

Nasty fucking crew they are. I'm running the flag and fuck you all.

———◦══⟨∽∽⟩══◦———

SUMMARY OF CONDITIONS: I found the prisoners to be well nourished and of sound mind. Prisoners appeared distressed on waking and have trouble sleeping. They did not require bathing. Prisoners experienced dry skin, chronic pain and halitosis.

All normal for this report.

Oscar Webster

WILLIAM BUNTING: THE TIME BALL TOWER KEEPER'S REPORT 1932

They can't move far, this lot, but they can do it if they have enough time. I arrived to find them at the door, arms raised to drop a heavy object on my poor head. The effort of it meant they couldn't move another inch, though, and I knocked them down easy.

They blamed the woman prisoner.

Of course they did.

"Her idea," they reckoned their words so slow I could cook myself a boiled egg by the time they finished two words.

"She fucken hates you," they said.

So I showed her.

To my future keepers: if you find a chicken bone carved like lace, think of me. But it might be you're looking in a place you oughtn't.

Beware. Never underestimate an opponent, even one you consider worthless, as good as dead.

They'll judge on your look, call you Pigface. It never hurt me; not a single word of it.

Most of us get over here and before long think about helping the prisoners.

"So long ago," they whisper. "All that happened so long ago." Sometimes it sounds like rustling leaves. They whisper, "We can forgive. We sit here and let it wash over us. We're a peaceful lot. Listen to the waves pounding the arse of the Time Ball Tower and let the past wash away."

SUMMARY OF CONDITIONS: I found the prisoners to be well nourished and of sound mind. Prisoners bathed successfully. Prisoners appeared distressed on waking and have trouble sleeping. Prisoners experienced dry skin, chronic pain and halitosis.

All normal for this report.

William Bunting

George Manning: The Time Ball Tower Keeper's Report 1933

It does seem to grow. My heart aches with longing for home. I only hope they will understand there. Otherwise, I will turn to stone.

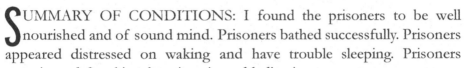

SUMMARY OF CONDITIONS: I found the prisoners to be well nourished and of sound mind. Prisoners bathed successfully. Prisoners appeared distressed on waking and have trouble sleeping. Prisoners experienced dry skin, chronic pain and halitosis.

All normal for this report.

George Manning

Arthur Harcourt: The Time Ball Tower Keeper's Report 1934

The Time Ball Tower rarely catches the attention of the press. It's better that way; you never know how the public will take a thing.

Sleep. Salt. Breathe well seemed to mollify the interviewers when they wanted to know Burnett's secret. It gave them something to report and made them look like they knew something. No one believes anything without proof anymore. We were a fluff piece. A joke. "Longest lived people in Australia." But how long has he been in the paper like this? That is proof enough. He was old, back in 1912 when they did the first story.

The subheadings, always, said: "The secret to long life? Sleep a lot." Or, if the reporters felt they hadn't been treated well, if they found our town annoying and unpleasant, "Be lazy."

Sometimes they would be sidetracked by the cleverness of our clocks and watches. They loved the tiny hole in the wall shops, with people inside fixing timepieces. If they stayed the day, they'd watch the ball drop at 1:05. If they were observant, they would see the town come to pause. Our daily rest.

Sometimes people decided Burnett was interesting, until they met him. He was a dull man; everyone thought so. And meeting him, most thought he was a liar. He had no birth certificate. He did a good job of making skeptics of people.

SUMMARY OF CONDITIONS: I found the prisoners to be well nourished and of sound mind. Prisoners bathed successfully. Prisoners appeared distressed on waking and have trouble sleeping. Prisoners

experienced dry skin, chronic pain and halitosis.
All normal for this report.

Arthur Harcourt

Leo Heath: The Time Ball Tower Keeper's Report 1935

I've asked the prisoners and they say no. They can't hear any strange noises.

SUMMARY OF CONDITIONS: I found the prisoners to be well nourished and of sound mind. Prisoners bathed successfully. Prisoners appeared distressed on waking and have trouble sleeping. Prisoners experienced dry skin, chronic pain and halitosis.

All normal for this report.

Leo Heath

Max Heath: The Time Ball Tower Keeper's Report 1936

If I train the binoculars just so, I can see people coming and going from the Club. Well, not so. But I can see them turning into the street that turns into the street the Club is in. It won't be long, and I'll be there, settled into an armchair, a lovely glass beside me and all I ever wanted at my fingertips.

Not too long.

SUMMARY OF CONDITIONS: I found the prisoners to be well nourished and of sound mind. Prisoners bathed successfully. Prisoners appeared distressed on waking and have trouble sleeping. Prisoners experienced dry skin, chronic pain and halitosis.

All normal for this report.

Max Heath

Ernest Muskett: The Time Ball Tower Keeper's Report 1937

My brother's done well since 1927. Doctor of great renown. Some marvelous research into the things that ail us. We both have a fascination with history, especially about the physical nature of evil. He knows more than any man about Baron Ungen von Sternberg. That man said, "Did you know men can still walk when flesh and bone is separated?" He ordered grotesque killings; leaving a man naked on ice or causing him to be torn apart by wild animals or dragged behind car.

My brother's got his eye on a wife, but he knows I'm keen on her too. Frances. She's lovely, she is, and just right for one of us at least.

I suppose I might become a doctor, also.

SUMMARY OF CONDITIONS: I found the prisoners to be well nourished and of sound mind. Prisoners bathed successfully. Prisoners appeared distressed on waking and have trouble sleeping. Prisoners experienced dry skin, chronic pain and halitosis.

All normal for this report.

Ernest Muskett

Frances Styles: The Time Ball Tower Keeper's Report 1938

Even on the boat over, I hadn't decided if I'd be quiet or loud. Weak or strong. Act big or act small. Would it matter there? It felt quite freeing to know I could be anything. My father gave me no restraints. It was an obsession with him. I think in stark contrast to the way he held my mother, with a tight rein, until she bounded away, onto the street, into the path of a speeding truck.

He tells me she had time to gaze at me, when I was delivered there, on the street.

But I know that's not true.

He's just being kind.

We'd sit together gazing at the Time Ball Tower. He longed to go back. I couldn't wait to get here.

He'd told me nothing about being a keeper. I had no idea what to expect. But that's how they play it, isn't it?

I'm luckier than most. I grew up without the confines of two parents. Only the one, albeit a griever who sometimes looked at me sadly because I reminded him of his great lost love, his departed darling, his wonderful Ruby.

My mother.

How do you make a girl feel bad for looking like her mother?

Will I ever have a fellow look at me that way? I know the Muskett brothers are both keen, the older and the younger. More decisions to be made on return.

I took delivery of a prisoner today.

The boatman dropped him off. "You'll be right, mate," he said. Like he was the stork delivering a baby.

This prisoner was skinny, lucky for me, in soft clothes that felt sticky and I wouldn't have touched him if I didn't have to. He snuffled at me, sniffing deeply as if getting one good one in. Reminded me of Clyde Blue at school, who stood close without touching and you always knew he was there because of the breathing.

He arrived trussed. Confined. Some good knots there. I put him in the box for a while.

The fresh prisoners talk a lot. Everyone says so. They figure out they won't be able to talk for long and want to get the words out. And the old prisoners are so desperate for new words, they will listen to anything.

His file came with instructions to keep him well chained.

He sniffs. He is obsessive about the way things smell. Certain scents set him off. Even a hint. But a deep lungful works better.

Smell of orange peel is one.

I put him next to Number Twenty-two, the one who kept prisoners, one in each room, and each one in a state of terrible disease or infection. Wounds rotting, and eyes dying in their heads. They say he kept a record, that it was something he thought important.

He's here, now.

That's good.

I set a tallow candle beside them all. The others reached as best they could, but the new one swore at me. "I don't need a candle."

I ignored him. Months later, I saw him in tears, his chest rising and falling. There was an awful sound. He was sucking on the tallow candle like the rest of them.

It made me ill.

I wore the scarf all my family and friends helped to knit, even the fellas. A glorious, crazy thing. Once the horrors tried to grab it, though, so I keep it on my bed, neatly folded, like a welcome mat to my only really private place.

I hated that they touched it. I would have washed it but who knows how long it would take to dry? I hate the smell of wet wool. I imagine everyone does.

I'd been my father's daughter so long, that's who I was. They saw something else in me, I don't think it was really there, but they saw it anyway.

SUMMARY OF CONDITIONS: I found the prisoners to be ill nourished and of unsound mind. Prisoners' baths a nightmare. Prisoners appeared distressed on waking and have trouble sleeping. Prisoners experienced dry skin, chronic pain and halitosis.

All normal for this report.

This should not be normal.

Frances Styles

Robert Bunting: The Time Ball Tower Keeper's Report 1939

Frances beat out a lot of young men for the privilege of going to the Time Ball Tower. I know there were some who wanted to use the Time Ball Tower as excuse not to go to war. They are called weak and pathetic and cowardly.

She did an okay job.

Too soft, though.

SUMMARY OF CONDITIONS: I found the prisoners to be well nourished and of sound mind. Prisoners bathed successfully. Prisoners appeared distressed on waking and have trouble sleeping. Prisoners experienced dry skin, chronic pain and halitosis.

All normal for this report.

Robert Bunting

Kim Adler: The Time Ball Tower Keeper's Report 1940

I'm dreaming every night of custard and stewed apple. What a sorry thing that is! But somehow it makes the pain go away.

It doesn't keep the ghosts quiet. They whisper *take me, take me*, and they whisper *I'll make a lovely baby boy* and *I'll love you all your life*.

Thing is, we've been unlucky. Gilda and me. We don't know if it's her or me or the two of us not matching.

But we've always wanted them, kids. We'd love the holy hell out of them.

So I took three ghosts in a jar, captured them by leaving the lid off and a little mix of me in the bottom.

I'm going to have her breathe them in and then we'll see. We'll have babies chuckling within a year.

SUMMARY OF CONDITIONS: I found the prisoners to be well nourished and of sound mind. Prisoners bathed successfully. Prisoners appeared distressed on waking and have trouble sleeping. Prisoners experienced dry skin, chronic pain and halitosis.

All normal for this report.

Kim Adler

George McCarty: The Time Ball Tower Keeper's Report 1941

They never warned me about the headaches.

Solid, like a living thing, like a growing creature at the back of my neck stretching up with long fingernails.

Summary of conditions: I found the prisoners to be well nourished and of sound mind. Prisoners bathed successfully. Prisoners appeared distressed on waking and have trouble sleeping. Prisoners experienced dry skin, chronic pain and halitosis.

All normal for this report.

George McCarty

Joe Madden: The Time Ball Tower Keeper's Report 1942

"No one unaccounted for in this awful display."

I say that to them every morning and they don't know what I'm talking about.

"Did you hear about Nikolai Yezhov?" I asked them. They call him the Bloody Dwarf. He had a million shot!

And of course, that makes them cry at the unfairness of the world. But it's unfair to them.

They don't care about the million dead.

And there is the monthly delivery. Oranges!

SUMMARY OF CONDITIONS: I found the prisoners to be well nourished and of sound mind. Prisoners bathed successfully. Prisoners appeared distressed on waking and have trouble sleeping. Prisoners experienced dry skin, chronic pain and halitosis.

All normal for this report.

Joe Madden

RUEBEN POTTS: THE TIME BALL TOWER KEEPER'S REPORT 1943

There was Number Fifteen, who'd poisoned his wife then sliced her up and fed her to school children. A dozen kids died eating her poisoned flesh. He didn't care.

SUMMARY OF CONDITIONS: I found the prisoners to be well nourished and of sound mind. Prisoners bathed successfully. Prisoners appeared distressed on waking and have trouble sleeping. Prisoners experienced dry skin, chronic pain and halitosis.

All normal for this report.

Rueben Potts

Linda Deeming: The Time Ball Tower Keeper's Report 1944

These great wastrels of space when men are dying. Men are dying, their hearts held silent and still. Men left where they lie, only a stone to mark their place.

And yet these ones sit here, safe and sound.

Fearless.

SUMMARY OF CONDITIONS: I found the prisoners to be well nourished and of sound mind. Prisoners bathed successfully. Prisoners appeared distressed on waking and have trouble sleeping. Prisoners experienced dry skin, chronic pain and halitosis.

All normal for this report.

Linda Deeming

Robert Potts: The Time Ball Tower Keeper's Report 1945

While men are dying.

I am dying myself, of shame because I cannot stop looking, cannot stop, where did these magazines come from?

I'm sharing them. I'm showing them and that makes me the worst person.

SUMMARY OF CONDITIONS: I found the prisoners to be well nourished and of sound mind. Prisoners bathed successfully. Prisoners appeared distressed on waking and have trouble sleeping. Prisoners experienced dry skin, chronic pain and halitosis.

All normal for this report.

Robert Potts

Lee Deeming: The Time Ball Tower Keeper's Report 1946

Shame for Richard Potts. He shouldn't have listened to these shits, though. That was his problem. Their entire aim is to guilt you, make you feel so bad you want to die and leave them alone, give them time to get down stairs and drown their pathetic selves.

SUMMARY OF CONDITIONS: I found the prisoners to be well nourished and of sound mind. Prisoners bathed successfully. Prisoners appeared distressed on waking and have trouble sleeping. Prisoners experienced dry skin, chronic pain and halitosis.

All normal for this report.

Lee Deeming

Gray Cook: The Time Ball Tower Keeper's Report 1947

Never met a snarlier bunch of bastards than this lot. I suppose it had something to do with the fact I got bitten by a fucken rat in the fucken basement when I went down to prepare the baths. Bastard got infected. Had to lift the flag. Man.

———◦═◍═◦———

Summary of conditions: I found the prisoners to be well nourished and of sound mind. Prisoners were not bathed due to rat bite. Prisoners appeared distressed on waking and have trouble sleeping. Prisoners experienced dry skin, chronic pain and halitosis.

All normal for this report.

Gray Cook

Peter Fenwick: The Time Ball Tower Keeper's Report 1948

They delivered another woman to me. Another Black Widow. Most women that kill get called it, don't they?

She's feisty.

Locked her in the box and all good after that.

Doesn't stop me jumping at the slightest sound, though.

I'm expecting to find one of them sludge one day. It happens. Someone preserved who shouldn't have been and it went wrong.

Another doctor, Dr. Marcel Petiot, is a perfect candidate. He posed as a member of the French revolution. Had a "safe house." Said he was immunizing people but was giving them lethal injections. Twenty-seven murdered at least, probably eighty or more. He gave hope to those arriving at his "safe house." Then killed them.

SUMMARY OF CONDITIONS: I found the prisoners to be well nourished and of sound mind. Prisoners bathed successfully. Prisoners appeared distressed on waking and have trouble sleeping. Prisoners experienced dry skin, chronic pain and halitosis.

All normal for this report.

Peter Fenwick

HOWARD DOWLING: THE TIME BALL TOWER KEEPER'S REPORT 1949

It's true. You do know them by the hardness of their hearts.

SUMMARY OF CONDITIONS: I found the prisoners to be well nourished and of sound mind. Prisoners bathed successfully. Prisoners appeared distressed on waking and have trouble sleeping. Prisoners experienced dry skin, chronic pain and halitosis.

All normal for this report.

Howard Dowling

ROBERT ANDREWS: THE TIME BALL TOWER KEEPER'S REPORT 1950

L ife is about choices and this is the one I made. It was either this or the sort of trouble that makes a man's balls shrink. Woman trouble. Can't help themselves in my vicinity. They're all over me. God knows how many children I've got running around the place. I had to get away from the women.

But there are women here, too. An ancient one, and some not quite so old. The best one, the juiciest, she's been here what, two years?

She's called the Black Widow, but she's a lot worse than that. Reading her file makes you sick to your stomach, what she did to those families. Those children. Gutless bitch, leaving them die, not even taking them out of their misery like a man woulda done. Letting those kids die in such terror. It's the worst thing you've ever heard.

Before I went in, people said, "Make her suffer." Her more than any of the others. So I dragged her into the middle of the room and gave her what she wanted. Shut her up for a while.

"Good man, good man," the prisoners chanted, sounding like a distant train. Noises are odd here. Different somehow and not always familiar.

You got to leave something behind. Cigarette lighter didn't work, anyway.

SUMMARY OF CONDITIONS: I found the prisoners to be well nourished and of sound mind. Prisoners bathed successfully. Prisoners appeared distressed on waking and have trouble sleeping. Prisoners

experienced dry skin, chronic pain and halitosis.
   All normal for this report.

Robert Andrews

Fred Webb: The Time Ball Tower Keeper's Report 1951

They will tell you terrible stories. It makes them feel better, miserable cunts. It gives them release.

Murdered children are never released. They will always suffer. Perpetual suffering.

And if a child is abused, even if they die as an adult, they'll haunt as a child, seeking expressions of regret, but nothing is ever enough. They'll wait until their molester dies then drag him to hell. Then they'll be free.

Can you feel the tug? They can sense weakness. The very hint of illness gets them going. And they know who's done what. If you can feel tugging, it means they know.

They'll fumble with your fly, tiny kid fingers not up to the task, but don't help them. You'll wake up with bites on your neck.

They hate the bath, don't they? They're like cats.

SUMMARY OF CONDITIONS: I found the prisoners to be well nourished and of sound mind. Prisoners bathed successfully. Prisoners appeared distressed on waking and have trouble sleeping. Prisoners experienced dry skin, chronic pain and halitosis.

All normal for this report.

Fred Webb

Patrick Curran: The Time Ball Tower Keeper's Report 1952

They always want to know; what happened to the keeper from last year? And you'll try not to let it out, but they are at you and at you and at you until you say, "He came back from the Time Ball Tower weak and anemic and he died soon after."

And they start talking about fingermarks in the dirt. They're picturing him holding on to nothing, trying to save himself. They reckon he'll drag himself out of the grave before too long.

He is not one who thought of the red flag.

Sometimes I think I can hear his fingernails on the window glass.

They ask about Robert Andrews, 1950, because he had as fine a patter as any they've known. Gift of the gab.

"How many children does that Robert have? Sowing his seed from near to far, he told us. How many little bastards set to end up here has he spawned?"

None, by all accounts. Unless he was successful out of town. In town, he was one to avoid. Girls knew this from the age of twelve.

All of us are "good men" and "good women." We have done many good things in our lives. And yet all of us are capable of something.

SUMMARY OF CONDITIONS: I found the prisoners to be well nourished and of sound mind. Prisoners did not require bathing. Prisoners appeared distressed on waking and have trouble sleeping. Prisoners experienced dry skin, chronic pain and halitosis.

All normal for this report.

Patrick Curran

John McKeown: The Time Ball Tower Keeper's Report 1953

I brought a girl here, thinking to get her all scared and needy.

Last shred of human in these men and they use it to say, "Fuck her here, in front of us."

It was tempting. "It's awful here," she said, tight as a limpet on my side. I could feel her pelvic bone against my thigh, she was grinding into me so hard.

She said, "Can they see or anything?"

I told her, "They've got all their senses. But they don't feel pain. Not much, anyway."

I showed her what other Time Ball Tower keepers had done. The cigarette burns. The names drawn into skin. She was shocked, but I had her to read the files so she wouldn't be sorry for them. This is how we can express that fury, all of us. We're looking after the worst of humanity so others can rest easy, knowing that crime is being punished.

She played with the oldest one.

His hair, brittle, long, white, snapped off it you lifted it. I gave her some to take home with her.

She sneezed all over them, my girl did. And you wouldn't believe it, but one of them got sick. Yes, he did. Not that you'd know the difference. Poor bastards.

Sick. It was pathetic to watch. Pitiful creature. They deserve all they get. No room for rehabilitation. Nothing. They deserve to suffer.

They say you change out here. That if you don't change, you did it wrong. Wasted your time.

Did I change? If I did, it was because of her. But she left. She was so full of vim and vigor and she left, leaving me again with them. Those almost fleshless skull heads leering at me, knowing more about me than they should know.

The storm was like the wrath of God came down upon us. Watching the storm from the top of the Time Ball Tower, I could see a vast expanse. Planning. I wondered how any of us would survive. Water up to the windows, just about.

I had to shift the prisoners about, all except the one who came in 1938. The orders to keep him chained were never rescinded. I hated to touch him. His clothes were soft and sticky, like an insect's casing. The only thing that gets him going is a new smell. Even my soap can set him off. He said to my woman that he could smell her cunt and she better watch it or it would rot from the inside out.

Honestly, he did say that.

Once he said that I couldn't bear touching her again. And I thought I was tough.

SUMMARY OF CONDITIONS: I found the prisoners to be well nourished and of sound mind. Prisoners bathed successfully. Prisoners appeared distressed on waking and have trouble sleeping. Prisoners experienced dry skin, chronic pain and halitosis.

All normal for this report.

John McKeown

Michael Carroll: The Time Ball Tower Keeper's Report 1954

John McKeown killed himself drinking acid. Wanting to suffer in the most unimaginable way.

I told this lot; didn't think it through because, boy-oh-boy, did that news make them happy.

"Happy for him," they're telling me. "Because he has blessed release."

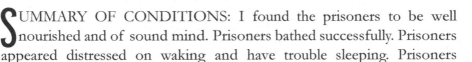

SUMMARY OF CONDITIONS: I found the prisoners to be well nourished and of sound mind. Prisoners bathed successfully. Prisoners appeared distressed on waking and have trouble sleeping. Prisoners experienced dry skin, chronic pain and halitosis.

All normal for this report.

Michael Carroll

BART CARROLL: THE TIME BALL TOWER KEEPER'S REPORT 1955

They make me think of the Huli description of ghosts; they keep aging. Their hair goes white, their limbs stiffen, cataracts form. Eyes like milk. Who wouldn't be a scholar, to learn this beautiful stuff?

SUMMARY OF CONDITIONS: I found the prisoners to be well nourished and of sound mind. Prisoners bathed successfully. Prisoners appeared distressed on waking and have trouble sleeping. Prisoners experienced dry skin, chronic pain and halitosis.

All normal for this report.

Bart Carroll

Donald Rouse: The Time Ball Tower Keeper's Report 1956

If Bart Carroll's a scholar, then I'm the Emperor of Japan. Didn't even talk about Tithonos whatsit and the long life and all the rest of it.

Some people have no idea how to educate.

SUMMARY OF CONDITIONS: I found the prisoners to be well nourished and of sound mind. Prisoners bathed successfully. Prisoners appeared distressed on waking and have trouble sleeping. Prisoners experienced dry skin, chronic pain and halitosis.

All normal for this report.

Donald Rouse

Brian Webster: The Time Ball Tower Keeper's Report 1957

The routine is a killer but also a life saver. Follow your head, not your heart. You can listen to your heart when you are back at home and the world is safe for you.

Do not listen to them. They will tell you things. You are made of stone, they'll say, and perhaps it's true. Who knows?

Still. You do what you have to do and that is not up to them at all.

I watched them all find God and lose him again. The Preacher still preaches, but everything that comes out of his mouth sounds filthy and degraded.

SUMMARY OF CONDITIONS: I found the prisoners to be well nourished and of sound mind. Prisoners bathed successfully. Prisoners appeared distressed on waking and have trouble sleeping. Prisoners experienced dry skin, chronic pain and halitosis.

All normal for this report.

Brian Webster

Nathan Bunting: The Time Ball Tower Keeper's Report 1958

I'd been led to expect they'd be happy to see me. Instead, all they do is try to spit with their dry, sad little mouths.

SUMMARY OF CONDITIONS: I found the prisoners to be well nourished and of sound mind. Prisoners bathed successfully. Prisoners appeared distressed on waking and have trouble sleeping. Prisoners experienced dry skin, chronic pain and halitosis.

All normal for this report.

Nathan Bunting

Frank Ross: The Time Ball Tower Keeper's Report 1959

Before I came out here, I checked out all the buildings named for my predecessors, built with money donated by keepers. As Burnett said, live long enough, anyone can become a billionaire. You just have to be patient. And money buys recognition like street names. Park names.

———⊶⚬❀⚬⊷———

SUMMARY OF CONDITIONS: I found the prisoners to be well nourished and of sound mind. Prisoners bathed successfully. Prisoners appeared distressed on waking and have trouble sleeping. Prisoners experienced dry skin, chronic pain and halitosis.

All normal for this report.

Frank Ross

Stephanie Brennan: The Time Ball Tower Keeper's Report 1960

Don't even want to think about what they told me at the Club. Cheeks burning at the thought. They said, don't be agitated. They meant; don't be horny! Couldn't believe it. Dirty old men talking about sex.

But to be honest, they pick up on it, these creepy little things. Sniffing away. I've been having more showers than is good for the skin. I have very sensitive skin…

SUMMARY OF CONDITIONS: I found the prisoners to be well nourished and of sound mind. Prisoners bathed successfully. Prisoners appeared distressed on waking and have trouble sleeping. Prisoners experienced dry skin, chronic pain and halitosis.

All normal for this report.

Stephanie Brennan

Luciano Costello: The Time Ball Tower Keeper's Report 1961

Boredom is your greatest enemy, not the prisoners. Some days seem to last a week. Others will last an hour.

I say—bring a project to complete. Do not come here unless you have a novel to write, a symphony to compose, a village of idiots to carve. I'm trying with driftwood and the awful blunt knives we've got out here. Note; bring knives.

I discovered a use for the many bricks left over from the building. A scientific use, if you will.

How many bricks does it take to flatten the arm of a man over one hundred and fifty years old?

A new one arrived, and I chucked him the box. Creepy little shit he is, too. Bathed the others.

They tried to distract me from it; really, you'd think they'd be happy of the distraction themselves.

Bathing changes everything. I'm glad they warned me not to go too far down. Jeezus. Still I hear it. Clickety clickety click.

SUMMARY OF CONDITIONS: I found the prisoners to be well nourished and of sound mind. Prisoners bathed successfully. Prisoners appeared distressed on waking and have trouble sleeping. Prisoners experienced dry skin, chronic pain and halitosis.

All normal for this report.

Luciano Costello

ROGER HEATH: THE TIME BALL TOWER KEEPER'S REPORT 1962

Do your research, my history teacher always said. Make sure you know your facts before you dive in with both feet. And yes, we said, but you don't dive with your feet, and that made us all laugh. But still, he was right.

Who deserves to be out here? Who deserves this punishment? Here's a list. But really it only makes me think; are these really the worst? Do they really deserve it?

These are the things that happened in the twelve months before I came here, into the Time Ball Tower. ONE SINGLE YEAR.

1961

March 20 Trial of Stephen Bradly who kidnapped and murdered Graeme Thorne.

April 22 Trial of Adolf Eichmann.

April 20 Five hundred hacked to death in Angola.

Sept 24 Wendy Mayer was murdered by John Maltby. He drowned on this day.

November 6 Leonard Lawson raped and killed sixteen-year-old girl at Collaroy (they always describe this as "killed and raped," not the other way around. Which is worse?)

November 16 in the Congo. The bodies of thirteen Italian UN soldiers are sold in a market.

1962

Feb 11 In Elliott, Northern Territory. School of eleven children, six white. White parents pulled them out, demanding aboriginal children be removed. "Worried about hygiene."

I think those parents deserve a spot in the Tower.

October 31. Robert Peter Tait. We've got him, here. He's the newest one. Luckily, he arrived before I got here so he's already been boxed.

Sir Henry Bolte wanted him dead, but an insanity plea kept him alive, so Bolte went for Ronald Ryan.

Some say Bolte is a long time secret supporter of the Time Ball Tower.

Tait is described sexual psychopath. A friendless alcoholic, sexual deviant in the extreme.

Wears several layers of women's underwear.

Killed and raped Ada Ethel Hall, eighty-two, a vicar's mother.

He was on parole after assaulting a church worker.

The Time Ball Tower doesn't care if they are sane or insane.

They'll all be insane before long, anyway.

He was due to die on 31 October 1961, but we got him instead. His grave was already dug. He told the others and me, "I seen it. It was this close. Me grave."

The longer you spend here, the more you understand the importance of the keepers. I'm a vicar's son, and would be a vicar too, one day. Always is, always has been. There is a certain inevitability about it all, something I enjoy greatly I know I can help people. I have the ability to listen.

I will baptize them. Down by the water. If God means them to go, he will take them from my arms.

I left that skinny little shit who was delivered in 1938 chained up. Who am I to change things? Music upsets them if you think they are getting the upper hand. Especially the trumpet, God knows why.

Roger Heath

LEE HEATH: THE TIME BALL TOWER KEEPER'S REPORT 1963

No flag was run up for two days, so they sent out the boatman. Roger was found face down in the water, massive dent in his head. Long dead, weeks dead. One of the prisoners was caught underneath him. Not dead, although they say he tried to keep his head under water, tried to move so that he could drown, too. So we don't have a full report from Roger.

Sometimes you forget there's a world out there. Where people are alive, not like these things. Beating hearts aren't a trick.

SUMMARY OF CONDITIONS: I found the prisoners to be well nourished and of sound mind. Prisoners bathed successfully. Prisoners appeared distressed on waking and have trouble sleeping. Prisoners experienced dry skin, chronic pain and halitosis.

All normal for this report.

Lee Heath

MARIA DE SALVO: THE TIME BALL TOWER KEEPER'S REPORT 1964

It's been ten years since my sister disappeared. Home from teacher's college for my sixteenth birthday, she brought me the smallest radio anyone in Tempuston had ever seen. I was famous for that for a while. It had a clock in it and all.

What I've heard is there might be a clue in the Tower to where she is. Rumor has it that clues to many things sit out here. We just want to know what happened. Even if she's passed away and we won't see her again. Just so my mother can bury her.

One girl went missing in 1953. She was found quickly though, within a month or two, washed up. It was a mystery for a while because she was wearing a negligée, and no one knew how she got out there. When the keeper John McKeown got back, he confessed and then hung himself on the cypress tree.

Called himself a blossom; said in his suicide note, "Like Victor Fegeur, I wish to leave something behind."

Victor Fegeur was a man executed in the States. His last meal was an olive with the pit still in; apparently, he wanted to turn into an olive tree. Leave something good behind. I doubt it grew.

I have asked for olives in my next food delivery. They'll need to send away for them, but that is what I want.

Number Sixteen kept his sister in a dark small hole all her life. Their parents had died not long after she was born. His once-red hair sits in awful pink strands on his scalp. "Boat coming," he said. He rarely said anything else.

I found out he bled black and slow and if you kept re-opening the wound, it started to hurt him.

SUMMARY OF CONDITIONS: I found the prisoners to be well nourished and of sound mind. Prisoners bathed successfully. Prisoners appeared distressed on waking and have trouble sleeping. Prisoners experienced dry skin, chronic pain and halitosis.

All normal for this report.

Maria de Salvo

ED KEENEY: THE TIME BALL TOWER KEEPER'S REPORT 1965

The Black Widow, the second one, says I've got more spirit than any ghost she's ever met. I can't help but laugh at that one.

Weird thing, the way your laugh echoes here. As if there are ghosts, indeed, and they laugh when you laugh, cry when you cry.

I did cry and my god.

SUMMARY OF CONDITIONS: I found the prisoners to be well nourished and of sound mind. Prisoners bathed successfully. Prisoners appeared distressed on waking and have trouble sleeping. Prisoners experienced dry skin, chronic pain and halitosis.

All normal for this report.

Ed Keeney

CHRIS BUNTING: THE TIME BALL TOWER KEEPER'S REPORT 1966

It stinks of death.

And it sounds of silence.

I watched a kid paddle out here. Too eager to wait until he's old enough. But it doesn't do any good to be eager.

It does no good at all.

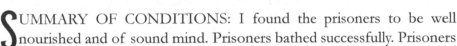

SUMMARY OF CONDITIONS: I found the prisoners to be well nourished and of sound mind. Prisoners bathed successfully. Prisoners appeared distressed on waking and have trouble sleeping. Prisoners experienced dry skin, chronic pain and halitosis.

All normal for this report.

Chris Bunting

Charles Peacock: The Time Ball Tower Keeper's Report 1967

Those at the Club make you feel welcome, that's for sure. I'm trying to remember that. Here, I feel like an outcast. It's ridiculous, but that's the way they make me feel. They are *masters* at destructive psychology. I should write a thesis on it.

———◦═◇═◦———

SUMMARY OF CONDITIONS: I found the prisoners to be well nourished and of sound mind. Prisoners bathed successfully. Prisoners appeared distressed on waking and have trouble sleeping. Prisoners experienced dry skin, chronic pain and halitosis.

All normal for this report.

Charles Peacock

Chris Penfold: The Time Ball Tower Keeper's Report 1968

Time moves on, the ball drops the ball drops the ball drops. Who would ever doubt that most of the men in this town are master clockmakers?

SUMMARY OF CONDITIONS: I found the prisoners to be well nourished and of sound mind. Prisoners bathed successfully. Prisoners appeared distressed on waking and have trouble sleeping. Prisoners experienced dry skin, chronic pain and halitosis.

All normal for this report.

Chris Penfold

EARL PENFOLD: THE TIME BALL TOWER KEEPER'S REPORT 1969

They warn us not to let the prisoners see "tumescence." Those old creatures aren't capable of erections anymore and the women have no juice, no matter how much they wish.

Mind you, being here. And what's out there. Is enough to dry anyone up. There's a place in the United States—and it's not the only one—where young kids are sent, to be "cared for" and there are dozens who never come out again.

Who could manage "tumescence" with that in your brain?

SUMMARY OF CONDITIONS: I found the prisoners to be well nourished and of sound mind. Prisoners bathed successfully. Prisoners appeared distressed on waking and have trouble sleeping. Prisoners experienced dry skin, chronic pain and halitosis.

All normal for this report.

Earl Penfold

MARTIN MUSKETT: THE TIME BALL TOWER KEEPER'S REPORT 1970

My mum crying on the shore, but it could have been the sea salt. You'd think we're an emotional town if you took any notice of all the salt or wind induced tears. Dad standing next to her, his arm reaching up around her shoulders.

He's got me sorted for every kind of medical situation. He's so uncool my old man. He has *no idea*. All I'll need is weed. All you need is weed, ladida di dah.

Mum gave me an ugly scare, like, you give it back now.

Crazy lady. She was never the motherly type, but I still love her. She's not big on the "world revolves around the children" idea but who cares? I know the world revolves around me and always will.

She's used to basking in Dad's adoration so isn't good with criticism.

He's not a man to give you a hard time, but he does have EXPECT-ATIONS. He will be so DISAPPOINTED if I don't make it. He's already on at me to have a dozen kids myself. Spread the word, spread the name.

That was about the first thing the prisoners wanted to know, my name. Yeah, I shouldn't have told them.

They figured out who Dad was, and then got out of me who Mum was.

"Those two? Made you? I wonder if he's doing it all? All the things he talked about? Anal, right? Do you think your dad and mum do anal? Course they do, that's why he's an only child." They laughed.

Every minute with them, I feel darker. Older. You know? As if they're sucking something from me I didn't even know I had.

I smoked a reefer and danced on their feet.

Someone has left a bottle of whiskey here. A note on it saying, in case of emergency break glass.

The look of it…doesn't make me sick. But it's a prop I don't need. I want to feel every minute I'm awake, to experience. I don't want to be deadened. Look at the Voyager disaster. Did the captain have a triple brandy before the collision? That will never be known. But I will not. I want clarity of vision, and the truth.

They are nothing. They never will be anything. They will achieve no more in their lives.

Me?

I can do anything.

SUMMARY OF CONDITIONS: I found the prisoners to be well nourished and of sound mind. Prisoners did not require bathing. Prisoners appeared distressed on waking and have trouble sleeping. Prisoners experienced dry skin, chronic pain and halitosis.

All normal for this report.

Martin Muskett

Jimmy Campbell: The Time Ball Tower Keeper's Report 1971

Jesus fuck my head hurts.

SUMMARY OF CONDITIONS: I found the prisoners to be well nourished and of sound mind. Prisoners bathed successfully. Prisoners appeared distressed on waking and have trouble sleeping. Prisoners experienced dry skin, chronic pain and halitosis.

All normal for this report.

Jimmy Campbell

Leo Adler: The Time Ball Tower Keeper's Report 1972

I've read my dad's report. He was here 1940.
  It's
  I'm not real
  Ghost
  What I've got inside me is not what other people have
  That's what I'll need to forget.

SUMMARY OF CONDITIONS: I found the prisoners to be well nourished and of sound mind. Prisoners bathed successfully. Prisoners appeared distressed on waking and have trouble sleeping. Prisoners experienced dry skin, chronic pain and halitosis.

Leo Adler

LEONIE HENNESSY: THE TIME BALL TOWER KEEPER'S REPORT 1973

It stinks. I'll never smell anything but them again. I'm desperate for perfume, any perfume, but the expensive kind. Chanel Number 5. When I get home, I'm going to buy perfume every single week and never be without it.

What these people did...they deserve eternal suffering. The skinniest one, pretty well a skeleton with skin stretched over it, he kept a daughter in his cellar for thirty years. Never taught her how to speak or read. All she knew about was oral sex and silent fucking. He brought men back for her and then he'd kill them. He was unrepentant. And there were the grandchildren, too.

This one, he's got a lean to him, as if his arse cheek hurts. Sometimes he'll push himself upright, but it takes him weeks, literally weeks. I like to tip him over again.

"Innocent innocent."

I wish they'd keep quiet. And those bloody women, too, wanting us to let them go. There was a child who rowed out here, way back when. God knows what happened to him and you don't want to.

All that classical study at school makes sense once you're out there, looking at them. Tithonos and all that. Was it always this way? Or did they used to be able to preserve the bodies as well? No one answers these questions. You're not even supposed to ask them.

Otherwise, everyone would do it, right? And the world would collapse on itself.

Look at them.

Like dried fruit.

Burnett Barton always said, "If you see ghosts, ignore them. It's only the evil of those men made manifest and best ignored."

You can say it's all stories. But I know what I saw. What I saw was real.

The place is infested with spirits.

I'm infested with spirits.

I'm never having children. I'm certain of that. I can't take the risk.

I crave oranges. I'd kill for one. I want oranges from Seville. I'll travel there. Travel the world when I get home; pack a bag and go on an adventure.

If I had my chance again, I would tell them nothing of meaning.

The biggest trick they'll play on you is to listen. This tricks you into believing they care, so you tell them more, and they keep listening, so you think they agree, and you keep on: blah blah blah. It's addictive.

"Men are base," they told me. "Never believe anything else. No matter what he says or does, he's thinking about fucking you."

They seriously said that.

But it's true. Don't tell anyone anything they can use against you. And don't trust a man to be thinking of anything but sex.

I didn't tell them I thought I was in love. That I'd met the man I thought I'd marry.

They didn't need to know that.

SUMMARY OF CONDITIONS: I found the prisoners to be well nourished and of sound mind. Prisoners bathed successfully. Prisoners appeared distressed on waking and have trouble sleeping. Prisoners experienced dry skin, chronic pain and halitosis.

All normal for this report.

Leonie Hennessy

Dale De Feo: The Time Ball Tower Keeper's Report 1974

The evil man's heart is like stone.

SUMMARY OF CONDITIONS: I found the prisoners to be well nourished and of sound mind. Prisoners bathed successfully. Prisoners appeared distressed on waking and have trouble sleeping. Prisoners experienced dry skin, chronic pain and halitosis.

All normal for this report.

Dale De Feo

Martin Todd: The Time Ball Tower Keeper's Report 1975

Nothing more delightful than a surprise delivery. Must have been the boatman. Don't know why he didn't call out hello, though. Could have done with a catch up.

Summary of conditions: I found the prisoners to be well nourished and of sound mind. Prisoners bathed successfully. Prisoners appeared distressed on waking and have trouble sleeping. Prisoners experienced dry skin, chronic pain and halitosis.

All normal for this report.

Martin Todd

Melanie Brooks: The Time Ball Tower Keeper's Report 1976

They told me the prisoners are dirty old men, but these ones don't seem the slightest bit interested.

Of course, I'm not, either. Never have been, never will be, don't get the whole sex thing, thank god. Life's too short for all that.

SUMMARY OF CONDITIONS: I found the prisoners to be well nourished and of sound mind. Prisoners bathed successfully. Prisoners appeared distressed on waking and have trouble sleeping. Prisoners experienced dry skin, chronic pain and halitosis.

All normal for this report.

Melanie Brooks

Rosalynn Brooks: The Time Ball Tower Keeper's Report 1977

Tait is begging for underwear, pathetic worm. If you wanted him under your thumb, you'd take plenty of undies. Wave them around, tease him. They're all pathetic. The awful baby starver says his nose is so sensitive, he knows what you had for dinner yesterday just from sniffing your arse.

———○━━◁○▷━━○———

SUMMARY OF CONDITIONS: I found the prisoners to be well nourished and of sound mind. Prisoners bathed successfully. Prisoners appeared distressed on waking and have trouble sleeping. Prisoners experienced dry skin, chronic pain and halitosis.

Rosalynn Brooks

Jim Glover: The Time Ball Tower Keeper's Report 1978

I never thought I'd say this, but I don't think of sex. I haven't thought of sex, of fucking or sucking or plucking or whatever "ucking" you want to mention—not for weeks.

It's so dry out here. It's like your juices dry up or something.

And yet they want to hear the dirtiest of stories, the filthiest of details, and they'll keep quiet if you tell them.

Poor bastards.

SUMMARY OF CONDITIONS: I found the prisoners to be well nourished and of sound mind. Prisoners bathed successfully. Prisoners appeared distressed on waking and have trouble sleeping. Prisoners experienced dry skin, chronic pain and halitosis.

All normal for this report.

Jim Glover

Rod Fenwick: The Time Ball Tower Keeper's Report 1979

I said to them, "We better write up your last words. Could be any day now. You want to be ready. Imagine waiting all this time and then finding you don't know what to say."

Never seen them so excited. Some of them almost sweating, if they had any sweat in them. Some laughter, some actual laughter, not the vicious squeaking they usually make.

Can't wait to tell them I was bullshitting.

Someone sent me a case of wine over. Nice of them! I've told the prisoners we're celebrating their imminent release.

Bastards'll believe anything.

SUMMARY OF CONDITIONS: I found the prisoners to be well nourished and of sound mind. Prisoners bathed successfully. Prisoners appeared distressed on waking and have trouble sleeping. Prisoners experienced dry skin, chronic pain and halitosis.

All normal for this report.

Rod Fenwick

Andy Hoff: The Time Ball Tower Keeper's Report 1980

Remembrance Day. I made them all wear poppies, and I recited war poetry, Wilfred Owen's *Futility* to them until they fidgeted about unhappily.

"Carry me to the sun.

Just for a short while.

Let it warm me."

"Carry me to the sun," Grayson said, quoting it back at me. Trying to get sympathy, make a connection, taking advantage of me in listening mode. "He wants you to try to free us and you will stay with us forever," the old priest said.

I said, "Burnett says war is for fools."

"Burnett! That evil fucker, that fucking evil fucker, he never went to war. Ask him how his village burned down."

"It drowned."

The Councilor said, "What will you give me if I tell you what really happened? The truth of Burnett's lost village, his broken place, his vanished home." This from a man who had systematically murdered his entire village. "How much do you want to know?"

How much indeed? It wasn't something my life depended on, but the tenets of all we did rested on the truth of his beginnings.

"I'll move you under the window, so you can get that tiny bit of late sun." I lifted The Councilor and he leaned into me gratefully. Once I had him settled, with that warmth surrounding him, he said, "What he tells you is not the truth. He tells you snippets, all designed to make him seem like the good guy. In truth, it was his lust and greed that saw the village burn down, not drown. The screams of the children, and the cowardice that filled him like the juice of an orange let sit for months in a jar. He saved his own skin and nothing else. This is a man who clearly did not go to war. Didn't fight for our country."

"Who of you went to war?" I asked, although I knew. "Does going to war makes a man good?"

Number Twenty-one, the cannibal, said, "If you haven't been, you can't know. The desperate hunger. A man will eat anything if he is starving."

"Yeah, but most of us won't eat human flesh and they most definitely will stop when the war is over." A normal company would have agreed with me. From this lot there was silence.

Another said, "Fighting a war doesn't make you a good man. Only momentarily helpless."

SUMMARY OF CONDITIONS: I found the prisoners to be well nourished and of sound mind. Prisoners bathed successfully. Prisoners appeared distressed on waking and have trouble sleeping. Prisoners experienced dry skin, chronic pain and halitosis.

All normal for this report.

Andy Hoff

Louis La Rocca: The Time Ball Tower Keeper's Report 1981

You know what would be handy? A lie detector. I know they lie all the time, but maybe they're telling the truth, too. I know there are secrets. Secrets concealed by the fact we don't believe a word they say.

God, I want an orange.

I'd kill for one right now.

I've asked, and I hope they send some with the next delivery.

SUMMARY OF CONDITIONS: I found the prisoners to be well nourished and of sound mind. Prisoners bathed successfully. Prisoners appeared distressed on waking and have trouble sleeping. Prisoners experienced dry skin, chronic pain and halitosis.

Louis La Rocca

Susan Mosse: The Time Ball Tower Keeper's Report 1982

You know what I want? A plate, a tray, of tiny little triangles of cheese on toast. White bread. Tasty cheese right to the edges and perfectly brown.

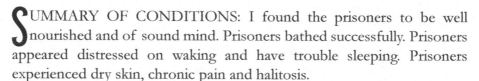

SUMMARY OF CONDITIONS: I found the prisoners to be well nourished and of sound mind. Prisoners bathed successfully. Prisoners appeared distressed on waking and have trouble sleeping. Prisoners experienced dry skin, chronic pain and halitosis.

All normal for this report.

Susan Mosse

Matt Glover: The Time Ball Tower Keeper's Report 1983

It'll probably bring down a curse or something, but the boat guy had to spend a couple of nights out here. The storm was insane. We watched the pier smash up, just shatter like matchsticks.

He went back when the sun shone. I could see him wading through the water, trying to keep hold of his boat, and no one there to help him.

The prisoners begged him to take them home. They're saying, mistaken identity! It isn't us! Some idiot in the past had told them about the Sharon Tate murders, and the innocent kid who was arrested at first for the deed.

He was a white kid and they let him go pretty quickly.

What if they'd been stubborn? Insisted on keeping him as their suspect? If he'd been a black kid? Then who knows what the Manson family may have done. Who knows? The prisoners use this an example. "See? The police make mistakes."

There are no mistakes here.

They're building a new pier, back on shore. It'll take months, the rate they're going. Wish I'd had a camera on it, to capture the build.

SUMMARY OF CONDITIONS: I found the prisoners to be well nourished and of sound mind. Prisoners bathed successfully. Prisoners appeared distressed on waking and have trouble sleeping. Prisoners experienced dry skin, chronic pain and halitosis.

All normal for this report.

Matt Glover

Vicki Fenwick: The Time Ball Tower Keeper's Report 1984

The boatman looked at me sidelong. I didn't like it.

SUMMARY OF CONDITIONS: I found the prisoners to be well nourished and of sound mind. Prisoners bathed successfully. Prisoners appeared distressed on waking and have trouble sleeping. Prisoners experienced dry skin, chronic pain and halitosis.

All normal for this report.

Vicki Fenwick

Rick Manning: The Time Ball Tower Keeper's Report 1985

I was told they can't get it up anymore, but I tell ya, if I tell them stories about death and destruction, they're getting it up all right.

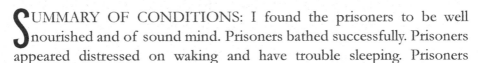

SUMMARY OF CONDITIONS: I found the prisoners to be well nourished and of sound mind. Prisoners bathed successfully. Prisoners appeared distressed on waking and have trouble sleeping. Prisoners experienced dry skin, chronic pain and halitosis.

All normal for this report.

Rick Manning

Suzy Dowling: The Time Ball Tower Keeper's Report 1986

The boatman was silent for the journey.

"Any tips?" I asked. "Anything to help me out?"

His shoulders lifted as if he was trying to block his ears, and he said nothing. I tried the same when I was out there. I don't mind noise, when I know what it is. But footsteps when you shouldn't hear them?

SUMMARY OF CONDITIONS: I found the prisoners to be well nourished and of sound mind. Prisoners bathed successfully. Prisoners appeared distressed on waking and have trouble sleeping. Prisoners experienced dry skin, chronic pain and halitosis.

All normal for this report.

Suzy Dowling

CARLO ZOMPARELLI: THE TIME BALL TOWER KEEPER'S REPORT 1987

Like others, I am disturbed by the journey out here. Perhaps better not to have to row out, a new man each year, but one boatman serves all? I can only imagine how distressing it will be when I have to return. The boatman needs to imbue a sense of positivity, not deep despair.

We call them The Bones. If I could get hold of enough vinegar I'd pickle them like a chicken bone and tie them in knots.

SUMMARY OF CONDITIONS: I found the prisoners to be well nourished and of sound mind. Prisoners bathed successfully. Prisoners appeared distressed on waking and have trouble sleeping. Prisoners experienced dry skin, chronic pain and halitosis.

All normal for this report.

Carlo Zomparelli

David Costello: The Time Ball Tower Keeper's Report 1988

I love the journey out and back. It's like being in limbo. I'd be happy to do it over and over again.

Love to keep the boat clean.

Love being on the salty water, so fresh.

So clean.

No one tells lies on the water. Out there, every last one of them is a liar. Every last word out of their mouths.

SUMMARY OF CONDITIONS: I found the prisoners to be well nourished and of sound mind. Prisoners did not require bathing. Prisoners appeared distressed on waking and have trouble sleeping. Prisoners experienced dry skin, chronic pain and halitosis.

All normal for this report.

David Costello

Sebastian Heath: The Time Ball Tower Keeper's Report 1989

There is beauty in most things. I say that as an artist, or as a wannabe, more like. An artist should be able to see beauty wherever he looks.

And yet…she was a baby farmer. How many newborns did she kill? I saw my little sister born. I know how absolute she was from that moment. Needy, vulnerable and a real person. This one took them from their parents and killed them.

I'd interfere with her if the thought didn't make me sick. Instead, I draw her in a state of unpleasantness. The things that others have put *inside her* I've drawn placed around her, a reminder of who she is and what she deserves.

I hope to give her shame.

During the bathing, I feel as if they opened up to me. As if the simple addition of water cleanses us all. I felt great pity for them, and great sorrow that I was not in touch with them earlier in their lives, before it all began.

I love solitude.
Patterns.
The form of shapes.
These things are beautiful.

SUMMARY OF CONDITIONS: I found the prisoners to be well nourished and of sound mind. They did not require bathing. Prisoners appeared distressed on waking and have trouble sleeping. Prisoners

experienced dry skin, chronic pain and halitosis.

All normal for this report.

Sebastian Heath

Jerry Butler: The Time Ball Tower Keeper's Report 1990

L ook at him. The Greyhound. Cannot leave himself alone. Disgusting.
   I called him the Greyhound because he used to own them, and because his dick is so long and thin it looks like a whippet.

S UMMARY OF CONDITIONS: I found the prisoners to be well nourished and of sound mind. Prisoners bathed successfully. Prisoners appeared distressed on waking and have trouble sleeping. Prisoners experienced dry skin, chronic pain and halitosis.

   All normal for this report.

Jerry Butler

Rod Glover: The Time Ball Tower Keeper's Report 1991

I was good at science at school, but I hated the experiments. I'm not that cold. Then you get the extreme, our guy here. He liked his subjects fresh from the womb. Somehow he had that power. He's aborted these babies and then kept them. It's the worst thing I've ever heard of.

———◦══⟨∞⟩══◦———

SUMMARY OF CONDITIONS: I found the prisoners to be well nourished and of sound mind. Prisoners bathed successfully. Prisoners appeared distressed on waking and have trouble sleeping. Prisoners experienced dry skin, chronic pain and halitosis.

All normal for this report.

Rod Glover

Tyson Keeney: The Time Ball Tower Keeper's Report 1992

I've collected playing cards all my life. Only odd ones, found on the streets, whatever. Others pick them up for me, too.

I was the picture of health when I got here. But near the end, not so much. Not sure if something was triggered here. Maybe I breathed too hard. I don't know. Maybe it's their breath, filled with poison.

I've covered a wall with my playing cards. I hope someone gets something out of this.

This all seems strange now, but when I get back, things will make sense. It's an indescribable feeling, that knowing. And that belonging.

I asked Burnett why he chose eternal life.

"They did it to me," he said, "even though I didn't deserve it."

"Who did?"

"Don't know to this day. May you never choose it."

"Why would I choose it?"

"The temptation to see the future."

"Is that what you wanted? The chance to be alive through the centuries?"

"Nobody cares what I want."

"Why would they do this to you?" I asked. "Why did they hate you so much? And who?"

"Not hate. Love. Fear of losing me," he said, but it was clear to us both this was not the truth.

I awoke to the sound of crying. The prisoners can sometimes muster a weak mewling when they're feeling particularly sorry for themselves, but that noise is an irritating one you can easily to ignore.

This was the sound of newborn babies.

I followed the noise; it became louder the more steps I climbed until there they were, newborns, but slithering across the floor, eight, ten of them, naked, covered with blood, their cries digging at me like thorns. I couldn't comfort them all. I couldn't comfort even one. As I reached for him, he turned to dirt in my fingers.

I wouldn't let these evil creatures see me cry. I wouldn't. But they knew.

"How many babies have you killed?" they said.

I shook my head.

I know, I know, that we should ignore these ghosts; that it is only the evil of these men and women made manifest.

I know that for an actual fact.

And yet they crawl.

Burnett Barton says, "Ignore ignore ignore what isn't real." Which is all very well.

Who are they, these desperate babies? Do they really belong in my conscience? Are they mine? Is this the truth of condoms and masturbation, that there are real children lost, that there is a future adult destroyed? Surely not.

I've always had a sensitive nose. In the city, it was people washed and unwashed. The cooking. The smell of rubber, of the trains, and I could smell cats always, terrible stench of them.

I couldn't smell rain, or the sea, or corn growing.

Smells of the Time Ball Tower. Rock. Old food. Leather. Heated glass. The prisoners smell like coconut some days, animal fat others.

Right at the top, if you fold the window open, you can kneel on the sill and stretch your head out. You'll get some sun on your face that way.

I call them the ghosts. Tethered to life, incapable of real physical activity, bitter and twisted.

What made me think reading Dostoevsky here would be a good idea? Jesus. Makes me think too hard about crime and punishment and what these losers beg me to do. "Release us, kill us, release us."

How would I kill them, anyway? Every Time Ball Tower keeper must consider it.

Surely the crimes are paid for by now, comes the thought. Shouldn't they be given the blessed relief of death?

Not so. They chose this. Eternal life over the death penalty. They were tricked, of course.

Three things stop me from setting them free. These same three things have stopped all before and will stop all after. It's our job and what we're paid to do. They deserve it for what they did. And the town would fall apart if we had no prisoners to look after. Once that money goes, the town is done for.

The radio said, "Batten down the hatches, there's a storm coming."

The boats went in, struggling against the waves already. I love a good storm. I know you're not supposed to, but there's something primal about it, the way storms have been witnessed by people for as long as we've been walking the earth.

I lined them up along the stair windows so they could look out. You're not supposed to move them, but I wanted to share with someone. They'd seen storms going back a hundred years. Longer.

The sky lit up, and I imagined I could see people in the town. It looked to me as if the council office was burning, but perhaps that was wishful thinking.

Never been a fan of bureaucracy.

I could hear screaming.

The ghosts said, "Can you hear them? That's what death by burning sounds like." They speak so slow you almost forget what they said at the start of the sentence by the time they get to the end. They told me to keep the lights down low, avoid fire. I know they're manipulating me, but I'm not sure why and not sure I care, either.

These people are no longer people. No wonder I call them ghosts. Cold, full of mist, no heart.

I managed to burn my own arm badly on hot fat, and I say that scar is a reminder that I could have died if I wasn't doing my duty over here.

"Let me help, I was a doctor," the abortion doctor said.

As if I'd let him anywhere near me with those fingers.

Another one, his business was traveling the country, was supposed to be selling new and improved washing machines. He did that, but he also molested every child he came across and cut their throats, or he cut their vocal cords, so they couldn't speak.

He'd be in more trouble these days, now that kids as young as five can read and write.

I layered my playing cards, layer after layer after layer. Was it worthwhile? Who knows? But I attained a great deal of satisfaction from it.

Statistically, 5% of us should have cancer. Far as I know, I'm the only one. Just my luck. Was it something I did? Do I deserve it? I don't really care. I'm only glad I haven't got any kids to leave behind. Couldn't cope with them suffering. The world's an awful place. Full of dangers. I couldn't keep them safe and I couldn't bear them suffering.

SUMMARY OF CONDITIONS: I found the ghosts to be well nourished and of sound mind. Ghosts were bathed. Ghosts appeared distressed on waking and have trouble sleeping. Ghosts experienced dry skin, chronic pain and halitosis.

All normal for this report.

Tyson Keeney

Alex Rouse: The Time Ball Tower Keeper's Report 1993

On return, Tyson found it was his house burned to the ground, his mother dead, his father dying. He thought it was punishment for being too kind, for not taking full advantage, *heartfelt* advantage, of his situation and from then on, he tried to fill the hearts of keepers-intended with despair.

"Don't let yourself be warm to them. Or you'll be cursed like I am." He had said this to me; the others had laughed at him.

He told me not to ignore the troll. That was important.

SUMMARY OF CONDITIONS: I found the prisoners to be well nourished and of sound mind. Prisoners bathed successfully. Prisoners appeared distressed on waking and have trouble sleeping. Prisoners experienced dry skin, chronic pain and halitosis.

All normal for this report.

Alex Rouse

Steve Andrews: The Time Ball Tower Keeper's Report 1994

Rumor always had it that there were missing women out here. Most people know that those women ran away; they got tired of Tempuston and left. We just can't cope with the idea that they'd leave us without ever calling home, but that's what happened, all right.

No argument there.

SUMMARY OF CONDITIONS: I found the prisoners to be well nourished and of sound mind. Prisoners bathed successfully. Prisoners appeared distressed on waking and have trouble sleeping. Prisoners experienced dry skin, chronic pain and halitosis.

All normal for this report.

Steve Andrews

Nikki Curran: The Time Ball Tower Keeper's Report 1995

efore I left, Tyson Keeney thought he was giving me a boost. He's a confused, conflicted man. He freaks out a lot about imaginary things. Hears things that aren't there. He hasn't coped well. He failed out here, somehow. I'll figure out how and fail differently!

I won't fail.

There are questions I'd like to address. I figure the answers will make me famous.

Ideas of sexual desire in the very old. Does it fade in most? An examination comparing the reactions of the experienced versus the sexually inexperienced.

What role does memory play?

What role does past exposure, both to actual experience and to varying levels of pornography play?

The boatman didn't know what I had in my cases. He would have stolen some if he could! They all tell you to take porn out there, but this was a shit load.

Did they like it?

Did they ever.

I spoil ya, I told them. It was true.

But did it cause an actual physical reaction? And could they then develop their own fantasies, or were they reliant on the information provided in the magazines?

Are men stimulated by the presence of sexual need? Does sexual need fade?

I'm looking out at the shore, and the children there. The innocence of them. One of them at least will be here in a few years; I hope the prisoners treat them well.

SUMMARY OF CONDITIONS: I found the prisoners to be well nourished and of sound mind. Prisoners bathed successfully. Prisoners appeared distressed on waking and have trouble sleeping. Prisoners experienced dry skin, chronic pain and halitosis.

All normal for this report.

Nikki Curran

Nick Webster: The Time Ball Tower Keeper's Report 1996

I found their medical records. They were well out of date, but most of them had suffered obvious illnesses. The Traveling Salesman's file noted, "Blinded by German Measles." What would it be like not to see for hundreds of years? All the others caught up as their cataracts took hold. He would gain some power, being used to the darkness. His file didn't note he'd been dangled out the window in 1908.

SUMMARY OF CONDITIONS: I found the prisoners to be well nourished and of sound mind. Prisoners bathed successfully. Prisoners appeared distressed on waking and have trouble sleeping. Prisoners experienced dry skin, chronic pain and halitosis.

All normal for this report.

Nick Webster

Frances Webb: The Time Ball Tower Keeper's Report 1997

Could anything be more perfect? One year, unmolested by those who think noise important, to read and investigate the works of Dickens. There was a set of books out there, very old, which I couldn't wait to get my hands on. But I wanted to take my own set, too, plus my notes.

Dickens does tragedy so well; I feel he understands me. We lost my older brother, didn't we? We shouldn't have. But we did. Trying to save him and destroying him in one.

You can't do that to a loved one.

SUMMARY OF CONDITIONS: I found the prisoners to be well nourished and of sound mind. Prisoners bathed successfully. Prisoners appeared distressed on waking and have trouble sleeping. Prisoners experienced dry skin, chronic pain and halitosis.

All normal for this report.

Frances Webb

Luke Harcourt: The Time Ball Tower Keeper's Report 1998

Put the lot of them in boxes and leave them there, I reckon. That way we wouldn't have to look at them.

SUMMARY OF CONDITIONS: I found the prisoners to be well nourished and of sound mind. Prisoners bathed successfully. Prisoners appeared distressed on waking and have trouble sleeping. Prisoners experienced dry skin, chronic pain and halitosis.

All normal for this report.

Luke Harcourt

Gary Lawrence: The Time Ball Tower Keeper's Report 1999

Geez, it's dry out here. I'm playing music as loud as I can, and the booze helps, trying to lubricate, as they say. *Lubricate.*

SUMMARY OF CONDITIONS: I found the prisoners to be well nourished and of sound mind. Prisoners bathed successfully. Prisoners appeared distressed on waking and have trouble sleeping. Prisoners experienced dry skin, chronic pain and halitosis.

All normal for this report.

Gary Lawrence

Jill Brooks: The Time Ball Tower Keeper's Report 2000

Gary Lawrence was the one who showed me around the Club. The place was murky and kind of unpleasant, bit like Gary himself. But at the same time there are benefits.

SUMMARY OF CONDITIONS: I found the prisoners to be well nourished and of sound mind. Prisoners bathed successfully. Prisoners appeared distressed on waking and have trouble sleeping. Prisoners experienced dry skin, chronic pain and halitosis.

All normal for this report.

Jill Brooks

Kenny Campbell: The Time Ball Tower Keeper's Report 2001

$1315 PER DAY
$54 PER HOUR
90c PER MINUTE

SUMMARY OF CONDITIONS: I found the prisoners to be well nourished and of sound mind. Prisoners bathed successfully. Prisoners appeared distressed on waking and have trouble sleeping. Prisoners experienced dry skin, chronic pain and halitosis.

All normal for this report.

Kenny Campbell

Johnny De Feo: The Time Ball Tower Keeper's Report 2002

On the list of those who should be here: Jeffrey Dahmer. He'd be able to gnaw on a leg bone here, an arm bone there. He'd be right at home.

SUMMARY OF CONDITIONS: I found the prisoners to be well nourished and of sound mind. Prisoners bathed successfully. Prisoners appeared distressed on waking and have trouble sleeping. Prisoners experienced dry skin, chronic pain and halitosis.

All normal for this report.

Johnny De Feo

Tracey Campbell: The Time Ball Tower Keeper's Report 2003

Don't tell Mum, but I bonked my way through Perth. Don't tell anyone! Not pregnant, though. Certain of that. It's given me things to think about here, all alone. Why am I here?

I'm going to flag it.

I definitely am. Fuck the money.

SUMMARY OF CONDITIONS: I found the prisoners to be well nourished and of sound mind. Prisoners bathed successfully. Prisoners appeared distressed on waking and have trouble sleeping. Prisoners experienced dry skin, chronic pain and halitosis.

All normal for this report.

Tracey Campbell

Lee Stewart: The Time Ball Tower Keeper's Report 2004

I'd say Rudolf Hess experienced something of what these creeps experience. Imprisoned in isolation for decades.

SUMMARY OF CONDITIONS: I found the prisoners to be well nourished and of sound mind. Prisoners bathed successfully. Prisoners appeared distressed on waking and have trouble sleeping. Prisoners experienced dry skin, chronic pain and halitosis.

All normal for this report.

Lee Stewart

Michael Todd: The Time Ball Tower Keeper's Report 2005

I know, I'm an idiot. Conspiracy believer, fool, dummy. But I had to look, didn't I? Just in case they were here, all the bad guys of history.

I didn't find much. Some chittery little mouse noises down in the basement. Signs that maybe someone else comes in here, someone we don't know about. That's about it.

It was disappointing, but to be honest, the ones we've got here are evil enough.

I gave them all a turn in the box. Two at a time. Sometimes three.

They didn't like that.

SUMMARY OF CONDITIONS: I found the prisoners to be well nourished and of sound mind. Prisoners bathed successfully. Prisoners appeared distressed on waking and have trouble sleeping. Prisoners experienced dry skin, chronic pain and halitosis.

All normal for this report.

Michael Todd

Eric Peacock: The Time Ball Tower Keeper's Report 2006

Cutest thing; a kid on the shore as I left, taking photos like her life depended on it. I went to school with her brother Cameron. She's a little cutey, all right. Not the brightest spark, our Phillipa, as Cameron used to say, but she'll be a looker when she's old enough.

SUMMARY OF CONDITIONS: I found the prisoners to be well nourished and of sound mind. Prisoners bathed successfully. Prisoners appeared distressed on waking and have trouble sleeping. Prisoners experienced dry skin, chronic pain and halitosis.

All normal for this report.

Eric Peacock

JAKE STAUNTON: THE TIME BALL
TOWER KEEPER'S REPORT 2007

The history of the tower, with all the prisoners eating each other, chilled me and reminded me of the island of Pulau Tengah, where three hundred dogs were dumped. They ate each other. The people who dumped them said they didn't imagine the dogs would do such a thing, but dogs want to survive as much as humans do.

SUMMARY OF CONDITIONS: I found the prisoners to be well nourished and of sound mind. Prisoners bathed successfully. Prisoners appeared distressed on waking and have trouble sleeping. Prisoners experienced dry skin, chronic pain and halitosis.

All normal for this report.

Jake Staunton

CAMERON MUSKETT: THE TIME BALL TOWER KEEPER'S REPORT 2008

Phillipa spent every last minute with me before I left. She's more obsessed with the tower than any of us. I'm like, "Sis, live your life until you get there! Don't just wait around!"

There's an innocence about her most people don't have.

She loves all our lists, though. Our bizarre family tradition to list the monsters. Like Alfred Stroessner, who recorded the screams of torture victims to play to their families. The families of murdered "dissidents" had to pay to take the remains of their loved ones, if they wanted a proper burial.

Dad loves the lists, too. It's like his greatest time was out there in the tower. I feel sorry for him, in a way. He never achieved the greatness his father thought he'd achieve. Failed medical school over and over again, year after year. I guess that's why he turned to booze.

Loser.

SUMMARY OF CONDITIONS: I found the prisoners to be well nourished and of sound mind. Prisoners bathed successfully. Prisoners appeared distressed on waking and have trouble sleeping. Prisoners experienced dry skin, chronic pain and halitosis.

All normal for this report.

Cameron Muskett

Nate Deeming: The Time Ball Tower Keeper's Report 2009

Kids are shits and always have been. Kids'll tease you until your heart breaks and you wish you were dead.

They didn't think I'd have to guts to come out here. I didn't think I'd have the guts.

But here. I can feel something almost magic. Being amongst these prisoners, it's like all they've ever known, all they've ever done, it's going to help me be a better person.

Such a difference a bath makes.

SUMMARY OF CONDITIONS: I found the prisoners to be well nourished and of sound mind. Prisoners bathed successfully. Prisoners appeared distressed on waking and have trouble sleeping. Prisoners experienced dry skin, chronic pain and halitosis.

All normal for this report.

Nate Deeming

Kate Hoff: The Time Ball Tower Keeper's Report 2010

I'd been warned about them. Desperate, creepy, incapable, frustrated. It was kinda fun, actually. Playing games you wouldn't get away with on shore.

They knew before me, which is just...weird. I did not imagine for one second I could be pregnant, but there you go. Sucks. Well, not sucks. Sorry, sweetheart, if you're ever a keeper and read this. I love you! I kept you!

But sucks because I only got six months in the tower.

Because I think there was more to know.

SUMMARY OF CONDITIONS: I found the prisoners to be well nourished and of sound mind. Prisoners did not require a bath. Prisoners appeared distressed on waking and have trouble sleeping. Prisoners experienced dry skin, chronic pain and halitosis.

All normal for this report.

Kate Hoff

Peter Mosse: The Time Ball Tower Keeper's Report 2011

There was always talk amongst the young ones about innocence and guilt. "Who's to say what anyone deserves? Who's to decide?"

I had no problem answering.

"The law decides. That's who. That's what it's there for."

As we approached, I could see that the walls were caked with sea creatures, sea plants, the splattered bodies of a million insects, the shit of ten thousand birds. It was craggy. Untended. Bleeding rust around the bolts.

I made myself some cheese on toast. Mum always made it for me. She'd make tiny little corners with perfect crispy cheese. I couldn't make it that well. The prisoners thought it was hilarious.

"Who would eat in front of living corpses? What sort of man?"

The sort of man who'd record every noise they made.

I played back part of my recording. Mostly it was moaning; the men were in constant pain. I heard them complaining to each other, whining voices, each louder than the next.

They cried out, "He's not going to help us. He's like the others. He won't help."

"St Peter allowed St Agatha to die, a great release after her terrible tortures," the priest said. "You have a blessed name. And yet you won't help us."

I fiddled with the controls to make music out of their voices. I was so thrilled by it, I couldn't wait to play the results to them.

"That's us! We didn't sing but we're singing!"

"He's a bloody magician."

"I'm just a musician." I knew how fake the humility sounded, but I didn't care. I played my guitar for them, the time passing so quickly it was more than an hour before I stood up.

"You know where there are wondrous sounds? The likes of which you'll not find elsewhere? Up above. Up top. Spend a night up there and you'll be surprised. Music of the gods. Of the stars. Music of the sea and of the dirt. Music of the air. You'll hear words you thought long lost, hear notes never heard before."

They wanted to help me, but I knew they were mostly trying to ingratiate themselves. It wouldn't work. I wished I was recording the words, because they were the most poetic lyrics I'd heard.

SUMMARY OF CONDITIONS: I found the prisoners to be well nourished and of sound mind. Prisoners bathed successfully. Prisoners appeared distressed on waking and have trouble sleeping. Prisoners experienced dry skin, chronic pain and halitosis.

All normal for this report.

Peter Mosse

Damian Muskett: The Time Ball Tower Keeper's Report 2012

We've always listed the monsters at our place. I don't know if my parents thought this would make us immune to them? Or if they just like talking about it. Anyway. It gave Phillipa nightmares, but she always had nightmares. The sort she didn't remember, but we all did. She'd scream the house down.

Course that meant it was easy to freak her out, too, and you can't blame a brother, can you?

I figured out pretty quick the prisoners love the dirty details. I love the dirty details, too. I told them about Shipman, the doctor who killed hundreds. "Mercy killing!" they're all like. "Good man, he's a good man," they say, because they love to judge, this lot. They'll go through every keeper, good, bad, good, bad.

Don't know what they'd call me. I wouldn't let them know much.

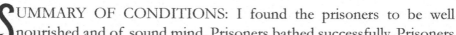

SUMMARY OF CONDITIONS: I found the prisoners to be well nourished and of sound mind. Prisoners bathed successfully. Prisoners appeared distressed on waking and have trouble sleeping. Prisoners experienced dry skin, chronic pain and halitosis.

All normal for this report.

Damian Muskett

Max Glover: The Time Ball Tower Keeper's Report 2013

Mostly what I think about is women.

I'm too young to be here. I've told them that. I should be over on the mainland, enjoying myself. Instead, I'm here.

But it's okay.

But my arm hurts. Fucken protestors cut me. Sliced my arm as if it'd stop me going out. The prisoners want me to show them. They haven't seen a wound in a long, long time they reckon, but they do that side eye thing, where you know they're keeping secrets.

Everyone keeps secrets. They've told me shit…just ridiculous shit about the keepers and all the people back in the town that make me understand *nothing* is real, nothing at all and you can't trust a single soul.

Weird. I thought I saw Phillipa Muskett. Just her shadow. But I went downstairs and there was nothing, unless there was a disturbance in the dust, which there might have been.

I'm jumping at everything.

I never used to do that.

Summary OF CONDITIONS: I found the prisoners to be well nourished and of sound mind. Prisoners bathed successfully. Prisoners appeared distressed on waking and have trouble sleeping. Prisoners experienced dry skin, chronic pain and halitosis.

All normal for this report.

Max Glover

Phillipa Muskett: The Time Ball Tower Keeper's Report, 2014

Goodbyes?

Hate them. So much fuss.

Someone handed me a velvet bag full of small parcels. All labelled, gifts for the prisoners. Many of them barely knew which family member was even out there. It was an inherited duty, something they did without thinking.

There was a tally kept. If no bad behavior was reported, a small present could be sent. Things like cigarettes, handmade blankets, small portraits. The town prided itself on ensuring all gifts reached them, even the bottles of rum, the money; the things other people may have stolen.

Max hugged me. Gave me a box of chocolates. "Don't save them. Eat them all in one go. Indulge. Don't worry, they're not poisoned." He had a bit of a thing about poisoning.

He helped me into the boat which bobbed at the end of the New Pier. It's been here thirty years, but we still call it the new one.

The boatman took my hand, helped me to settle, then sorted out all my belongings.

"All set?" he said.

I faced the tower; already it seemed as if no one existed on the shore. They cheered as we set off.

The boatman kept up a steady, blurred patter which I could barely distinguish from the sound of the waves.

"I'm the first to do this job permanent. Not sure how many reports you've read, but you'll see how shitty it was before. We needed a permanent boatman and I'm it. Continuity," he said.

He was in his mid-forties but seemed much older.

Apart from being boatman, he watched the coastline, kept the beach clear of litter, was a self-appointed lifeguard. If he'd saved a couple of young women who didn't really need saving, if he'd squeezed tits, run his hand over arses, then he'd saved others for real and perhaps it was a pay-off. He never did it out of the water, nor did he touch the children. And he wasn't bad-looking, so maybe they didn't mind it, but he'd never admit it, not even at confession. He never did it to me.

"Best advice I can give; don't listen to their weasely words."

"I'll keep my headphones on so I can't hear."

The boatman nodded. "Good plan. They'll whisper to you. They'll whisper whatever they think will set them free. By which they mean, kill them. Or tuck them in the boat and take them home. Can you imagine? Who would look after them?"

He looked up at the top of the tower. "Well, I'd do it. I've got the space. Shame my missus'd never allow it."

Did he want a response from me?

"Burnett would be glad of the company."

"Yeah, nah. They're where they belong. Punishment's what they deserve. They'll tell you stories. We don't repeat them. If you never repeat them, you will forget them. That's one good thing. Remember that."

I understood punishment. As a child, I'd been caught once stealing a chocolate bar from the shop. I was tied, as many of us were, to a rock overlooking the Time Ball Tower. Left there past midnight. They said that if the moon shadow of the Time Ball Tower reached you, you'd be damned to eternal life, eternal wandering. The longer you spent near the Time Ball Tower at night, the longer its moon shadow.

It helped keep the teenagers indoors, or at least away from the water. Not me. I loved everything about the Tower, even its shadow.

Many's the night I'd visited Burnett at dawn, sneaking in after a date.

The boatman began to hum to himself.

I had waited for this trip for most of my life and didn't want to miss a second. Should I look to shore and watch it shrinking? Should I look to the Time Ball Tower, watch it getting closer? Look for the troll?

The day was very bright, the sun reflecting off the water and off the sides of the Time Ball Tower.

"You'll go quiet in there. We all do. Wanting to be sure about them.

You'll listen when they talk. You'll start to doubt. That's when you read the files. There are details the general public don't know. Only we get to know. Then you'll be sure."

The crimes of the prisoners were well known to us all. I was looking forward to these details, to having information others didn't have.

"Keep reading the reports as well, so you'll know you're not alone. Keep busy."

"I'm a photographer," I said, holding up my camera. 'I'm going to be doing that most of my spare time.'

"Good to have a project."

"What was yours?" I asked.

"Cataloguing. Keeping a record. I'm not very creative."

I'd seen a lot of the projects, on display in the Club.

One had read the so-called Great Books of the Western World and produced an artistic impression of each book.

One had counted the number of sins committed in the Bible.

There was a framed needlework; amazing detailed stuff, a remake of the Bayeaux tapestry.

There was a ship's model and a model of the Time Ball Tower itself.

There were heaps of books, mostly self-published, some quite successfully and there were animal prints and carved things made of ivory. Not the sort of thing you'd see elsewhere.

We traveled in silence. Then he said, "Before people sailed over the edge of the world, the sea horizon seemed endless. Eternal. If you sailed your whole life, you would never reach the end. Even if your life was eternal."

Too soon we were there. Up close, I could see white bones, caught in the rocks. Sticking up like tiny masts, seaweed caught on them. He maneuvered the boat through the whirlpool like water.

"Last chance," he said. "I can take you back if you like. But don't. This is an experience only a few ever get a chance to live. You'll never forget it."

"Of course I'm staying," I said.

We unloaded my boxes, and he handed me a silver bag. "Just something to help." Inside were large supplies of painkillers and sleeping tablets. "Don't overdo it or it'll be on me, but you might need these."

He settled the last of my things on the rocks. "I can help you carry it all upstairs. Help you get settled in. I'm in no hurry."

They'd warned me.

"No, it's fine. Thanks."

"Get your things inside away from the weather, but take your time getting it upstairs. Don't kill yourself. You'll be bored shitless in a while and this will seem like a useful thing to do. Get yourself settled before you see to the prisoners. Put your things away, make yourself a cuppa tea. There's always whiskey under the sink. All being well, I'll bring over some fresh goodies for you in a month. Keep a list, they reckon. Of the stuff you like. Other than that, you'll be heading back with me in a year."

"Or sooner, if I decide I need a break!" I was sick of his voice. Dreaming of quiet.

He shook his head. "If you have a break, you're done. No one ever goes back.

"You'll love it there. All your favorite foods waiting for you, a bit of peace before the media onslaught begins." I'd seen this, the excitement to get a keeper's story when they returned from the tower. "Gives you that time to acclimatize. Because you'll be a bit crazy when I pick you up and it takes a while to wear off."

"I'll be fine."

"Everyone thinks so. And it's nothing permanent. But I haven't picked up one single soul at the end of a shift in the last twenty-five years who wasn't gone with cabin fever." He hung his head slightly. "I'll tell you what I tell everyone. I've seen 'em in and I've seen 'em out again. I know who copes the best. You'll be right."

"How do you know?"

"You've got the right nature."

Later, I would understand what he meant by this.

I waved him goodbye and watched as he sailed away. I wanted to experience this alone, in isolation. I didn't even want to hear his boat motor.

Then I turned and faced the tower.

The base was mosaicked, as were the steps leading to the door. I wonder who'd done that one, or who inspired it.

Painted across the door was, "Never Forget." There was also a sign saying, "The Breatharian Institute." Funny!

I pushed the door open. It was stiff on its hinges but swung open okay. I raised my hands protectively, in case they'd gathered themselves and were ready to attack, but nothing. The front door was shiny on the inside. This was one of our duties, to keep the metal shining.

The ground floor was grimy, with leaves around the edges, dirt up the walls. Watermarks? It had once been tiled, but most of these had long since lifted. There were glorious patterns left behind that I'd photograph once I got settled. A broom sat by the door and I quickly swept the worst of the mess out before I found the generator and set it going. The last job would be to fill that generator with fuel, ready for the next keeper.

I followed the boatman's advice and dragged all my things inside. I'd suss out the place before taking it all upstairs but grabbed the small suitcase which held the things to fulfill immediate needs. Food. Drink. Toothbrush. My camera.

The stairs were steep. I wouldn't want to climb them too many times a day, although it'd definitely improve the leg muscles.

The original plan was for two or three keepers at a time to stay in the Time Ball Tower, so three tiny bedrooms were built. With only one keeper, most kept clothing and other belongings in one, and used the second as a study or storage room. There were suitcases in the storage room, and boxes with names on them. I'd been told to only take what I planned to carry home, that there was no more space, and that was clearly true. So much crap left behind. A stuffed cat with a name tag ("Mittens", which made me laugh) and a vase painted with roses and a plate with Queen Elizabeth II, raised, in faded paint. Piles of books, boxes of collected shells, broken furniture and some old electrical things I could not even identify. A pressure cooker? A bread machine? The floor was carpeted, thick, expensive, slightly sodden.

Most keepers had slept in the third room, kept clear and uncluttered.

I unpacked some clothes. Laid my grandmother's scarf on the end of the bed. I stroked it a couple of times, then I took my supplies to the kitchen. I had a freezer bag full of food, including plenty of dried chili, and lemons and limes in all varieties. Fresh, juiced, preserved.

"You don't want to get scurvy," my mother had said. She sniffed each lemon before she packed it. "Make sure you eat them. Lack of vitamin C can lead to weird visions."

I made coffee (instant for now. I'd get proper stuff sorted soon) and opened up the chocolates Max gave me and ate my way through the top layer.

I climbed to the top, to see the Ball. We'd been warned not to touch it because even the slightest bit of sweat might throw it off balance, but I planned to ignore that. I did pull on a pair of gloves, though.

I opened the last small door, which was stiff with salt, and propped it open with a large, heavy rock that sat waiting. Wind blew in, but there was little to damage in the tiny foyer. I climbed the ladder, glad I was wearing gloves, because I could feel the chill of metal even through the leather.

The ball was even larger than I thought it would be. A wonder of science.

I could put my arms around it and only reach a third of the way. It was smooth but not perfectly so, and there were odd patches of warmth. The wind nearly blew me over, and I was glad of the cage up there. They needed the cage. Too much risk without it. Too easy to jump off.

It was a beautiful thing but marred with fingerprints and greasy marks so I wasn't the only one to ignore the rules. I rubbed at one, then another, and I was lost in awe of this glorious object.

It took about two hours to clean and polish. I had a lot of breaks for warm drinks (wine) because my hands would freeze up.

I took a hundred photos. People would pay good money for shots like these.

Then I heard the whirring and realized it was about to drop, so got myself out of direct earshot. Even so, the noise of it shuddered through me like an earthquake. I had a headache, a dull one that was not quite painkiller worthy.

I wanted to sleep. To eat. This was the moment, though. The reality. So had I had a quick vodka and lime.

Then I went upstairs, to where the prisoners sat.

They were behind the door. As much as I thought I'd prepared myself by spending time with Burnett (and the oldest of them were not much younger, one hundred and eighty or so), knowing the way he smelled, the way he spoke, here there were many of them. And Burnett was cared for whereas they were neglected so their decay would be worse.

Would I see evil rising off them, like heat waves or petrol fumes?

I checked my hair, checked my clothing. I didn't want any loose threads, too much cleavage. I didn't want to trip or have hair in my eyes when I presented myself. They would pick up on any flaws.

I carried the bag of gifts, thinking to disarm them that way, focusing them on the gifts rather than on me, while I assessed them.

I wiped eucalyptus oil under my nose, a tip I'd taken from the Club, and pushed open the door. I did it quietly, hoping to watch them for a while before they noticed me.

It smelled like a guinea pig's cage. They were lined up along the two walls, very little space between them, but enough walkway space that I wouldn't trip over their outstretched legs. They had no beds, no pillows. They sat on the floor, resting their backs against the wall.

There was a buzz; the prisoners murmuring, or perhaps simply breathing.

They were dried up, like shrunken heads, tongues protruding and slightly black. Nostrils broader than they should be. Eyes dull, opaque. Arseholes? I hoped not to see those.

Their fingers were clenched over, and some of them had nails grown into the palms. I once saw a documentary about a paralyzed, dying woman, and she had towels in the palms of her hands, to stop her nails digging in. Nobody had put towels in the hands of these prisoners. I was supposed to cut the nails for them, but seeing the piles of the previous clippings made me feel ill. Yellow piles of hard calcium.

"Here—he—is!"

The voice was slow, low, grating.

I walked slowly through them. The smell was intense and made me gag. Like rancid coconut oil.

The prisoners showed signs of illnesses; some were a mess of lesions.

I felt pity and sorrow for them. I knew that wasn't what should be expressed, that I couldn't show the slightest empathy or emotion. Did working in the dementia ward help prepare me for their almost inhuman appearance? Possibly.

I backed away, thinking to settle myself more before engaging further. I felt unsure. I hadn't expected to feel such an attack of pity.

"Come—back!—We—don't—bite!" I heard. "Come—on,—mate!—Tell—us—your—name.—What—family—are—you—from?"

"I'm not going anywhere." And I stood there and faced them. "You don't need to know my name. You can call me Keeper. Family...none of your fucking business." I hoped my voice sounded strong, that it wouldn't crack.

"She.—She.—It's—female."

"Yep, female," I said. My voice echoed in the room, felt impossibly loud, and they cringed.

"You—look—like—a—man—from—behind.—Muscly—bitch."

I'd been warned often enough not to let them know how I felt about anything, so I kept my smile to myself. I hate being identified by gender and enjoyed this confusion, even if they thought they were insulting me. One of them masturbated constantly; he always would. Keepers called him the Greyhound.

"What—year—is—it?"

Over their heads were written the dates of their birth and their arrival, with a hyphen between, like the dates on a tombstone. Beside that, each one had a small picture. In the retirement home, the residents' pictures showed them with their favorite thing. A boat, a cat, a horse.

These pictures depicted the prisoners' terrible acts.

"No need for you to know," I said. "You don't need to know about time. Unless you've been counting the ball drops."

One wall had I REPENT written over and over many times, by many hands. I REPENT.

"What—family?—Who's—your—father?—Your—mother?—Are—you—married?—Are—you—a—virgin?"

Questions coming at me so slowly that I lost track of them.

"I have gifts. Who deserves a gift? I've heard that none of you do."

"I—do.—I—do."

They were disappointed. The gifts were bland, meaningless. A packet of tea. A plain notebook. A squeezy stress ball.

"We—used—to—get—real—presents.–Nude–photos.—Underpants.–Carved–things.–Real–treasures.–Now.–Crap.–We–used–to–get—messages—too.–Letters."

"Those people are all long dead. Anyone who cared about you is dead." My voice came out sharp, hard. I had worried it would come out a whisper.

And while they knew this very well, still it made them cry. The men had few items beside them, things perhaps once meaningful but now disintegrated, pointless. A small book. A dried rose. A rusted tin.

"All–our–good–things–are–in–boxes.–Away–from–us.–Ring–of–three–golden–metals.–A–silver–serving–dish.–A–prayer–bowl.–All–gone."

Later, I explored the storage room, looking for the treasures the prisoners spoke of. But anything of value in the named boxes was long since stolen or lost and replaced with bottle tops, scraps of paper, plastic toys, small broken pieces of stone.

This was hypocrisy writ large.

I found a box of the nude photos and underwear that women had sent in for the prisoners, but didn't delve into that; it was clearly collected for masturbation purposes.

The keepers would never admit to this. But I'd seen some of the stuff they described; under the portrait of Keeper 1872. I knew that's what it was.

I also found stacks of porn in a cupboard, going back seventy years. I wasn't too keen to touch the magazines themselves, but it was fascinating to see the changes and the similarities over the years. I considered adding a *Photographer's Weekly* to the pile.

Time passed. The Ball dropped. It sounded so different from the inside. On shore, it was a hollow thud, a distant reminder, as regular as the tide. Here, it was like my heart dropped with it.

Each time it dropped, I jumped and that never changed. Time passing. Time passing. Time passing. And so loud, so mind-numbing loud.

I felt a weird gnawing hunger, but the idea of food made me feel sick. Still, I climbed to the kitchen to raid my supplies. I opened a packet of biscuit-and-dip, ate that staring out the window. Quick couple of brandies on the side.

I hadn't touched any of them, but I felt filthy.

I showered, water tepid, a lot of soap.

That night, I slept badly. It was the noises. I didn't know good from bad, and kept imagining them crawling up to me.

The Ball dropped.

I spent three hours scrubbing the kitchen. It wasn't really dirty, but there was a memory there of others. Then I sat down with coffee and biscuits and reports. I left the originals alone, not wanting to damage them. Plus, I liked Burnett's snarky notes. I tried to make an index, so I could look back on it. Surprised no one had thought of this before.

I listened at the door for the prisoners. They were mostly quiet, with the occasional call of pain. They felt nothing, we were told, but had the memory of doing so.

The baby farmer (baby farming bitch) called out to me.

I stood and stared at her. I'd felt disturbed by the 1919 report, with its simple listing. I didn't know what it meant, but understood that there was something secretive about it. Private. Simple listing, then the description. "Baby farming bitch."

The woman begged me. "Please–as–a–woman.–Men–make–it–worse."

The woman hitched her skirt up. Her knees were apart.

"Give–us–a–look," one of the men said, and I took his gift away on the spot.

The stench was terrible. I have never smelled anything like it. Like the rubbish tip, but far, far worse.

"Whatever–they–liked,–it's–shoved–in."

I gagged. Had to cover my mouth and nose. It stank.

"I–got–some–out–but–not–most."

She said, "Help–me,–woman.–Girls–together."

But I had work to do. I took up the broom and swept around them, the smell of waste rising. It was old, awful, and I needed to go downstairs, outside, when I was finished.

We weren't supposed to help, or show any acts of kindness.

I was told, if you ever feel sorry for them, read their files. I'd been ambivalent about doing this. I knew parts of what they'd done; the basics of the crimes. We all knew that. Did I want to know the details? Would it make me judge them at a personal level? I'd been told, "Once it's there, it stays. Like cancer. Like a sleeping ball of death at the base of your skull. It doesn't seem to do anything, but it is so near you can almost smell it." But I wanted to know about this woman. What she did. So I could stop myself from helping her.

She'd suffered plenty, I knew, but I didn't understand the reality until I saw the woman. The reports were mostly vague, and misleading, except for the one that graphically described the "sexual encounter" as he'd called it, with the inmates chanting, "Good man, give her one, good man, give her one."

He was going in time with them, he said, and he wondered if sex would ever work again without that chant.

The keeper of 1950 wondered *who are good men and women?* It gave me pause, as well. Being called a good man by this lot? That's not something you'd boast to your mother about.

My mother. She never wanted kids; she was terrified of the idea. I don't want to think about how we happened. Did Dad trick her? How? Get her drunk? She's so disconnected most of the time, but she loves us. She really does. More than he does. Sometimes I think he only had us so he could send us out to the tower.

So I did it. I read her file.

In our family, we talked about the monsters all the time. Around the dinner table, on long drives, all the time. So really, I knew. But there were details in here no one ever told me.

She had been here since 1901. A baby farmer, a woman who had taken orphan babies, and children unwanted, taken large fees for them, and, if she couldn't easily find new (paying) homes for them, killed them. None of this was disputed.

It was far too tempting not to read the rest of the files. The cover on them read, "These are the nastiest arseholes of their time. Think Stalin. Think genocidal maniacs. Think baby-biting freaks. And worse. Read the files, but remember, you'll never be able to wipe them from your mind."

I glanced at them to begin with, trying to reconcile the husks I saw with the representations of the worst human beings in the world in the files.

I helped the baby-farmer, coming back with gloves and some tongs from the kitchen.

Pencil knife fork rolled up paper stick stone fingernail clipping toenail clipping no bacon rind for fear of stench wool straps, seagull feather egg shell cigarette butt match stick dried tea leaves china doll arm washed up at shore, same piece of shoe, suitcase handle fishing net fishing line tin label hair ribbon with strap, some watch fittings, rusted nail pennies cigarette lighter. I found all of these. I found a carved chicken bone: 1932.

I thought of the portrait of 1932. A big man with a face something like a pig's. I could see what his family might have teased him about.

His signature was tight, small, easily readable and I thought perhaps he was the same.

I threw them out the window when I was done, all the things I found and the tongs as well. I pulled her dress back down, tucked it under her. Modesty far too late.

I took some photos of the items before I threw them out. Just for the record. Mostly, my photos are of things. If they're of people, I've usually objectified them. It's my way.

"Professional Time Ball Tower keepers need to rise above it. Not be affected by what they see and hear, not pass judgment." That's what I'd been told.

But of course, we do pass judgment. It was impossible not to, once I'd read the files and seen the inmates. The keepers inflicted damage. They left notes filled with hatred and fury for the prisoners.

"Thank–you.–Thank–you," the Baby Farmer whispered.

"It's not because I like you," I said. "I despise you. How do you do that to children?"

"Are–you–a–mother?–Mothers–are–always–the–tenderest.–Did–you–leave–children–behind?"

"This is my job."

"You–left–them–behind?–Poor–mites–need–their–mother."

"You'd all know, right? Every last one of you brought up in a loving home."

I felt in control. They would only know what I let them know. "Every–last–fucker–here–was–abandoned–by–a–mother."

The Ball dropped.

I ate the last of the chocolates Max gave me. Started a list of things I wanted delivered. Chocolate. Oranges. More coffee.

I breathed the salt air deep, watched seagulls, daydreamed Max and me together.

The prisoners all showed symptoms of scurvy, but I was loath to donate any of my lemons to them. They were lethargic, had spots on their legs. They had spongy gums. They were pale (though of course they had been without direct sun for decades), yellowish, and their teeth were mostly gone.

One seemed even weaker than the others. Even less human. He groaned constantly.

"Are you in pain?"

"Why,–you–got–painkillers?"

"Not for you."

"My–head–aches.–It's–a–terrible–burden–to–me."

"He never stops," another said.

This was Grayson Alexander, the youngest of them all, who was only fifteen years old when he was locked up. His teeth were sharp, like the victim of untreated syphilis, the only one of them with any real teeth left.

"I'm–only–here–because–people–want–"youth"–locked–up.–But– I'm–nearly–the–same–age–you–are.–I–was–fifteen–when–they–did– the–thing–to–me–and–I–stopped–living–the–moment–they–did.–I'm– still–that–age.–They–stole–my–life–away."

I remembered my younger brother at that age. I couldn't imagine my brother having the…maturity to commit the crimes this boy had committed. His file said he was born in 1907. He came to the Time Ball Tower in 1925.

His crime was the long-term, horrendous mutilation of children.

He said, "Do–you–want–to–know–this?–You–have–kids–yourself.– Don't–judge–me–on–that."

"I don't have kids," I said. Shit. He got me. I'd have to be more careful. "Don't–believe–the–files."

"So you're saying the files lie?"

"The–files–are–full–of–nightmares–from–which–you–will–never– recover."

I read out his charges to him, hoping to disgust him, but he liked it, got a kick out of it. The rest of them, too.

"That's–me!" Grayson said. Delighted. "I've–suffered–the–greatest–loss– of–all–of–them.–Not–much–life–lived–before–being–in–here,–so–my– only–memories–are–of–childhood.–They–all–got–to–live–a–life.–I–was– only–trying–to–beautify–those–children.–Beauty–is–Power."

"I must be powerless, then. You are not a good man," I said. "Doesn't matter how old you were."

"I'm–innocent,–I–am,–I–never–did–it."

I knew the motto.

Heinous, unrepentant, undeniably guilty.

"Your file says you were caught. Pants down. In the hole you'd made in the girls…"

I stopped, distraught. It was too much. The image of it broke me.

"Her–stomach!–You–ever–fucked–a–stomach?"

I wanted to break his neck, but that was it, wasn't it? No end to their suffering. Instead, I lifted him up. His mouth came close to my hair and I felt him trying to suck it.

I carried him upstairs. "No," he said. "Not–the–box."

The box was on the top floor. Long enough for a tall man, wide enough so that if you were capable of movement you could turn from side to side, it had three drilled air holes.

I folded him into the storage box and shut the lid. Let him feel buried alive. It was a punishment they all hated.

I lifted the lid. "Just hope nothing happens to me. No one would ever find you in there. You'll be there until the world turns into a black hole."

"Make–a–note–where–I–am."

"No, I won't."

It was cruel, but I couldn't bear to hear him talk. To know that, given the chance, he'd do the same again, made me feel vicious and full of the need to punish.

I was glad I'd read the files. I needed to feel this hatred.

Taking this action made me feel more powerful than I would have liked. No matter what they said, I was stronger. More alive. There was something tempting that the other keepers hadn't resisted. I would.

At the same time, I wished I hadn't read the files. The images gave me nightmares and I found it hard to think of anything else.

I focused on food. Keepers are great fans of slow food. All in the pot, cook it for hours. Our Keeper's Recipe Book said, "You don't want to be running up the stairs to check on anything. Make and forget, that's the way."

I put up a beef stew, starting with a tinned soup base. I opened cans of beef, poured dried herbs, tipped in some chili, and set the slow cooker going. We are the experts at turning canned food gourmet.

I walked back past the gallery. My portrait was a photograph, not the first. I hung it next to 2013, my friend-with-benefits Max, who showed no signs in the portrait of the paranoia he now displayed. None of them did. I thought I'd like to see before and after photos, but no one had ever made it happen.

There was other artwork, too, like the entire series by my great grand-father, Rossiter. Theirs was such a beautiful love story. He became obsessed with "capturing" his wife Ruby, my great-grandmother. Painted her portrait a hundred times or more. On teapots and teacups. Everywhere. He'd drawn her on walls, even the toilet wall. Along the stairs. Everywhere, she peered at you. I wasn't sure if this was romantic or creepy, but I leant towards creepy. Obsessive.

I admired Rossiter's dedication, to keep trying, to persist in getting to the tower over a number of years. There was a teenager, when I was young, who had failed his physical, or his mental, or something. Some said he had a relative imprisoned out on the rock and that's why he wasn't allowed. He committed suicide because of his failure. I always thought that was the worst thing. If Rossiter had given up like that, maybe he wouldn't have married Ruby. Maybe I wouldn't even exist.

I wondered about myself. Would I change? I couldn't imagine being any different from the way I was now. Not in a year, anyway. I could see myself well in the future, a real adult, settled. But now?

There was one titled, "The Stones of Little Cormoran." It was signed Eugene. I'd seen some of his art in Burnett's room, and it all had this same naivety about it. Almost outsider art. On the back of the painting, someone had drawn a family tree. He was my ancestor Harriet's brother.

Burnett spoke about him in his *True and Honest History of the Time Ball Tower*. That book had been part of my life for a long time.

Burnett Barton's *True and Honest History of the Time Ball Tower* is a thousand pages long and growing. He's had a long time to write it. He doesn't mind moving slowly, although sometimes it makes him cry because he knows he'll never be done. That he'll never again see the places he's chronicling.

And that, perhaps, the pages will turn to dust while he still lives, a husk, a living skeleton, an almost inanimate object.

Much of the text was written in the early days of Tempuston with the more recent works, of fifty years or so ago, mostly consisting of "I Wish" and "I want" with nothing else. Sometimes, "Tired." I'd transcribed a lot of it. You could see the progression of my handwriting, from the large, round, careful letters of an eight-year-old to the drawn-out, rather beautiful scrawl I used now.

We started on the day I'd fallen and hurt both knees. My mother didn't care less; she didn't even notice. So (and I'd already learned this), I went to the old people's home for sympathy.

They handed out peppermints and marshmallows and you gained a lot of brownie points just for walking in the door.

Our living cautionary tale Burnett Barton's room was at the end of the corridor. I hadn't met him at that stage.

"Don't pull back the sheets. Underneath he's just a skeleton with some bits hanging off it. The only thing left is his head and his bones." That's what we'd been told.

I followed my favorite nurse down there, wanting more care, my tears now forced and starting to annoy me.

"Look who I've brought. It's Phillipa. She's dying of a scratched knee!"

"Two!" I said, my voice a whisper as I stared at the horrifying sight. I'm used to it now, but I still remember thinking, *how is he even alive?*

"You never sank into the ground while sitting on a church pew," Burnett said. "You never drowned in your own church. It was an act of the devil, drawing us down to hell because he couldn't get us any other way. No matter what the temptation, we resisted."

This page appeared to be tear-stained, but Burnett's sweat was very salty so it could be that. Burnett would never see Little Cormoran's stones again.

There was nothing left of his village, as far as he knew. It found no mention in the history books. There was no record of the town's demise. No memory beyond his own. That is all he has left to trust.

I had a lot of questions about his history, now. As a kid, I accepted it all. But now, I know more. Now, I have questions.

I asked the prisoners. They said they knew everything.

"So tell me about Edna."

"He–killed–her."

"Mercy–killing."

I imagined corners of his mouth twitching. A smile.

His father's promise.

"How can Burnett say people were not sorry that Harriet disappeared?" I didn't see how this could possibly be true. She was a loving mother and grandmother, a loving wife, and from all I'd heard, all I'd read, she was greatly missed. Why would she leave them? Why would she leave the town she'd helped to create?

I was most curious about Harriet. She sounded like an amazing woman, like my grandmother. I wanted to be like them, not like my mother. Harriet was full of anger and determination to make change, have an effect on the world. That was clear. And that was good. If you're not angry sometimes, you're not being honest with yourself.

Did Burnett love Grace or Harriet? Or both?

They didn't answer any of that.

Something crackled, as if glass was heating, or plastic shifting. I'd been away from them for long enough. I'd done all the chores expected of me, but if this year was going to mean anything, I had to engage. No matter how sympathetic I felt. How much pity.

The files helped a lot. They didn't help my headache, though, so I swallowed some painkillers.

The smell of meat cooking reached me, making me hungry. Slow-cooked tinned beef, done to perfection.

Already I craved a bowl of steamed broccoli. A green salad with fresh tomatoes. Stir-fried beans with garlic and spring onions. It made me think of home, and the family meals we'd shared, all of us around the table laughing, eating wonderful food, and our dad telling his stories, and our mum loving us so very much. She's telling us stories of her world travels and we talk about our adventures, our travels, and what a great family we are.

Did I?

Did we?

What is it about this place? I'd noticed it in the reports. Some delusions. Some forgetfulness.

"**C**an you smell that?" I asked the prisoners.

There was an exhalation of air, those sighs they expelled when filled with regret.

"A–mouthful–each.–A–taste–for–us."

"It'll make you sick."

"Is–your–cooking–that–bad?"

In the end, I did give them all a spoonful, if only to prove I wasn't greedy. I wasn't bullied or tricked into it. I believed it was the right thing to do.

I waited three days, though, when there were still leftovers and I couldn't face them anymore.

I spooned a mouthful for each of them. When I went back a day later, half of them still had food in their mouths.

"Saving–it," they said, "savoring." I yawned. I wasn't sleeping well. It was a mistake to let them see that. I wouldn't tell them about the dreams, the constant dreams of my teeth falling out.

"**Y**ou–got–sleeping–tablets?–Take–'em.–Share–'em.–I'll–take–a–baker's–dozen."

Me too, me too, they all said, until I threatened to lock them in solitary. That shut them up.

Burnett was in solitary, effectively. But he could hear everything that went on in the rest home. Catch glimpses of the pathetic real world going on outside his door.

The Ball dropped.

I swept the floor. I'd get used to it, but it still made me retch.

"We–make–you–sick,–do–we?" This was Number Twenty-two. He'd kept people in his ten-bedroomed rooming house. Chained them, let them starve, photographed it. "Show–us–your–camera.–It's–a–beauty."

Some awful part of me wanted to see his photos. He was the weakest of the lot. He slumped, barely able to lift his head. More dark depression than anything else.

He started crying. I opened the fold-out stool I'd discovered in the store room and sat next to him.

"What's up?" I said, not really caring, but not wanting things to spiral out of control, either. Others had started up.

"I–like–your–hair," he said.

I laughed. Sure, it was blonde, but I looked more like a poodle than a model. I thought, anyway. It surprised me when people thought I was sexy.

"Thanks," I said. "Is that why you're crying?"

"I–just–can't–stop," he said. "You–got–painkillers?"

We didn't give them painkillers.

"Don't–you–feel–something?–Anything–for–me?"

I shook my head.

"You–bastards–never–do.–They–say–we're–the–evil–ones.–But–you–bastards–feel–nothing."

"None of us? You reckon we're all the same?"

"Most.–Most."

So there. Was that it? I was chosen more because I was capable of non-feeling than for anything else? Renata always pushed me to show compassion; I could never see the point.

To shut up his crying, I took Grayson out of the box, squeezed this one in. I took a photo.

As I carried him back downstairs, Grayson clung to me.

"I–was–dreaming," he said, "and–dreaming–and–dreaming–and–dreaming–of–you."

I put him back in place without responding, then went upstairs to see if Number Twenty-two had any belongings. I wanted to see those photos.

He had one small box. Inside, an old photo, possibly of his mother. Someone had superimposed a knife over it. There was a tin wedding ring and a piece of leather and nothing more.

I checked the sawdust supplies and collected driftwood to make more.

They said I moved too slow at Tech, but why is their pace the right one? So what if I didn't get work done in their time frame?

I checked the time ball mechanism. It was a beautiful thing, oiled, perfect. I could watch it shift for hours.

I grabbed my camera and went to the prisoners. I wasn't tired of it yet, although they didn't like the flash in their eyes and asked me what I was doing.

"I'm immortalizing you!" I said, but they didn't think it was funny. They didn't think much was funny, unless it was the suffering of another. They were too angry, or perhaps too tired, to laugh most of the time.

I went through the routine of sweeping between them, and they complained about the dust rising. They sneezed if they could.

"Stay–a–while," Grayson said. "Don't–go. Stay–a–while. I was lonely in that box, dreaming of you."

"It's time for my next job. Busy, busy," I said. Stick to the routine, do not vary it. If you have the routine, you have control.

Keeper 1877 established the routine we still mostly followed, all of us realizing the importance of routine to sanity. Though it was 1873 who'd set up the systems themselves. The idea that we could remain in control was his.

1877 said: *It's habit. Unthinking habit that gets us through each dull day. If we have to think too much about each dreary choice, we would not survive.*

Reading the reports helped mitigate the monotony of the routine, although I didn't mind the dreariness of it too much (7:15 turn on generator two. 7:18, turn on kettle) because it freed my mind up to think elsewhere. The tasks didn't feel Sisyphean, because there was a point to them, even if that point was, at times, simply maintaining the status quo.

The Ball dropped.

The Ball dropped.

I swept up the old sawdust and made new from driftwood that caught in the rocks, using the large grinder in the corner under the stairs. I hadn't noticed it on arrival. Someone had written over the grinder: Fee Fie Fo Fum.

I had books of photography and every issue of *Time-Life* on my iPad. I found books, diaries, notebooks, belonging to the prisoners or left behind by the keepers, and they were them both dull and dusty and full of juicy gossip. Some a summary of conditions, others a graphic description of sexual fantasies. I never knew which until I looked inside.

I woke up early every day, snapped the sunrise.

At 7:45, on alternate days, I was to check on prisoners. Allow food as required. I disliked the feeding while at the same time being fascinated by it.

What they loved was tallow candles. Even the newer prisoners.

"Give–us–one–to–suck,–love."

"Go–on.–It's–time.–Give–us–a–treat."

There was a store of them in the lower room. They smelled faintly rancid and made me think of the time I'd helped clear out an old lady's fridge and found ancient roast lamb, sitting in a solidified pool of fat. Not exactly a rotten smell, but almost.

I handed out the candles.

"You're–a–kind–lady.–Just–like–your–granny."

"We–knew–she–was–a–good–one.–We–could–smell–it."

They all sniffed the air like dogs.

"She–wore–a–long–scarf,–remember?–So–long–we–grabbed–hold–of–it.–Could–have–choked–her–like–Isadora–Duncan.–Bet–she's–still–got–it–

to–remember–us–by.–Bet–it's–a–family–heirloom."

"Wisht–she'd–left–it–here–for–us.–Felt–nice."

I'd found a box of wine, still good, and sat there sipping it. I must be used to the smell of them.

"I–remember–that–scarf," the abortion doctor said. He did it for profit, but he did it for pleasure, too. He told women their fetuses weren't viable. He said, they won't have a life and neither will you. But most of them, those babies, there was nothing wrong with them. "Could–have–used–it–as–a–bandage."

"I–remember–the–smell–of–it," the one I call 1938 said.

"Oranges,–and–gentle–sweat.–A–man's–cologne.–Sunlight–as–well."

I reckoned they'd be able to figure out what that sensitivity to smell meant, now. They'd give 1938 a syndrome to manage. No doctor had ever been out there, though. Never would, most likely.

I had the scarf on my bed. I wouldn't be letting them near it.

I was glad to have the scarf. I wouldn't wear it in front of the prisoners. It was my private thing.

One of the punishing things was that they remembered everything clearly. There was none of the kindness of forgetting, of pain easing. The happy things they remembered too, but this brought a sense of great loss. They knew all they'd missed out on. They remembered birthdays, heroes' returns from war, sex they'd never have again, meals when their tongue could still taste, and the freedom of walking.

I hated them for this remembering, though, thinking of my grandmother and how her mind was going. It pissed me off that they had such clear minds and she didn't. And they didn't preserve history in any meaningful way, whereas she could share so much. I was angry with myself for not ever taking the time to listen to her. I bet she's been locked up by now. I should have made Dad promise not to put her in a home while I was away. I knew enough about those places to know how much she'd hate it. Dad would have done it in a heartbeat, but I always stopped him. He said the doctors said she was a menace.

A menace. So she gets lost and shouts at people. Big deal.

"I–remember–another–scarf,–made–of–twisted–leather.–Stretched–so–gentle–around–the–throat–that–they–didn't–even–know–they–were–dying." That was the priest.

"Go–on!–Details!" one of them said. This evil old man, the Grand-father, I'll call him, is Renata's family. The one whose imprisonment had formed her existence. So much of her life, her family's lives, were tied up in his rights.

And he was as bad as the rest of them here.

He egged the others on to boast, to tell of the terrible things.

He didn't deserve the belief his family had in him.

I'll never tell him she's a friend of mine. He doesn't need to know that. I had the wooden puzzle she'd asked me to give him in my room; I didn't want to hand it over.

I recorded some of his words, and I'd tell Renata about his file, how awful he was. I also scavenged about in the pile of belongings, looking for evidence that might set Renata free from caring.

I found a book with the grandfather's name on the front page. This was Renata's ancestry.

"Aged 11," it said in fading ink, and his name.

"Look at this!" I waved it at him, giving in to curiosity when I shouldn't have. The book was over a hundred years old. Dusty. Discoloured. He remembered everything about it.

"That–was–before.–When–I–could–have–had–a–good–life,–a–different–life.–At–eleven,–I–was–an–innocent.–I–could–have–been–a–policeman.–A–priest.–I–could–have–been–loved.–A–good–father.–Instead,–my–grandfather–taught–me–the–same–shit–I–taught–my–kids.–Best–get–it–from–home,–right?–He–gave–me–this–book.–I–wore–my–old–shorts–my–mother–hadn't–darned–yet–and–a–scratchy–brown–jumper–knitted–by–my–grandmother–for–my–grandfather.–She–hated–him.–I–think–she–stitched–burrs–into–that–jumper–because–it–scratched–like–a–vest–of–thistles."

"You remember so clearly."

"We–remember–everything.–But–the–last–ten–minutes–are–a–blur.–I–remember–what–I–had–for–breakfast–on–my–twelfth–birthday,–but–not–what–you–wore–yesterday."

This wasn't abnormal. People on death row often have no short-term memory, either. They don't want to lay down new memories when they know they'll die soon. They don't want fresh memories, so they don't make any. And the tedium of prison, the pounding sameness of it, doesn't help.

Although the prisoners remembered very well what was said to them.

They knew every piece of gossip, all the information.

As to what happened two days earlier? Nothing. Because nothing ever did.

I understood this. Could barely remember myself what I'd had for breakfast, or if I'd slept well.

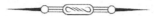

I dusted and cleaned all the exhibits. All the past projects of the keepers, like the cards all laid out by 1992. I sang as I worked; good to act cheery.

I shifted them all slightly, as per instructions. Most of them felt so loose and weak they were like dolls, but Grayson was more agile than the others. Younger by decades than most of them, his skin still had a kind of pliancy.

"I was only three years younger than you when they did this to me. Still a kid! Still at high school and they never understood me. I wanted to be an architect," he said, his eyes shifting slowly. I thought he was talking more quickly, but maybe I was just used it it. That was a bit scary. "But they wouldn't let me. They said I couldn't. You can't even imagine the things they said to me. I wanted to make affordable houses for poor people. Because I was one of the lucky ones. Don't you think that would be worthwhile? Don't you reckon it's a waste, me being here?"

"I've read your file."

"Don't read it! Pack of lies!"

"But you confessed!"

They all laughed at that, especially the priest.

"Confession is nothing but camouflage. Distraction. Confess one day, there's a different truth the next."

Burnett had often called for a priest, wanting to confess. "What did you confess?" I asked him once.

"Don't remember. It's a habit from a young child. All those small things you think are important as a young person. A sharp word to my mother. Lack of loyalty to my father. Those things."

I watched his eyelids slide closed and wondered if he was telling me the truth.

T he Ball dropped.

The Ball dropped.

The Ball dropped.

I'm beginning to think I should have chronicled sunset, not sunrise in my photographs. I hate getting up so early. Although, it makes me get out of bed each day, which is a good thing. You need something to make you get out of bed or you'd start to mimic the prisoners and just...lie there.

It really is tempting.

There is an incredible glow as the sun rises though. Watching the sea appear, the rocks, the islands, sometimes with kids camping out, and the town. So much less isolating than sunset, when it all disappears into darkness and the sense of isolation is intense. A few lights in town, flickering like min-min lights in the outback.

I made the mistake of mentioning this and the prisoners tried to convince me the lights get closer every night. "Just like the min-min lights do," the washing machine salesman told me.

"No one's ever proved they exist," I said.

"Who needs proof?" he said. "You've got sightings going back a hundred years, love. They're coming for you."

"Make sure you close the windows and doors. Tape the cracks. Or one night they will seep into the Time Ball Tower." The Washing Machine

salesman considered himself a moral philosopher. That was his excuse for
all he'd done.

"And what?" I said. "Lights? What can lights do?"

"Possess you. Each one the ghost of an angry man. Look."

And he pointed to the scientist, whose face was set in a permanent
scowl.

"He was possessed at seven years old, never a moment of love since."

I didn't believe them, but the lights did fascinate me.

"If you ever feel as if someone is watching you, they are. While you
sleep, and whatever else it is you do. We know it all. He comes and tells us.
His ghost waits at the door, but he can't leave the confines."

"Who is it?"

"It's the ghost of the first man out here. He hasn't mellowed, but perhaps
he's weakened, which makes him even angrier."

I shook my head at them. "No such thing as ghosts," I said.

Grayson called out, "Your hair is so shiny, just like you."

"Don't listen," Wee Willie Winkie whispered. "He hates you, I heard
him say it. He said he'll kill you then row home and fuck your mother. He
was laughing; he nearly choked at the idea."

I looked at the arm of Wee Willie Winkie and it was flattened, the
texture like rubber, the bone flaccid inside as if it had turned to a thick
jelly. I'd read his file; a foul list of vicious crimes. He was a sadist, no
doubt, and I bet he hated it turned on him.

"You don't know, you trust too much. Your best friend? A friend like
that is poison and she'll damage you for life, probably already has. What's
she doing back there? What's she saying? You should shut her up the
minute you get home. We'll help you if you help us."

"What is it you want? Ask me directly and you might get it. I hate being
manipulated."

"Freedom."

"Death."

"Forgiveness."

Who said that? 1938, who'd let his children starve to death. The others
think they have paid. Been forgiven.

"But what if there is a hell and you're not absolved?" I said. "Isn't it
better to pay now?"

That set them wailing, or as close to wailing as they were capable. "We've paid a thousand times over, and again," Wee Willie Winkie said.

To quieten them, I told them whatever would throw them off guard. Sexy stories. They loved to hear these more than most.

They were mesmerized by me, and that way I controlled them. They kept me talking and I didn't mind. I knew what they were doing, but I liked telling the stories. They listened when most people in my life didn't really.

"Did I ever tell you about the time I took the train across the Nullabor Plain?" I said.

"No, you never did," the Executioner said, but I wasn't sure if he meant I hadn't told them, or if he didn't believe I'd travelled close to two thousand kilometres, from one side of the country to the other.

"Go on," Grayson said.

"I was only eighteen at the time," (none of them questioned the time-frame, which is good), "and quite the innocent kid. Growing up in Tempuston you have your fumbles with the boys your age, the groping in the dark, the feels and kisses and all that."

All what, they said, come on, give us the details.

"I'm not telling that story now. If you're good I will."

They sat up straighter, if that was possible, and the grandfather managed to lift his finger to what was left of his lips: Silence!

"There were families on board, and businessmen, and a school group, kids about eight I suppose." I regretted that addition; half of these evil shits would want that story instead.

"It was hot," I said quickly, distracting them. "So I was wearing a loose, thin white dress. I wore white underwear so it didn't show as much but I'm sure there was nothing left to the imagination."

I let them think for a bit.

"The teacher was so handsome. He was only about twenty-two, dark haired, clear brown eyes, the strongest jaw I've ever seen on a man. I like a good strong jaw."

Half of these prisoners had no jaw left at all.

"He and the other teachers would put the kids to bed by around nine, but then have to patrol half the night, making sure they stayed in their cabins. Eight-year-old kids are pretty naughty. I slept like a log on the first night, enjoying that rhythmic rocking of the train. I enjoyed it differently on the second night."

Grayson's breath seemed faster, and the Executioner had his eyes squeezed shut. I hoped some of them might start crying and I could steal their tears.

"On the second night, I couldn't sleep, so I went and sat in the bar carriage. I didn't talk to anyone, too shy, but I sat and drank brandy for hours, looking out into the dark, listening in to conversations. After a while, probably around midnight, I was finally alone. The barman had closed up for the night, but he'd left me half a bottle, charged to my room, which was nice of him."

"Didn't he want to fuck you, though?" the Priest asked.

"If you're good I'll tell you the story of the third night on the train," I said. "For now, I sat there, almost nodding off but not quite, thinking about what I'd do in Adelaide, who I'd find. What adventures I'd have, things I'd see, what I'd eat and drink and what all that would feel like. Then my heart started to race and I didn't know why. It was a scent in the air, something exciting to me. And there was the teacher, standing there beside me.

"'Sorry to sneak up on you,' he said. 'I've been trying to be quiet, not to wake any of those darn kids up.'

"'There's a lot of them!' I said. He said there was and we spoke a bit about that, but I couldn't get over how good he smelled, and he must have been the same because he said, 'I don't usually do this, but you smell amazing,' and he leaned over and kissed me so hard that he pushed me back in my chair. I had to brace myself! He tasted like oranges, sweet oranges, and maybe a bit of brandy as well. All I know is I felt dizzy with it and I knew I wouldn't say no, not matter what he asked me."

"What did he ask you?" the cannibal said.

"He didn't say anything at all, not in words. But he took my hand. Actually, I think I took his hand first. And we went to the end carriage, where they stored all the stuff, like the spare luggage and things like that. And he kissed me again and before we knew it we were stripped off and we could make as much noise as we wanted, shouting into the scream of the train, rocking into the rhythm, and no one has ever, ever fucked me as deep as that man did."

"You're not like other women," the grandfather said.

"Women are like me, these days. You'd know that if you were out there."

The first Black Widow said, "One of them came out here preggers. Took her a while to realize. We were the ones who told her in the end, weren't we? I knew it early on. Pregnant women have a nasty little lean to them."

That would have been the female keeper who'd helped me. Kate Hoff, 2010. She came back early, because of the pregnancy.

"You're not preggers, but you're fertile. You won't have trouble once you decide you want children."

"You know that if you fuck three men in the same week, you'll get the strongest baby known to man. It's a fact. Fuck 'em all for the sake of the baby. But don't think about the baby when that big cock is heading up the velvet path. Don't think of it," the second Black Widow said.

None of this embarrassed me.

I missed my sex life. Thought of boyfriends I'd had, and of Max. But less than I thought I would. There was nothing sexy about the Time Ball Tower and the dryness that seeped up from the insides. The smell of them. The thought of them. They heard everything. If I moaned in my sleep, they asked me if I'd had a sexy dream. And if I snored? "We thought you had a man up there."

"Actually, it sounded as if you were being murdered," the Executioner said.

They were trying to rattle me, like my brothers did, telling me I had nightmares when I remembered nothing.

"Maybe I did have a man in. Maybe I summoned one up to see me right."

"Tell us about him." And I did, luring them in once again, making them slaves to me. They remembered everything; no pain was lost, no good thing. All of it made them suffer. I showed them a couple of pictures on my laptop. Sexy half-naked men who I said were my lovers.

"Show us more pictures."

"Show me family," Wee Willie Winkie said.

Information about their descendants was handed out as a reward and I supposed he'd earned it, warning me about Grayson. He hadn't abused me or tried to disgust me with stories.

"Why do you even care? You never did."

"We've had a lot of time to think about it," Grayson said.

I open a new screen. The information was all there, ready to be doled out.

"Okay. The Winkies. Last count, direct descendants of your parents, two hundred and one."

"My children?"

"Nothing on record of yours."

He asked every year, apparently. There was a certain pleasure in watching his face fall.

"So none of these are yours. But they did come from your sisters and brothers. They're almost yours. Three died recently. One a stillbirth. Baby unnamed, it says. They called him Wee One, but I doubt for you. One ninety-eight-year-old, died peacefully in bed."

"Bastard," he said. "Fucking cunny bastard."

"And one was drunk, smashed his car into a tree. One's a novelist. If I'd known, I would have brought his book over. If you're good, I'll tell the next keeper."

"Me next, me," they all whispered, "me, me, me," their voices whistling through broken teeth, gaps, those foul gums hard and yellow.

"You do good things, you'll hear good things," I said. I had footage of some families, stuff from the internet. A couple of news clippings. Families lost and broken. "Although I've very little good to tell. Sins of the Fathers. What you did has set your family back. If you'd been a good person. If you weren't locked up. Your family would be in a different position now."

Did they care at all?

The grandfather still begged for news.

"What do I get for it?"

"A story. The true story of my crimes. My confession."

Burnett had told me, *all we have is our storytelling. All that's left to us is our voices.*

I got my stool.

"You look at me and see an old man. A grandfather. It wasn't always the case. Once I was young and handsome. That's why I have this air of confidence about me. You never forget being good-looking, even when you're old. I had 'em all over me. They thought I was a catch. All you had to do in those days was not be a rotter and you were ahead. I'm sure that's the case today as well. Older women—unpleasant to me, but I worked my chops on them. It's the little ones who were my friends. Somehow it was better if I knew them. You want details?"

"Go on then," the others called out, nasty bastards, but I didn't want to hear it.

There are some things you don't need to hear.

He did so with relish, egged on by his room-mates. They all loved the nasty. None of them wanted a happy ending. They wanted stories about serial killers. How many, and were the bones all found?

Do people's faces change when they confess? I took his photo, time-lapse, clicking away many times looking for that moment.

"My granddaughter came out here in '21, took a boat herself and came to see me. She believed I was innocent. We are all innocent, she believed. We paid our debt and should be allowed to die. She was ahead of her time. She still is, I'm sure."

"If she was still alive."

I would never tell him about Renata.

Some of them had tiny tear beads on the cheeks; some had them on their chests. They were quite firm, opaque.

The things were so beautiful I wanted them to cry more.

"Do you ever think you'll get out of here? What's the time frame?" I asked, knowing there was none. "The FBI keeps fingerprints for ninety-nine years then destroys them. I wonder if that would be right?"

"Then we should be released after ninety-nine!" they said. "We should!"

"You'll never get out. You never will," I said, and this did make them cry more, those lovely crystal tear drops.

"My children?" It was the man delivered in 1938, when my grandmother Frances was keeper, and he moaned louder than the rest.

"Your children? The line ended when they died. You're at the end."

His wife was deep in catatonic depression. They never spoke. He walked past the children's room daily for four months without ever going in.

He's not the only one who killed by starvation.

I squatted by him, trying to get a glimpse of the man my grandmother had described: *This prisoner was skinny, lucky for me, in soft clothes that felt sticky and I wouldn't have touched him if I didn't have to. He snuffled at me, sniffing deeply as if getting one good one in. Reminded me of Clyde Blue at school, who stood close without touching and you always knew he was there because of the breathing.*

There was nothing left of that. Nothing.

"I read your file. You say, "I was a bad father." That barely covers it. It doesn't show you let your two daughters starve to death because your wife wasn't fucking you and you were annoyed at her."

"Not just that. She never spoke to me. I was like a ghost. She never washed or cooked, and we never said a single word to each other."

"What did you think your children were eating?"

He shook his head.

"Do you know how long it takes a child to starve?"

"They were quiet. If they'd cried, I woulda done something."

"They were too weak to cry. Waiting and waiting for someone to feed them."

This was the whole point of it. The justification, the reason. The guilt he felt. Every day, for eternity, because anything else wasn't enough.

His wrists were thickly calloused and partly cut through from so long in chains.

"Take them off. I'm so weak now, I'm no danger."

After the death of his children, he'd killed many more, each time, he said, hoping for relief. He said, each time hoping someone would stop him.

"Leave them on!" Wee Willie Winkie said. "He'll strangle you the moment he gets the chance." Laughing. They don't really look out for each other, although they showed each other affection when they could. Desperate for physical touch. It must have been so much worse when they couldn't even see each other. You'd think their sexual desires would be long gone. Only a memory. But they still want it, although I haven't noticed an erection amongst any of them. Makes them cross, as it should. Things change, and your standards slip. That's the way it is. Any port in the storm, as they say. They used to keep the female prisoners separate, but it's hard to tell them apart now, isn't it?

"Leave them on. You know what he did? If he killed you, you wouldn't be the first."

"You can talk!" the man in chains said. "That Tristram Barton never fell down the steps. Those bastards slaughtered him like a hog. Not me. They dragged his stupid fucking basket out, to keep up the impression he was still alive. Meanwhile, he was lying dead and rotting. But they got too slow and couldn't get to the basket in time."

Then they were all at it, with their slow, infuriating voices, accusing each other, trying to make me believer that one of them was better than the next.

I drank a bottle of wine. And part of another.

Nothing worse than wanting a party and there's no one to party with.

Why did they hate trumpet music? I played some on my laptop and it did agitate them. Made them moan and fidget.

"It's Gabriel, blowing his judgment."

"Releasing all the sinners from Hell."

"And we're not there. No release for us to Heaven."

"Cruel."

"We want an ending. We want that."

They would wink out to nothingness, if they were ever forgiven.

I promised to stop if they answered some of my questions. I asked them about the so-called "secret" prisoners. The evils, the awfuls. Hitler, Mussolini, the ones I'd been told never died at all.

"No such things," they all said.

"Maybe it's you lot." I was bored that day. "You're Hitler, aren't you? And you're some other arsehole." I went down the line, re-naming them all. I'd read about a leprosy hospital where the first step was to separate them from reality by giving the patients new names. I think they rather liked it.

Mr. Madden, first told me about Hitler and the rest. But he wrote such a boring report. I was disappointed. He'd seemed quite philosophical and I thought he might give me some insights.

I went upstairs before I gave in to the temptation and picked one of them up to dance.

Shocker of a hangover.

I had a sudden thirst. Desperate for a beer. Hair of the dog that bit me. I thought of the whiskey upstairs but didn't want that. They didn't need to smell it on me. Didn't need to know I liked a drink. They'd use that if they could. There was the wine, too, and that I couldn't resist.

The Ball dropped.

The Ball dropped.

The Ball dropped.

I swept the floors, up and down. So much dust gathering.

It was time to attend the troll. *Don't let the troll's outline wash away. We contain it this way. Control it. This means what we see is not imagination, it is truth. Reality.*

There were buckets of charcoal and a suction ladder that would cling to the wall outside. I headed out there to do my duty. Every profession has its superstitions. This was one of ours and I wasn't the one to break it without good reason. I really was bored, anyway.

I placed the ladder beside the troll-like stain and climbed up. I thought I could hear breathing but knew it was the wind wrapping around the Time Ball Tower, so loud out here. I began the outline. The edges didn't shift, I knew that, and the troll image wasn't spongy. This was not a real thing. It was imagination. It was like a giant itself, and I remembered what Burnett had said, that the tower was a giant. He wouldn't like to see this up close. I outlined the troll in anti-fungal paint, first.

The sun darkened. A storm was on its way so I worked faster, wanting it done before the storm so that there was less chance of it washing away, singing to myself, looking out to the mainland hoping someone was watching me. That someone cared.

"Oh, please," the wind said. "Please, please, please."

I finished the outline, climbed down the ladder and pushed the door open. Inside, it was dark. I knew it was the storm coming, but I felt as if the troll was growing over the windows, blocking me in.

I was covered in coal dust, could feel it in my hair, gritting in my eyes. I had to secure the prisoners, but I wanted to shower first. Really there was little to be done; strap them down, make sure the windows were barred shut, the shutters down against the wind.

"How is our troll?" Grayson said. "Does he send his regards?"

How did they know? I didn't answer him.

"Your fingernails. They always forget the fingernails. Dead giveaway that you've been talking to the troll."

Coal dust rimmed them, black, filthy.

"You shouldna climbed the ladder drunk. Might have fallen off. Watch out he doesn't leak in. He does that in bad weather. Leaks in and then you'll never be done with him," the second Black Widow said.

"He likes the ladies. Remember in 1953? The keeper took a woman in here. She saw too much. You can look her up. She was dead in a month. One of those unexplained accidents," the grandfather said.

The wind picked up, and I could hear water gushing down from the roof.

He winked. "Keeper couldn't get it up until the troll took him. Then he couldn't stop. But he knew she'd seen too much."

Did I feel different after being up close and personal with the troll? Time would tell.

"Storm coming," I told them. "Sun showers mean the worst storm."

"Move us to watch. Let us see it." They were desperate for the slightest entertainment.

"Let us sit underneath where at least we might feel a drop, a wisht of wind," said the Councilor, who missed the open air.

They talked sometimes of nature, as if it were a dream dimly remembered. The rustle of leaves. The shape of the clouds. The change of seasons.

I tried to move him, and a piece broke off. Some had a small pile of broken pieces behind them, a reminder to be gentle.

I'd move Burnett when I returned, set him in a place where he could see all. A high house with a view. He deserved that at least.

I shuttered all the windows. *Let us see*, they called, *it's all we've got*, but that wasn't the way. I had books, candles, torches, music on downloaded, print-outs of my photos (all paid for. We had a budget of thousands for our project. Some of us wanted to use the money for other stuff, but it wasn't transferable. You used it, or you lost it.)

They whimpered to me, stay, stay, and there was something about being needed like that.

"I'm going to get cozy upstairs," I said. "Hot drink. Things to do."

The Executioner pushed himself up slightly. "But I want to change my last words. Write it down for me so I don't forget." He knew the value of last words. The importance of being ready.

"Can you still read?"

"You can read it to me."

I knew it was a delaying tactic, but there was something chillingly good about the way these people worked on their last words as if anyone would care.

"Okay, then." I sat beside them, pen out.

No person in history has had as long to think about it.

We sat in silence. "Come on, then!"

"I can't think of anything. Give me an idea," the Executioner said.

"I don't want to sound like an idiot," Grayson said.

"Or a lunatic or lost soul."

"I can't write your last words for you," I said, but I fetched a book of famous last words a keeper had brought over. That helped. I almost enjoyed myself and so did they

They got there in the end and I updated their last words on the laptop. ("Into thine hands, Oh Lord" and "May the loved ones forgive me" and "This is my fate, thank you Lord") I updated the photos, too.

"Look at her, looking at her flat box," the Executioner said. He had thick strong thumbs. He'd strangled many more. He'd described strangling a kitten and a child. It was like he was reciting a poem.

"They all make the same gurgle at the end.

"Doesn't matter the age.

"A little gurgle before it's over.

"I'll make it nice for you," he said. "If you've ever thought you'd had enough. I can help with your passing." He was too weak now. He said, "There are some who ran to me, so keen were they."

The Ball dropped.

The storm came over at last, having threatened for days. I watched the village through my telescope, and saw the empty streets, a few foolhardy teenagers out testing the wind. So empty. It made me think I was seeing into the future, when our town inevitably died. I watched cars blow over, trees uproot.

I hid in my room, updating photos.

There was no damage to the Time Ball Tower, although the entrance flooded, and I had filthy mud to clean up. It seemed an endless task, and I was tempted to go, to signal with a flag and to leave it behind.

But I thought that would make a victory for the prisoners, that they would feel they were better than me because they had toughed it out, choice or not.

So I stayed. I thought about my boyfriend who I'd dumped. And the other men on the mainland. I thought they'd seem ordinary after these long-termers. But beautiful. Very beautiful and alive. I'll want to touch their skin, just for the suppleness.

Would I be able to understand people, or would they talk too fast?

I would lack patience for them all.

They would annoy me, and I'd want to smack them, want it white hot.

Wee Willie Winkie said, "You can't imagine how satisfying it is to watch the blood spill out and that annoying person silenced. It's a beautiful thing. I wasn't always the oldest, you know. The other one died. What was his name?"

But no one knew.

The storm lasted for two days.

I felt a flu coming on and wanted to be home desperately. I wanted my doctor who knew me since a child. I felt suddenly homesick.

Not so much I wanted to run the flag, though.

I cleaned the kitchen, scrubbing out the oven, washing the floor. It didn't really need it, the cleaner had done a good job, but it was on the list, so I did it. Am I an order follower? I guess so. Other people have always made decisions for me. For us. Makes for a less stressful life.

In glorious clear and calm after the storm, I swam down amongst the rocks, but it wasn't really swimming. I loved the water over my head, though, loved the silence it brought.

Those rocks had taken the life of one child in my memory. He'd been out there showing off, displaying no fear and he'd slipped between two of the rocks.

His friends said the rocks chewed like a giant's teeth. He was mangled, but no adult blamed anything but the surf and the rocks.

I tripped over the wet stones and banged my head. Momentary black out.

I woke up chilled to the bone.

How long was I out? Had they moved me?

My thighs were parted.

How?

Had I moved them that way myself?

Surely. I felt with my tongue; a tooth loose.

Weird then that I saw a cigarette butt and a pink rubber glove. They didn't look washed up…weird. I photographed them but didn't remove them. They were too high to have washed up.

People would pay well for my photos of the Time Ball Tower and the prisoners. People love that stuff.

I hoped for silence, but they made shifty noises like mice scratching at the wall. "Quiet or I'm boarding up the windows for good and taking out the lightbulbs and you can spend eternity in the dark."

It drove me crazy and made running the red flag tempting.

I touched the red flag. I could do it, run the thing up and I'd be home in a day. Then I thought of the keeper saying, "If you ever feel like running the red flag, run the yellow and promise yourself absolutely you can run the red the next day if you still want to."

The red flag was stiff with disuse, its folds dusty.

I ran up the yellow. If two days passed with no new flag, they'd send out the boatman.

I didn't want to be one of those pariahs. Those losers.

The red flag was there, always there. It helped me sleep at night, helped me not obsess or freak out. I can always run the flag up, I thought. In an emergency. If I was injured, not so much.

The Ball dropped.

The Ball dropped.

I ran the green flag.

I thought about the money.

The money.

The money.

And the fame.

And the success. People would call me brilliant. Like Madame Curie. Or Annie Lebowitz.

This was what I wanted for myself. This renown. This memory of my name. I didn't want to die unknown.

I printed out their last words for them, stuck them above their heads next to the photos of their atrocities.

"I never did what they said."

"May God forgive me and welcome me."

"Tell them to be strong and do not let the bastards get them down."

They weren't particularly inspiring. I read them aloud as the rain fell like diamonds in the bright sunshine outside.

I needed to add the last words to their medical files so hunted them down. I wanted to find the secret places, anyway. I knew there were some.

On return two days later (I had tired of their voices and needed a break), I found them desperate for attention, for me to notice them.

"We know stories," they said. "We can tell you truthy things."

"Anyone is capable of murder. We're just the idiots who got caught." The grandfather said this. I had realized he was the least repentant of them all. "Your lot are no better, but they get away with it. Look at the early days, where they killed each other and themselves. Proof right there. Killed others too. Lots of ladies."

I didn't want to respond to that.

"Lots of ladies. Didn't you ever notice? Young ladies leaving town and not going home again? All at the bottom of the ocean."

"A teacher once, remember? She's calling out names, all the children of the town, but that didn't stop him?"

"Stop who?"

They couldn't remember. She hadn't come home, that nasty fifth grade teacher, and no one had cared.

No one had looked for her.

The light came in, those few minutes a day when it did, and I took some quick snaps.

Photography's all about light and timing.

"It's a beautiful day," I said. "Look at the light out there."

One of them had been a photographer, but I didn't even want to think about what he'd photographed.

"Light has changed over the decades," he said.

We talked about it. A long, slow discussion.

Light and shadow are important to the photographer. Some of them will play with it for hours; I like to let it be what it will be. Whatever is, is. That's my idea of perfection.

The Photographer told me, "We remember light poorly. We know we were lit, but how? I remember it all. The Quality of Light has changed, as if the very air itself is different.

"How will light shine in the future? Will it glow from the ground, will it float particle-like in the air? Will I be able to see it or, by then, will my eyeballs have dried out, solidified?

"When I was a boy, we lived by the light of the fire and the sun, so we kept time with the sun and no arguments about bedtime.

"Each source of light glows differently. If it was possible to bring these lights to me, I could tell you what era we are in, simply from the form of it. The light. Some people are transported by smell; I am transported by light.

"We can all identify the sunlight of each season. Winter and summer. You know what season it is from the way the sun shines. I know what century it is from the glow of the light."

It was actually really interesting.

"You need compassion, though. If you are to be great."

"And you can show it now," they said. They clamored for the sun, "Let us in, let us in."

"You're too evil for the sun."

"We're not so bad. Look what people do now. What they do is far worse than anything we did."

I didn't tell them we had a list. The evil of men's hearts list. The wish list. I'd added to it myself, this list of names, famous and obscure.

I'd also brought a list with me of those who were supposed to be dead. But what if? What if they were here? I'd researched some of it and was surprised to find how many of these terrible people I don't know. Terrible things happening elsewhere that we have no knowledge of. Names mean nothing, faces the same, unless you know the history.

A man they called the granny killer was on the list and would have been here if he'd lived. Or was he one of them, the secret prisoners kept in isolation?

The texting girl who'd killed two pedestrians then texted, "2 drunk 2 care."

And the two men who adopted a child then put him into their pornographic movies. If they were here, I'd lock them in the box for months at a time. The photo I have of them is a good example; photos lie, big time. Last photos of murder victims smiling next to their killers. These two men look sweet.

The woman who poisoned her son with salt. So many characters. The child killers. The terrible kidnappers. No one would argue here.

Ariel Castro, who kept three women imprisoned for decades. Killed himself in jail, they reckon.

Even the gentlest souls want these people punished.

"We're better than that," the prisoners said. "We're here for political reasons. We're political prisoners, you know."

I really laughed at that one and they joined in. Like fingernails on glass. So awful I could feel it in my teeth.

"What do you think of that, Sugartits?" Grayson said.

"It's Phillipa. My name is Phillipa. If you won't call me Keeper, call me that."

"We would have called you Pip in my time," Wee Willie Winkie said.

I had a drink to drown out my idiocy in telling them my name.

The Time Ball Tower was supposed to be a deterrent, where you'll go if you commit terrible crimes. But the people who commit those sorts of crimes don't imagine they will ever get caught. That's one of the problems of the prison system. The ones it needs to influence don't think they'll end up in jail. The ones who are terrified of jail probably won't commit the crime anyway. And like Lucifer, most of them get worse after punishment and imprisonment.

The Ball dropped.

They said, "Did you wash the windows, Pip? Check the supplies? Change the ropes? You haven't, have you? Out of order! Out of order!"

The Ball dropped.

My stomach ached, and I wished I was hungry, to fill it with carbs or dried fruit or something. I craved fresh iceberg lettuce: crispy, juicy, flavorless.

I forced myself to rise. It was no good sleeping all day, as tempting as that might be. You had to keep occupied.

"Just one more hour of sleep," I said, the sort of thing you want to say to a housemate or a lover, a momentary whinge. I slumped in to the prisoners. Sneezed.

"Are you sick? Because we don't want it. Not unless it's life-threatening."

"I think it's just the sawdust."

"Come on, give us a kiss, ay? Give us a dose, Pip."

The prisoners convinced me to go back to sleep. "Good for you. Keeps your skin soft."

"You can sleep when you're dead," I said automatically, because we all say it.

"You can sleep after you're dead, too," they say. They were trying to manipulate me, overpower and force decisions on me.

"You only want an hour," the grandfather said. "You deserve it."

It stank in there. I needed to change the sawdust.

"Leave it for the other one," they said.

"You mean the next one? The next keeper?"

"No, the other. The cleaner. Comes in when you're asleep. Cleans up. Looks after the secret prisoners in the basement."

Were they distracting me? Lying to me? Hard to tell at times. Renata might know, but then she thought the best of everyone. Of most people. And if she was here, she would have done for them long ago. I wondered if I should have told someone what she was doing. It hadn't occurred to me before now. Some people, I guess, would have reported it.

I asked the prisoners if someone else really did come in, if it was just the keepers. If someone came in to replace the wine, the whiskey.

"The cleaner."

"Who?"

But they'd say no more.

This triggered a childhood memory. Another story we used to tell to terrify each other. I thought it was silly and didn't really understand it.

You had to stay clean. Keep your bedroom clean, because if the cleaner came he cleaned everything, even your blood, and that's how people get leukemia.

I didn't know what leukemia was. A boy at school was called Luke and he was a pain, but that was all I had.

Now the title "The Cleaner" gave me a chill. Who was he? And why was he secret even from the keepers?

To be cruel, I told them stories of the real world.

"You should see the restaurants. And the waterfalls. And the places you can go and the things you can eat and the movies you can watch. The lessons you can learn, the books you can read, the music you can listen to. Humans were meant for this. They are wasted otherwise."

The Ball dropped.

I drank the whisky. Too much. But there always seemed to be more, somehow, and my favorite blend, as if there was some magical fairy leaving presents for me.

The salt deposits on the window were beautiful. I'd taken over two hundred photos already, but there was no limit. I had some beautiful backgrounds. I had a brilliant idea for a business; provide these for people to place their own photos in front of. I pictured wedding parties with this beautiful background. It was a great idea.

I was lost in the beauty of it. The inmates looked more like ghosts in comparison. Slumped like ghosts. Gaunt, skull-like, skinny, ill, almost incapable of speech. Some keepers called them ghosts. Some called them the bones. I called them straifs.

My real project was to capture the nature of the Time Ball Tower. The slowness of movement. I took the prisoners in very slow exposure, giving them more chance of movement than I would otherwise get. I brought with me photos of the fossils found at Marble Bar, Western Australia. Some of them 3.5 billion years old.

They said, "That's us! We're old fossils!"

Another said, "Nah, we've always been this way."

They were liked trained dogs. Adoring, attentive, needy. It was good to be the master. On the mainland, it sometimes felt (looking back, from the tower) as if I was the one who was the dog, taking orders, doing as I was told.

The Ball dropped.

We are all shut-ins to one degree or another. The keepers in the Club, sticking to themselves. The prisoners and Burnett, without a choice. My patients, sitting in their too-soft vinyl chairs, their only pleasure the occasional fart.

It felt strange to know so much about the keepers. They were stony-faced, mostly, although they smiled after a few drinks. They joked around, they looked after their loved ones, they held down jobs. But there was very little "give" about them. Very little truth. So to have read their journals, to understand them, was odd.

The Ball dropped.

I headed down for a swim.

They begged me to take them downstairs. "It'd take you forty years to build a raft, the speed you go. And you'd drown yourselves, anyway. How about I leave a rope down there and you can tie a rock to your necks? That'd only take you a decade."

We didn't rely on electronic devices to tell us the time in the Tower. Just the ball dropping, and a paper calendar they'd sent with me. Each day, I awoke and checked the events marked by the day; birthdays, and dates of historical significance and arrivals.

So I knew when the new prisoner was expected.

They hadn't given me details. I wouldn't know who it was until they got here. I didn't tell the prisoners, although I was tempted to share. Gossip, guess, all that. I wanted someone to talk to.

Number Sixteen heard the boat first. He was obsessed. You barely heard from him unless a ship was passing. He's the one who'd kept his sister in a small dark hole.

"Boatman," he said. "Sending a replacement for you. They know how much we love you and want to punish us."

I'd never get used to hearing words like that coming from the mouths of husks, empty ugly cases.

I waited downstairs, desperate for a glimpse of the boatman.

He was the first real person I'd seen for a long time and he was beautiful.

He waved wildly. "Phillipa! How are you?" His voice seemed insanely loud, and he spoke so quickly I could barely understand him.

The prisoner was tied in a straitjacket. Gagged. Her eyes were yellow.

I begged the boatman for news, feeling like one of them as I did so, and he gave me over an hour. I barely spoke, just listened, but oh God I was tempted to go back with him. Forget all my stuff, just go.

But the money. And my project. The idea that this was my chance at fame and I might not get another.

I couldn't bear the thought of dying unknown. You might be remembered if you live in a very small town. But for what? And by who?

He unloaded two cases of goodies for me (I'd unpack them later, fresh stuff I ate locked away from the smell of the prisoners).

"Want me to carry them up for you? All I'd ask is a cuppa."

I remembered *don't let him in.* I couldn't remember why, though. And why should I listen, anyway? And he wasn't that old, what, mid-forties? And he looked good and sweaty and alive, and seriously I considered taking him up to my room.

But the prisoners.

We unloaded the prisoner and tied her tightly to a trolley. This one was so fresh, she still had pink skin tones and a heavy pulse at the temple.

"Fiery bitch," the boatman said. "Watch that filthy mouth of hers that she doesn't bite you. She reckons she's hungry, wants a bite of meat. I'd give her this, but she doesn't deserve it," he said, his hands cupping his genitals.

The woman struggled.

He offered me a cigarette; no thanks, and he lit it and smoked as he rowed away.

I dragged her up the stairs. She tried to talk, and the noise was annoying to listen to. Like my brother trying to talk while he brushed his teeth.

Like the constant crackle of the Time Ball Tower.

I was curious to know what she'd have to say, how she'd say it. The old ones were slow, unbearably so. This one was only in her thirties in the real world, only been preserved two months, so still fairly normal.

"Don't bite," I said. Would she actually have anything to say or just abuse?

I took off her gag, but she only whimpered.

"You'll have to learn to be more interesting than that." The woman was probably terrified; who wouldn't be? I didn't care, much. Perhaps I would have when I'd first arrived. Now, I felt almost nothing.

She'd lost a lot of weight, according to her records. Photos at her trial had her quite hefty, a fast food chip eater, a soft drink guzzler. Now I could pick her up quite easily, although by the second floor she felt heavier.

The most recent man punished in there I'd taken out a week earlier, so the box was aired.

The woman struggled when she saw it.

She'd been in one before.

"You'll be in here two months. Maybe three. Depends. I'll bring you something in a while." I was vague about this because I hadn't checked the instructions yet.

I stripped her naked. It was cleaner that way. I'd have to come back and pull out the base of the box every now and then, like a birdcage.

They'd given me a CD to play on loop. Children crying at that really annoying pitch. People telling her how much they hated her, how much of a worm she was.

She killed her daughter partly because she hated the crying.

Her one chance to talk and she said, "Mercy. Please. Mercy."

"No mercy."

"Put me next to Mussolini. Won't you?"

So she'd heard the stories, too. I closed the lid. Sat and listened to her whimper for a while. Then went and told the other prisoners about the new arrival.

"She says she wants to sit next to Mussolini. Who wants to be him?"

If they could have raised their hands, they would have.

I returned once a day to take a photo of her.

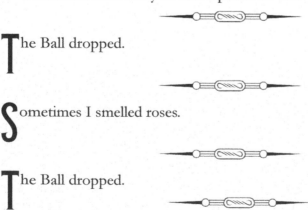

The Ball dropped.

Sometimes I smelled roses.

The Ball dropped.

They were due to be fed, but they could wait. A week or more, easy.
    I swam.

I found an injured seabird and took it inside to nurture. Kept it from the prisoners. They didn't understand tenderness.

The Ball dropped.
The Ball dropped.

My seabird recovered, and I set it free, watching it flap away in the wind, winding back once to the tower then away, away. You'd almost think it was symbolic.

My calendar told me it was time to pull the woman out. It was hard to believe, but there it was.

There were flakes of paint, dust on the lid. I found a dustpan and broom and swept them up, the strands of the brush leaving trails in the dust.

I lifted the lid, bracing myself for a possible attack, holding tight to a solid metal torch. You could crack skull or bone easily, they were so brittle.

She had shrunk, definitely. She rested easily in the box, where I had had to shove her down. She was asleep, her eyelids quivering. I poked her.

"Wake up."

"Not—

"...asleep."

Her voice had slowed. My own thoughts were slower here, had to be or I'd go crazy with the lack of speed.

She opened her eyes. They were still clear and yellow, although marked with red lines. She smelled like dried shit, the piles you see on a city street on Sunday mornings, even though all the shit dropped through to the tray underneath and I had tipped it out the window. There wasn't much in the tray. The first week, mere dry pellets, and with no food at all for six weeks, beyond the vitamin pills I'd left on a dish, the prisoner produced even less.

She was sufficiently weak to join the others and so grateful to be out of the box that she panted like a dog wanting to please her master.

"I'll be your friend, your best friend. I can stop you being lonely," she said.

"Only the lonely," they sang to me. They often did it.

"I'm not lonely. I've got plenty of friends. A boyfriend." I'd had one. I would have another.

"You don't like any of them, though. They all annoy the crap out of you and you know it," she said.

"They're all right. It'll be better once I go back to." I wasn't sure why I lied and said it was Uni instead of Tech. Pathetic, really.

Wheedling, sly, yet I knew what this woman had done. The crime so fresh it was still on her breath like bitter almonds.

I lifted one of her arms. It still felt meatier than the other prisoners, but I could carry her without the trolley.

I covered her head with a small black sack because she still had teeth and they'd been known to bite.

I carried her down to the others.

"Get your back into it," the Abortion Doctor said.

It was astonishing that a human would still have that intense need to survive. The body taking over from the mind, struggling feebly against death.

There was silence as I settled her in. They tried to shift, all of them making room so I'd put her down sit next to them. What did they want from her? Company alone? Or would they victimize her?

"Female," Wee Willie Winkie said. "A Vagina."

She struggled slightly.

"It'll be all right," I said. "They'll be gentle. Just like your hero."

She'd given her baby to a musician, a guy she adored. He was dead, murdered on the street and not a single person cared after what he'd done. She was the one paying the price, but it wasn't enough.

They got stuck in, talking dirty to her, and she gave as good as she got. But she went too far. It was good in a way; hearing her weasely voice describe just what she'd done made it very clear to me what level of evil she resided in.

The Ball dropped.

I missed the internet. The isolation was good in many ways, and the separation from all the shit that was transmitted, but still. It would be nice to catch up.

But there was a certain closeness about the Time Ball Tower, a completeness about it that made me lose interest in what went on elsewhere.

My head ached often, and I succumbed to a handful of aspirin.

"Watch your stomach lining," they said. The painkillers made me sleepy and the prisoners took the chance to ask me questions, prying into my personal life, wanting information about the real world, anything to alleviate the boredom and, in the end perhaps, help themselves to escape.

While I was not in any way charmed by them, I did come to enjoy their long life experience. No "callow youths," they always had a story. A conversation.

I took aspirin, kept hydrated, doctor's orders, even though I thought the doctor was an idiot.

The Ball dropped.

As I drank cold coffee, I found myself irritated by them, seeking fault. I walked the line with a clipboard, adding days for infringements.

"Your hair is looking unkempt, there. Three days added."

They all believed that somehow, some day, they would be released, that there would be an end to their sentence. Even an hour added hurt them.

The new woman wailed most of the time and the other prisoners tried to drown her out. "Ask us anything," they said. "Get her out of here, ask us anything, distract us from the bitch."

"Okay," I said. "I'll move her for a while, but you'll answer lots of questions for me."

I tied the woman up in a sheet, like a mummy, and carried her downstairs where I stashed her underneath the steps.

"Can you remember my mother? Father? Grandmother?" I asked them.

"Who? You all look the same after a while."

Was that true? Or would they remember, like people remember presidents or Prime Ministers?

"I'm pretty sure you remember every last one of us."

"You, we'll remember. All of us are in love with you," they said, as if I'd be flattered to be admired by this bunch of murderous, desiccated, malodorous people.

"Worst one was that Burnett Barton. Come out to gloat whenever he could. Look at me, look at you, he'd say. As if he was better than us."

"Why do you hate Burnett so much?"

"He didn't stop this," Grayson said.

The Strongest interrupted him. "He put us in here."

295

"Stop what?"

"Stop the process."

He was interrupted again. "That he started himself."

"Harriet, too. My ancestor. She was a smarty, they reckon. I was told it was her idea."

"Oh," they said, every last one of them fishy as all fuck.

The Ball dropped.

My job list said, "Bath time" and detailed the bathing order as well as the process.

"This is a rewarding chore, which you will discover if you stay alert," it said.

Grayson was first, moving down the ranks.

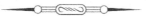

- Grayson.
- Wee Willie Winkie.
- Grandfather.
- The Executioner.
- The Strongest Man.
- The Baby Farmer.
- The First Black Widow.
- The Second Black Widow.
- The Scientist.
- The Priest.
- The Cannibal.
- The Washing Machine Salesman.
- The Abortion Doctor.
- The Councilor

And so on.

Bathing was done downstairs, in the basement, where water gathered. Really it was about pain rather than cleanliness, a reminder of what once was, a memory of being clean. A state they would never truly reach again. They'll fight it, I was warned. I realized later it was because they knew what came next. They knew what came after the bath.

"We don't need bathing. Don't go down to the basement. The troll will know it and step inside. You'll find all of us sucked clean out," Grayson said.

"He's not real," I said.

"He's coming in. Do something or you'll be lost. He'll take you as his mistress and he keeps them tied under the water. He doesn't care how they rot. As long as the bones are still together, he's in love."

"You'll do anything to get out of a bath," I said. I wasn't scared. I knew what they were up to. Like the Ku Klux Klan, who pretended to be the ghosts of confederate soldiers to terrify the people they vilified, these prisoners wanted me weakened with fear and doubt. I felt none of that. All I felt was curiosity.

Every last one of them fussed and fidgeted about the bath.

"It'll make you feel human," I said. "Almost normal."

They wriggled as much as they were able, as if that would stop it.

"Give us your undies," Robert Peter Tait, inmate from 1961 said. "Because you think you're not lovely, but you bloody are."

They all started in, then, talking about my underwear as if they'd seen it. Desperately, as if taking my mind off something.

I picked up Grayson and carried him downstairs. I'd forgotten about the woman there; I'd have to carry her back up soon.

The front door sat slightly ajar. It did that, swelling and pulsing out of the frame. I didn't shove it home, concerned I wouldn't be able to open it again.

"You should pile us against the door, stop that troll from leaking in. Once he finds purchase, you won't get him out."

I moved supplies off the trap door. And hefted it open with the aid of a short plank. It was heavy, creaking as it lifted, then falling backward with a thunderclap.

Someone had written on the underside, "Some are born to sweet delight. Some are born to endless night." I hesitated then. No one would know if I skipped this job. I could just say I'd done it. Nothing was written in stone, or law.

Down to the basement. I hadn't explored the place after the first quick look. It wasn't fear, exactly, although the keepers had warned me about it. Haunted by the true evil. The very epitome. It stank far worse than the rest of the tower. Stagnant water, and dark mold, and piss, as if every time they went it oozed down here.

Minimal lighting which was apt to shut down at any time, so I took two flashlights.

I'd worked myself up to believe they'd all be down there; Hitler, Mussolini, Pol Pot. Idi Amin. Or there'd be one left, on a pile of bones, fat, squatting, white, flaccid, hairless; a troll.

"Don't go down. They'll haunt you. Possess you. All the ghosts are there. I like you the way you are. Not possessed," Grayson said.

I headed down the rickety ladder with him over my shoulder.

At the very base, water had flooded in. It worked tidally and was at its highest point now. I peered over, but it seemed bottomless.

I stripped him, tied a rope around his shoulders.

This, I think, was the worst, most disgusting moment. Awful. I had a moment of realization how much my parents must hate me, to send me here.

"Imagine you're a tea bag," I said. I set my tiny travel alarm clock to ring in thirty minutes. "I'm going to look for dictators."

"It's not them. It's the ghosts. They'll bite and never let go." He wanted to keep me talking. The salt bath was good, although he'd itch for a week afterward. "You strip naked too, go on. Let me get a look at you. Most beautiful woman I've ever seen, dead or alive. Then or now. And I saw some beauties."

I didn't feel sexy.

He started to moan. "Watch me, oh god, watch me, please, it's all I ask." I was almost turned on, to my own disgust. "Let me watch you when you sleep, then. So I can imagine you when you're gone."

"Why should I?"

"I can tell you about a hidden prisoner. Like you're looking for."

"Who?"

"Let me watch you sleep."

I dunked him in the water.

He didn't want his head under, but I dunked him anyway. I was looking forward to the silence.

There were salty deposits around the edges and I photographed those.

I photographed the greasy oil bubble that rose to the surface.

I looked around a bit, but it was too cold and damp to venture far. I did notice markings of a broom on the sandy floor but hadn't seen any mention of sweeping in the job list. I wasn't doing it if it wasn't on there. It did say that what I needed was in the wooden box; I found that. Inside was a rough towel and what seemed to be a note. Nothing in my list spoke about that, although with the towel "dry them off before dressing or else mold will form in the creases."

I understood that this note must be part of the "reward."

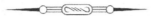

I pulled him back up. He was heavier; perhaps his porous skin had soaked up water, or it was the salt caked on him.

He spluttered, gasped, a deep, wrenching sound.

"You weren't drowning. It takes a lot longer than that."

He couldn't speak. He could do nothing but take those deep, slow, desperate breaths of a body still not ready to die.

I collected the woman under my other arm.

Upstairs, as I settled them into position, Grayson said, "Do you have any scent? I like that after a bath. A nice smell for me."

Wee Willie Winkie whispered into my ear when I picked him up. "You watch him, that one. He talks about you when you're not here. He's nasty on the inside and out even though he looked like an angel before he was a ghost."

Grayson's photo showed him as just this; a gorgeous man who could get away with anything with a bit of flirting.

"Nice of you to tell me." His tongue lolled sideways, dry, white around the edges, blackened in the center. I dropped some vitamin juice on it.

Wee Willie Winkie was the longest-serving and the oldest there, older even than Burnett, one hundred and seventy-two according to the records. I took my camera close to his eye, snapped the milkiness there. I wanted to see inside, but his eyes were too opaque.

He smelled of wax and of clothes dried too slowly. Standing close to him, I felt nothing. I wondered if I'd somehow "know," be able to "see" the evil in him. He was nothing but a husk, like Burnett. If I hadn't read his file, if I didn't know about him, I might feel pity.

I carried him downstairs.

He told me, "You think it's your precious keepers write about the whole truth? There is much they leave out. Many dead out there. Oh, those lost women. Oh, so many of them. Did it here, right in front of us sometimes. Didn't we just love it?"

I dunked him in the water.

I heard insects. A kind of chittering noise. I couldn't see anything. I thought of things hidden in the walls and didn't want to know. I wanted to read the note but would save that for later.

Bathing. Was it the worst thing I've ever done? Certainly close. Stripping them naked, seeing what remained of them. And the honesty, the begging, as if their souls were stripped bare as well.

They felt similar, each of them. One more knobbly than the others, one more pliable.

Even more, I could see the damage the years had wrought. Not only the years. The keepers. I could see here and there the marks of the people who went before me. I wasn't tempted to add to it. Not really. Inflicting physical pain…although I'd lie if I said I didn't enjoy the emotional pain I could dredge out of them.

I worked the Grandfather next. He was the easiest to manipulate. It was his family and his desire to know about them I could play with.

I picked him up.

"We don't need a bath. Nothing to wash."

And yet his skin was greasy to the touch, as if he'd been slathered with lanolin a long time ago. I looked around the basement a little more while he was under, but the corners of the place were far away and the whole thing gave me chills.

They fussed at me, begged.

It was too late, though. I had the feeling I had the information they were trying to stop me having.

The note detailed a hiding spot upstairs, "to your advantage," it said.

I climbed the stairs to the top of the Time Ball Tower. There was a small bookcase there, filled with crime novels I hadn't bothered to read. I really didn't like to touch most of the books left behind.

I pulled the books out and felt around until I found a knothole. I inserted a pinky finger and tugged.

Nothing at first but a bit of give, so I tried again.

The back came off, revealing a metal box set into an alcove.

It had a heart on it and I was concerned it was Keeper Erotica. I wasn't sure I wanted to read that.

Inside, was a thick wad of paper folded and held together with a piece of leather strap.

Was it really that simple? This is it?

No wonder they talked about the easy way.

I made myself comfortable at the top, sitting in the tiny bit of sunlight. I could see the shore, which comforted me. I could look out and see the ordinary and the normal.

If you are reading this, congratulations! Not only are you bright enough to become a keeper, but you have shown ingenuity and courage to find this note. You will not be disappointed if you can hold your nerve. Hold your tongue, regardless. No one can know of this, bar those who follow in your footsteps. You know there are consequences; you will have seen evidence of such. This is for your eyes only.

1912 discovered the heartstone quite by accident. I am certain Burnett Barton intended to keep the secret to himself, because he wants the power, doesn't he?

None of them had even hinted at this secret.

The Priest had been begging me for days to cut him open. Kill him.

"It'll only take a minute. Cut my throat, cut my gut and join the two. I'll barely bleed. You know that. It won't be disgusting."

He scratched his arm with a small, sharp piece of metal he'd found. Once upon a time, they'd do all they could to inflict damage on us. Now they want to hurt themselves.

I tired of it. He finally yanked my nerves so hard I snapped. I didn't cut him, but. I wasn't going to give that priest what he wanted, but this shut him up. He watched as if he was at the movies.

I cut the fella next to him, no loss at all. No loss. He was the one who murdered every black fella he could find, strung them up along the main street as if it was meant to be.

Inside him, it was not what you'd expect. There was little blood, and nothing pulsed at me.

And he was still alive, even with his guts out.

What I saw was this grey lump and I thought, that can't be good, so I plucked it out and sewed him back up.

The bastard lived.

In their chests, lies this heartstone. It grows and grows over the years. Take it out, it'll grow back. Take it out, you'll be lucky for the rest of your life. Even if you don't deserve it, you'll be lucky. You'll have it all. They'll be weaker for a while, but that stone will grow back. It won't kill them. This secret you must keep. And share it grudgingly. Part of the secret is selfishness.

If there are any witnesses to the reading of this, or to the process itself, they will die within five days. That is certain. If you ever tell anyone what you have read, the wrath of the Time Ball Tower keepers will come down on you. And we are a powerful lot. You know that. The heartstone is for us and for us alone.

The secret was almost lost when a long-lived, turtle-transforming man died in Little Cormoran. But the person who stole his heartstone knew what to do with it.

You've taken them naked to the water. You know how they feel. The touch of them.

Tap their chest to see who's got the biggest one. And take it. Place it in a jar and let it sit. It'll go to liquid. That's what you want. A single spoonful is all you need. Any more and you'll become like them.

I felt stiff. I hadn't moved in half an hour. Cut them open? Seriously? And find...what sounded disgusting.

Things fell into place, though. Comments made and withdrawn. That foul jar in Burnett's bedside table, that I always thought had lung oysters in it and therefore wiped from my memory.

Keepers had noted whose heartstone they took. They left messages.

Some years, no heartstone was taken.

I realized that this was why the man I called weakest man was so weak. He'd lost his heartstone often.

My father hadn't taken it.

Had he been too blind drunk, all the time?

Pathetic. It didn't make him a better man, did it?

As for my mother, she had a lot of classical literature on the shelves. I read them all. Amrita is the nectar of immortality in Swarga. Made by the churning of the milk sea. She made us drink milk a lot. Does that mean anything?

But she had four of us. No wonder she seemed scared of us sometimes. No wonder we had such a childhood. She thought we were ghosts from the Time Ball Tower. She hated most men. She thought they were base. She had passed this on to me. "So long as you know that, it's okay. Don't have any expectations beyond that."

I didn't want to think about my father that way, but the attitude explained a lot.

My mother was irreparably damaged by being in here. Agoraphobic, barely leaving the house.

No world travel.

My mother was absent most of the time, going about the daily business with her conscious mind not there but elsewhere. I stopped telling her about school or boyfriends because there is nothing worse than pouring your heart out to someone and have her say, "What's that? I didn't hear you." Infuriating that they don't care or understand.

Now I understood that my mother never wanted to think or speak of the Time Ball Tower.

We could talk once I got back, maybe. I doubted it would be a good conversation, though. I'd have to forgive a lot and I wasn't ready for that.

My art teacher said he'd bathed them, but according to his summary he didn't. Not sure what that was about. Because he did have a lack in him, something that stopped him from great success, even though there were sparks of genius in his early work.

I felt dusty. Dirty. I washed my hair and brushed it dry down on the rocks, loving the sun. The wind.

When I returned, they were silent, quieter than I'd ever heard them. Watching me, not calling out.

It was lucky for them that they were quiet. I felt more irritable than I ever had. Ready to snap at the slightest thing.

They'd tried all along to stop me finding the heartstone notebook. To avoid their baths so I wouldn't read the instructions. I didn't blame them. This was horrendous. I could barely accept it, make sense of it.

This was the secret, though. I'd figured it out, which gave me a palpable sense of relief and pride. I knew the secret Nate, 2009, had hinted at; I was truly one of them. I wouldn't write the secret in the report. No one did. We wrote, "Prisoners bathed successfully," and we knew what it meant.

My head ached. I felt snarled. Blocked.

Exhausted from the physical effort of getting them all washed, and the rest of it too, I collapsed into a chair. I dreamed that the Time Ball Tower was covered with slowly creeping rocks, and I was trapped inside. I was slow. I couldn't run, and I realized I had been preserved.

I asked Burnett once if he still dreamed.

He sighed. "Not in color. And only of the driest things. Flowers pressed in a book. Autumn leaves. Nothing more."

The notes sat on my bedside table until the smell (dank, sweaty) had me put them back in the hiding place.

Then I went to the prisoners. They didn't know I knew.

I stood looking at them all.

"Look at you, all flushed and sexy," Grayson said. "Are you all right?" He almost seemed to care.

I stared at them.

"Stop it," they said.

"I thought you liked being watched."

But they knew what I was thinking.

I slept then, and dreamed of a little boy, paddling over. Lost.

It was time to wake the prisoners. Sleepy or not, happy or not. I woke them.

"No! I was having a good dream." They often said this to me. I had vivid dreams too, full of detail and easily remembered.

"I was dreaming about a little boy in a boat," I said.

Grayson said, "I was dreaming I was a child, and I paddled and paddled and paddled until I reached an island. It was deserted."

I didn't believe he'd dreamed anything of the sort.

"He reminded me of myself, when I was a boy, before all hell broke loose," one of the prisoners said and I nodded. My mother had written about him: *he kept a daughter in his cellar for thirty years. Never taught her how to speak or read. All she knew about was oral sex and silent fucking. He brought men back for her and then he'd kill them. He was unrepentant. And there were the grandchildren, too.*

"Thank you. For listening. All we have is our voices. That's all that's left. All we have is storytelling."

"You're pretty bloody slow at it. Shocking bad," I said, although I was used to the speech by now. I thought of what he'd done, this man. How many lives he'd destroyed.

"We've had a lot of visitors. Some ladies, wasn't there? Come out to service us all."

I had to laugh at that. I said, "One of them drowned going home. The other tried to get you lot released before she forgot about you and pissed off. Everyone blames her for the school fire."

"You know who made that school burn down? Your Burnett. He's the one ordered it done. Send a message, he reckoned. Make sure no other bitch comes out. The man whose father did the burning told us. Not the only fire he ever caused, was it? Keep listening. You'll get to the truth eventually. He can't help himself."

They were agitated, moving about, so I turned them all face down for a bit.

All old people must have this forming in them. Those ancient husks, wasted and drugged, lined up like sardines in front of flickering TVs. All of them with this precious stone inside.

Burnett must have one.

I thought of those rare keepers who were not huge successes. Did they refuse to take a heartstone? The boatman, with his egg-producing chickens. His monotonous trips to the Time Ball Tower. His failure to thrive. I re-read their reports, and all of them, all the failures, did not bathe the prisoners. They didn't get the message. Missed the cue or allowed themselves to be manipulated. Distracted.

I didn't want failure. I wanted a future. Many successful people had a keeper in their background. Somewhere amongst the ancestors.

I walked along the gallery examining the portraits of the keepers. Who did it and who didn't?

Here were the successes, the hugely talented, the famous.

Here I wanted to be.

I was wiser, now.

I knew much more than I ever thought I would.

I could help my mother, if I did this. Help my father. Help them recover. If that's what I chose to do.

I don't want to die anonymous. Like the unnamed corpses used for medical research in Victorian England. Having achieved nothing. Nothing memorable about me, nothing to remember. I had family, so I probably wouldn't be buried in an anonymous grave. But I wanted people to care. I wanted a funeral full of grieving mourners.

I was skilled, but not that talented. As my father said, I was no genius.

I would never be the world's greatest photographer; I had neither the vision nor the originality for that. The same went for all of them. I'd heard some of Peter Mosse's pieces before he went into the Time Ball Tower. Before he took the heartstone, I guess. Sure, he was young, unpractised, but beforehand there was a lack of soul there. Nothing special. After? After he wrote some of the greatest music I knew. His "Time and Tide and Stone and Rust" went,

As we approached,
I could see that the walls were caked with sea creatures,
sea plants,
the splattered bodies of a million insects, the shit of ten thousand birds.
It was craggy. Untended.
Bleeding rust around the bolts.

Beautiful. I had the whole sequence downloaded and I listened to it often. It was relaxing, calming, and while it was more my parents' speed than mine I could see it was a work of genius. It's been said he was even more distant on his return, that he never connected with people, not really, losing himself entirely in his music. He was shit before, they'd say, and he came back a genius. No one argues with that.

Was my art worth it?
My head hurt, and aspirin barely made a dent.
I had been chosen for reasons other than I thought. I'd been chosen because they thought I was cruel enough, ambitious enough, and capable of taking the heartstone. I must have suspected this and perhaps been warned. But I realized that it was true.

I was no better than any of them.

I looked at my wish list, the photographers who were famous, who traveled the world for their art.

And there were the other lists, the sad, long lists. Of graduating photographers, all of them wanting fame and fortune, most of them hopeless.

I wanted to rise above them.

The prisoners said, "It's a trap, a test, a trick." Too many options, I realized. They were lying. Manipulating. "This will kill you. It will destroy you. You'll never have children." I also realized that all Burnett's talk of methods of preservation were a smoke screen. That when he clutched at his heart, when he spoke of a stone, he was talking about his very own heartstone, and he didn't want me to know it.

The Ball dropped.

The Ball dropped.

They hoped I'd forgotten, or didn't believe it. But every night I dreamed
of the photographs I could take if I had intensified vision. Because it
wasn't that the keepers got lucky, not that alone, at least. It was that they
grew skills and insights ordinary people didn't have.

I wanted that. But I had a sick twist in my gut about it. I knew it would
hurt one of them. And it seemed to me that if I took it, I was making a
decision about the sort of person I was. The sort of person who would
take something, take the heart of a person, for their own gain.

Still.

These were no longer people. Not really.

And I wanted that success. I'd always wanted it.

In the end, the decision wasn't so difficult.

But who? They wouldn't be unaffected by it; it was as bad as they could
feel in their position.

I walked past them pretending not to be deciding who but; "Which
one did I call you again?"

"Hitler. I'm Hitler."

"Are you?" I was bored with the game.

"I am Hitler. Please let me be."

I joked with them, and they didn't know I was assessing them.

"You can be Hercules. He killed his children, did you know that? Of
course they blamed it on Hera. She bewitched him. They always blame the
woman."

"That's because it's always the woman's fault," one of them called out, and they all found that hilarious, as much as they were capable.

"Did I ever tell you about the time I went for a job interview at a Canteen? Serving five hundred miners three meals a day, plus morning and afternoon tea."

I always waited for the question. Sometimes they wanted food porn. Sometimes something violent, blood and guts and fists. Sometimes it was pure sex.

"What did you cook?"

Food. As I assessed them, I talked food. "I cooked thirty roast chickens in one day. The men said they could smell it from deep underground, the skin roasting, the juices forming, the gravy. The onions. The potatoes, crispy on the outside, creamy on the inside." I walked the aisle, looking them up and down.

"She's getting ready to leave," one said.

"Leaving us."

"Don't go. We like you."

"We love you."

"No one will ever love you like we do."

Sadly, this was probably true. I sat at the very center of their universe, providing all.

Even a child has more than its mother. Even a tiny baby has other stimulants.

I'm joking with them, I'm telling them porn, I'm tapping on their chests as if I'm flirting.

They tried to pull away from me and I felt great sense of power; I was so much stronger than them.

"Not me," they said one by one. "Choose him."

"Don't choose me," Grayson said. "Don't choose me and I'll tell you secrets. I can tell you things you should know. I'll tell you about the secret prisoner, if you allow me to sit in your room and watch you sleep. I will tell you all."

I didn't trust him. Crazy stuff he wanted, and he'd ask for more, no doubt at all. Push push push until I'd want to cut his throat.

"You tell me, show me, whatever, and then we'll talk. I'm not taking you into my room for a dud deal."

He was stubborn, though.

"It doesn't hurt, taking the stone out. It does nothing to you. They told me."

"They also say cancer doesn't hurt. Have you heard that?"

In the end, I chose the man who'd arrived when my grandmother was there in 1938. It seemed apt. His chest had a satisfyingly hollow sound, with something solid at the center, and he had not been operated on for ten years.

"Not me. You don't want to do that."

"This is for your own good."

"No, it's not. None of this is."

"It's all for you. All of it is for you."

I put some tallow candle in his mouth. His dry lips caught my finger and the contact seemed soft and gentle.

I pulled his bedding backward, so he lay down flat. He tried to lift himself, remembering a time when he could do so, when he'd done fifty pull ups without a problem. Up and down between prison bunks.

"Don't do it," they called out. "You don't have to. Not all of them do. Even the ones who say they do."

"I know the ones who didn't. They're the losers. I'm not a loser."

I sat cross-legged beside him and exposed his chest. Tapped to find the place.

His chest rose and fell gently; it wasn't capable of anything more violent.

"Does anyone want to volunteer to take his place?" I asked, and they were silent, suddenly interested in the ceiling, the floor, anything but the reality of what was happening.

I lifted the knife. I'd spent ten minutes sharpening it, and had nicked myself with it easily, so I knew it would do the job.

I tapped.

Using my left forearm across his collarbone to anchor him, I sliced into his chest.

It parted easily, revealing pale pink flesh, spongy material. Very little blood. The stone was right there near the surface and I lifted it out. I wished I'd worn gloves because it was disgusting. Grey and lumpy. A soft, sticky surface, tacky to the touch.

I dropped it onto my lap and pressed his flesh together. Using the needle and thread I'd gathered earlier, I clumsily stitched him together.

He panted. "Leave me open. At least I might die that way."

I laughed. Chucked his chin. "Oh, no. You've got so much to live for," I said. Dissection was once illegal and considered a terrible punishment.

Is that what I was doing? Dissecting him?

I carried the heartstone in my lifted shirt, not wanting to touch it again.

Now I understood the furtive looks of the keepers. Not the boatman or teacher, the ones who didn't take the stone. They'll look you in the eye.

Because the taking of the stone was horrendous, violent, foul, vicious, wrong.

And yet I wanted what Peter Mosse had. What they all had.

The hard and evil heartstone.

It looked like tightly wrapped worms. Heads tucked into arses.

I settled the heartstone into a jar as I'd been told, and watched as slowly, slowly, it began to liquesce. The worms uncoiled. Pieces shifted off. Like a poo left in the toilet bowl.

The Ball dropped.

The Ball dropped.

The Ball dropped.

I added my notes to the secret notebook; whose stone I'd taken and what he looked like on the inside, and how he'd recovered.

Strange thoughts came to me. Solitary thoughts, the idea that everyone else had died and I was the last person alive. It was the isolation. And I heard the prisoners whispering while I slept, entering my dreams.

"Grind us up for sawdust," one begged me. "No one will know. Please."

"Leave us on the rocks. Expose us. That way you're not doing anything active, are you? Don't go, leaving us here."

1938 hadn't spoken since I took his heartstone. Some movement had returned, but his eyes were duller than they had been. Once, I thought, they'd lit up a little when I entered the room. I thought he'd enjoyed my company, thought about what could have been with me.

"You'll be able to go away and forget us. You'll look back every now and then and wonder about us, but we'll fade away."

"One of these days, a boatman will arrive to release you," I said. "When your sentences are done."

This wasn't true. There was no hope of release. But I enjoyed the deception.

The Ball dropped.

Children waited on the beach to be the first to say hello. I looked out with binoculars at them.

I waved, knowing they couldn't see me, but remembering what it was like to be on the shore, hoping the keeper could see you.

Nikki Curran, 1995, talked about looking out to shore. I felt a chill or a thrill reading that. It had probably been me, out on the shore. I spent most of my spare time there. It was supposed to be good luck if you were the first one to say hello to a keeper when they returned, and we'd hung around, waiting for the chance.

I saw three boys and two girls on the shore. One boy, blond, wearing a striped shirt and long shorts. Two boys, brown hair. One in jeans and a T-shirt, throwing stones. The other in shorts only, running in and out of the water. The sun glimmered on the water, so bright.

They waved at me. The two girls swam out as if trying to reach me. I shouted out the window at them, but there's no way sound carries that far.

Looking at them steeled me. They were fearless, like most children were, like I was once.

If you read this, kid, if one of you is the keeper, I was watching. I saw you wave.

I took a spoonful of the stuff. They'd told me that; a single spoonful, no more. One spoonful and the world was your oyster. Drink the glass and you're eternal. One of them.

Nobody wanted that.

The smell of it was foul. Bitter, rotten, sulfurous; a combination of all the worst things I could imagine. The taste was worse. I still considered the possibility of being preserved. Of accepting the disability that came with eternal life in order to see the future, where it all would go. Even after all I'd seen.

You'd be like a time traveler. Imagine the time-lapse photography. Fuck that "one year in the life," or even ten years. I could do a photo a day for a hundred years. Once I grew too frail, I'd get others to do it for me. I'd be rich by then—that's what happens if you invest wisely and live long, Burnett told me. Slow and steady.

I was starving. I ate a packet of plain, salty crackers out of the packet. I didn't even think about adding chili.

My chest hurt.

Heartburn.

But my headache was gone.

I changed my mind about my parents. They were not cruel and evil for sending me here. No one could have more self-understanding than a keeper. Having experienced this I understood it was a gift. Parents send us out here because every now and then there is a golden child. A great success. There are failures; but there are the golden ones. I'd be one of those.

That night, I carried Grayson to my room. "I didn't choose you. Talk."

He shook his head. "In the morning."

All night he whispered, porn, detail after detail.

I didn't mind it. If I blocked my nose. Kept my eyes shut. It actually wasn't bad. Some of it was my own stories told back to me. A lot of that came from dreams about my boyfriend. Far better than the real thing. Just thinking of his neediness, his desire for flattery, to be told how young he looked…ugh.

They were so easy to tame.

In the morning, I forgot Grayson was there. Had breakfast. Then remembered and went back to him. "Well?"

He raised his arm and held it over his head. Tapped the wall.

"In there," he said. "In the basement. Bring a knife."

"I'm not going to kill you, no matter what happens," I said.

For all I'd seen, all I knew, I still didn't believe it was possible. I didn't want it to be.

I made sure they were secure.

I picked up Grayson. He felt like a bag of sticks, hot from the fire, and he pressed into me with what little strength he had. I didn't want to take him, but even less did I want to wander around in the basement, searching alone.

"Down the steps," he said, bossing me. "Push the door open gently. You don't want a draught."

He directed me to the far left corner. The ground was progressively squelchy, and the noise of animals and insects increased. The chittering. The air was chill and full of dank. I was terrified. It's the worst person who ever lived, I thought. That's who I'm about to see.

He showed me the wall. I held up the torch to illuminate the outline of a small door, edges filled with gunk. I ran the knife along the edges then pried the door open. The chittering noise increased, and I was suddenly terrified. Absolutely terrified beyond belief.

It was a woman.

She looked worse than any of the prisoners upstairs. By torchlight she was so gray I could barely see her. She was almost bald. Her eyes were red. Wide. Her skin…the skin on her hands creeping, stretched.

Her mouth opened, and the most awful noise came out.

I screamed.

Slammed the door shut.

He was lucky I picked him up. I should have left him.

"Who is it?"

"We don't know. A lady."

I went back to my sunny spot. I had food but wasn't hungry. The sight of her broke me. I touched the flags.

No. No.

The Ball dropped.

I slept, and when I awoke imagined it had been a dream.

S ometimes I stood at the trapdoor, wondering who it was. Too scared to find out. The fury on her face.

T he Ball dropped.

I went downstairs, wanting a swim, a gentle, hold-on-for-your-life swim close to the edge. It refreshed me. Did I feel different?

I felt braver.

Brave enough to open the trapdoor.

Walk to the hidden door.

I lifted the trapdoor, folding it right back. I didn't bother weighting it down. They were far too weak to lock me in. They couldn't, even all of them together, lift the thing.

Salty water smell. My ears were attuned. I could hear the chittering, chitter, chitter, that Burnett hated so much.

I edged around the crack with my knife. Already, it was gummed with dust and sludge. So quick.

The chittering increased.

I pushed open the door. My knees felt wobbly, barely able to support me and for some reason I flashed to Mrs. Tingle, who worked at the library but was so fat she couldn't stand up. She'd say, "It's my knees, they can't support the weight," and I realized I was distracting myself from what I was doing, turning my mind away from it.

I had to know. I'd never felt such curiosity, such a need to know.

Things came to me. A teacher saying, "Where is your curiosity, your need to know?" and me saying, not in Ancient Greece. Whole class laughing. Renata most of all. She laughed so much, mascara smudged on her cheeks. In front of me…I could remember every single classmate. If I wanted to, I could go upstairs and list them.

But that was me, avoiding this.

Chitter

Chitter

The Ball dropped. I could actually feel the vibration of it rocketing up my legs.

Solid.

I pushed open the door.

This thing was tiny. Decrepit. Last remnants of hair white and wispy, eyes yellowed, skin mottled, loose, like a suede blanket.

The chittering stopped. Lips parted slowly.

Around its neck, a cameo.

A cameo.

Of a top-hatted man, bending forward to light a pipe.

I knew it. I'd seen Burnett's drawing of it.

Oh fuck.

Oh Jesus.

That thing.

Is Harriet.

To my eternal shame I ran back upstairs.

Shit, I did not want to go back down there. I felt a sense of doom, of disaster, but that was gutless. Too often I listen to that and then nothing happens. This was my moment. Beyond taking the heartstone. This was on me. Mine.

"Harriet?" I said. "Harriet Barton?"

The chin dropped to the chest.

She couldn't move beyond that. I stepped closer to her. Her head lifted, and she said, "I am." She spoke even more slowly than the prisoners upstairs, but I barely noticed.

God. She was one hundred and eighty years old.

She was barefoot, just as my grandmother had fantasized, but there was no freedom and never had been.

"Can I take you out?"

The chin lifted.

I felt such tenderness. It overcame revulsion. This was my ancestor; without her, I wouldn't be here.

I carried her to the doorway. It was going to hurt, being in the light.

She felt so brittle. She squeezed my arm, like the bite of a spider.

"Burnett?" she said. Three times, then four.

"He's still alive!" I said. "You might be able to see him, somehow. If I can get you to shore."

I felt pressure on my shoulder. She was squeezing, so weakly it barely registered.

I said, "He's not here. Keepers only stay one year. He's been gone a long time."

"Not a keeper. A prisoner," she said.

"Why?" That was only my first question.

"Does the cypress still grow?" she asked.

The cypress she planted in Tempuston.

"Yes," I said. "It's a beautiful thing and we all know where it came from. Everyone one loves it."

I thought of Sunday mornings after the night before, where the base was always littered with empty alcohol containers, cigarette butts, used condoms, vomit. The bark marred with knife marks. The branches festooned with stained clothing.

"I'm Phillipa," I said.

"You are my child?"

She seemed confused. She knew that time had passed, and yet I was called Phillipa.

"I was named for your daughter. My grandmother was keen on the idea and my mother and father went along with it."

My parents hadn't found her. No one had found her. *Why me?*

I thought back to some of the things Burnett said. The chittering, and comments about Harriet. He was giving clues to me. Because I listened?

Harriet began to disintegrate in the light. She wouldn't survive long. Her skin was peeling off and she'd be nothing but a living skeleton before long.

She cried. Thick, hard blobs, opaque, like old glass.

"L et me speak, then help me die."

"Do you really want to die?"

"Now I do. If I'd been free all this time? Not destroyed? I'd happily live forever."

Her tongue lolled.

"Then you will kill me."

She asked me about Burnett and what I knew of him. I told her all; his report, mostly.

"Let me tell you the truth," she said. And she did. It took days. Weeks? With her resting between times. I gave her lime juice with sugar and she seemed almost blissful.

I wrote it all down. I titled the report "Being the True and Actual Story of Burnett Barton (née Smith) collated by Harriet Barton (née Turner), with the knowledge and assistance of Edna Noyes and Grace Barton (née Charney). Also, some information from Burnett Barton which must be taken with a grain of salt."

There was something about Burnett the girls didn't trust, and they'd trust anyone, near enough. They trusted the sailors who came through, the travelers, the adventurers. But they didn't want to go near Burnett, even though he was handsome and charming. He came after me with great dedication, like a dog, and me only twelve.

So, he called upon a girl who might; she was sixteen, but with the mind of a ten-year-old. She was a willing partner, in his eyes. Didn't she show him her project, the one the teacher asked them to do? A drawing of the sun rise. "It's lovely," he said.

She had bled; in our town this information was shared.

He was clumsy, glad he was practicing on her before a real girl. She'd remember nothing, say nothing. She babbled, singing foolish songs, and she felt loose about him, making him wonder very hard about the other men in the village.

Regardless, the sensation was a delight,

until it was over.

Burnett now understood what his friends were talking about. The sensation was strong.

She clung to him, wanting him to "tickle me some more," but her face now seemed sharp and ugly and he couldn't bear her neediness. He tells the story as a tragedy, that she choked on a knot of wool. She was knitting him a cardigan a matching one for the baby she had growing.

That was her level of naïvety. That she thought a baby would be welcomed.

I say he strangled her. He was strong once.

Then Grace came to the village.

Grace was the most beautiful girl for many miles, with a sweet nature and a joy about her that made people want to be near her. Her parents had been looking at husbands for her since she was five, knowing the decision would be difficult, so many to choose from, so many presenting themselves in the best possible light. She was too much of an innocent to manage well herself.

Burnett considered himself a contender, but she never did. He was a malicious man when she admired kindness, a small man when she admired great size. Her favorite of all was the man they called Samson for his size and strength. His name was Milton Carlisle.

Her parents weren't sure he had the dedication, so she set him the task of moving the rolling rocks of Little Cormoran.

He trained for months, practised rolling rocks off the cliff, uphill, over bumpy ground. It was entertaining, particularly for the young women. More than one said to him, "I'll have you if she won't," yet all he did was smile shyly and continue.

The day came to roll the rocks. Burnett, of course, whined and wailed, threatening the destruction of the village and all around it, the wrath of God, the death of them all.

Samson rolled the rocks. Perhaps there was a creaking noise, and a ground shaking.

Grace watched, always smiling.

He asked for her hand in marriage and all would have been happily ever after it if were not for the dark, vicious heart of Burnett Smith.

Burnett could not, would not, give it up. He didn't care how he had her; have her he would.

Before her family understood what was happening, he'd arranged for her to be preserved. He had what he considers a wedding, at the bedside, and they experienced their wedding night.

What he calls the wedding night.

Others would disagree strongly.

He did the speaking for her, announcing formally "a marriage by way of consummation."

They say it took three men to hold Milton Carlisle, the strong man, her real love, back. Why didn't they let him go, have him beat Burnett to death? Imagine that. All that we know would not have come into being.

There would be no Tempuston, no Time Ball Tower, no prisoners, although I cannot deny my role in any of that, may God forgive me.

They held Milton Carlisle down because they did not want to see him hanged over such a weak, pathetic man.

And Milton was the victor; Grace agreed to marry him. Really, she had loved him at first sight, but that is how some girls are, isn't it? They like to play the game. If he would take her as she was, then he was a good man. There was nobody who considered her marriage to Burnett valid.

Burnett tried to hound Milton Carlisle out of town.

"He rolled the rocks, he brought a curse."

Three young girls had lost babies in the womb and this was the curse. Burnett? Did he invite those ladies for tea? Did he brew it himself? Yes. He did all that. It was no use, though. We knew. We every last one of us knew who and what Burnett was.

Although I was not so sure until the years passed, and I understood.

Burnett burned them all.

He ensured Grace was safe at home. That Milton and his supporters were in the church.

And he burned them down.

We smelled smoke, my brother Eugene and I. Home sick. Allowed to stay home from church.

We heard screams, muffled by the walls and by the roar of the fire. We thought little of it.

We were too young to understand.

They were burned to death. All that was left were the bones of the immortal, shaking and clinking as the last of life left them over a torturous number of hours. The carcasses still breathing.

Burnett had told me he confessed much to me. But this was far beyond anything I imagined.

Burnett always said it was an act of God.

We went to Edna. Burnett thought she admired him, but she deeply despised him.

He agitated for departure, but Edna needed to talk to us, "the ladies," she said, but really she meant for Grace and me to stand guard outside the door for prying ears.

Finally, Burnett tired of it (and she was an unpleasant woman; true) and he insisted we leave her. He set her up in an inn, told us to go ahead while he dealt with the bill.

Again.

Who can say?

Still, we had her jar.

Onboard the ship, Grace was presented as his crippled wife, no matter what he says now. He presented that she adored him; that she loved every moment with him. But she most certainly did not. Every minute with him was hell to her, and each night, she would cast her eyes at me, begging me to help.

What could I do? I was a child. They were ostensibly married. What occurred between them was private and none of my business.

I regret every night I let him have her.

She said to me, "Thank the Lord I am beyond being able to have a family. I cannot bear the thought of him as father." The sea air revived her somewhat, as it did for all of us.

I nodded. I was an innocent girl, born to Christ and not much more, and I understood little of what was happening. And yet, she told me that it meant she felt a failure as a woman. That she would be unaccomplished in every way.

She did not talk to anyone else of this. It was her own dark secret. Her loss, her failure, her regret.

I was distracted, meanwhile, by the glorious Louisa. Burnett was deeply in adoration of William Barton, a man some might say was impressive to other men like him. And then our long journey.

I am so very grateful for the limits to which he kept this deception.

Much as I admired Phillip, I did not think him particularly intelligent. He was perhaps too honest for that. I, at least, had learned from Burnett the importance of limited information. That you can control what people know of you, if you are cautious.

Phillip was so obvious in his intentions to take over the family. To protect us from Burnett. Burnett grew very quiet, never a good sign. He allowed Phillip to make decisions along the way, which Phillip took as victory, but which I knew to be manipulation. A test as to how far he would go.

On this journey, Burnett decided I should act like his wife. That Grace was now the elderly aunt, almost dead.

He wanted to keep things as they were. He

wanted nothing to change. He didn't understand that no matter how long he kept me, I would never be his.

I would only tell the truth.

One morning, when we were not far from what would become Tempuston, I awoke to a clamor. It appeared that Phillip had left us, taking some of our precious belongings.

I didn't believe this for a second.

Burnett had killed him.

Burnett could not manage him, and knew that Phillip would be ever stronger.

So he destroyed him.

I don't know how. I will not ask.

But I said to Burnett: you do that to me? You destroy me? I will haunt you forever. And I will haunt the streets and the schools and the scholars and the fools and tell them *my* story.

I will tell them the truth, tell it from the grave.

I hate to think of him abandoned in the desert. Eaten by ants or others.

When I'm safe, when we are somewhere close to people who might listen, I will take Eugene and we will run.

She never did, did she? No matter what people thought.

Grace and I decided together to preserve Burnett. Hoping for his very great suffering. Burnett thanked us for giving him the treatment.

"After it's done, you won't be so grateful. You'll see. Even hell would be a relief to you."

He drank the heartstone juice from Grace.

After the treatment, he felt invincible. Untouchable. As if he could commit any crime or sin and there would be no repercussions.

I did do this; I held Grace under water for hours and hours and hours until she finally died.

I could do that for her, at least.

Edna always said to cut nice.

I could do that, also.

I watched for thirty minutes, but the tension of watching as the bubbles of air periodically rose was too much. I went inside, glancing out every now and then.

An hour later, the bubbles seemed to slow.

The air is fetid and as one last large bubble broke, the stench was so intense I felt it sinking into my skin.

Burnett pretended to be happy, but of course he wasn't. He wanted her forever, just like he wants me forever.

He doesn't like anyone to leave him.

He was the first prisoner in the tower; I was the first keeper. But still his power held.

Still he managed to change things.

They are coming now, I think. He is angry. He wants to silence me. Wants me to suffer this fate worse than death.

He wants to own me forever.

Tristram is an evil man, almost as evil as Burnett. I failed, didn't I? Failed to protect others from him. I will pay for that.

My very own son.

He says mine is the sacrifice that needs to be made.

That I am the one.

Oh Lord, help me. It is disgusting.

I will write while I can write.

And now I am here. Like them. May God have mercy on his vengeful soul.

I wanted to hold her, but she was too brittle. Instead, I told her stories, building her legacy into something greater than it was.

She'd never know otherwise.

She said, "Do you understand who Burnett is, now? He loves you. He will keep you."

He would if he could. She was right. I doubted he had the power, though.

Harriet said, "He wanted me forever in his power. He wanted me to be quiet. He couldn't kill me. He'd lost courage. And he did love me in his own way. He wanted someone else to remember Little Cormoran. If there are two left it stays real. And I had told him I would haunt him and many others with the truth. That terrified him."

I left her resting on my bed, weak sunlight on her face.

"Upset. Our lady is upset." The prisoners had missed me, even the one whose heartstone I'd stolen.

"What's happened? Know something see something hear something?"

"Found something." The loneliness of my position struck me more at this time than any other. I wanted to talk but to who? And even on land there was little for me, no one really who would understand.

Burnett was lost to me; I could never talk to him again, not now I knew the truth of what he'd done. He had committed enough crimes to deserve his punishment.

These prisoners were all I had. No others.

"Found what where?"

"Who," I said. "I found someone in the basement. One of you but not evil."

"We're not evil. Not anymore."

I'd hurt their feelings, saying that.

"She's been there a long time."

"The cleaner," Grayson said. "He's the one. He looks after her, doesn't he? That's what he means when he says, "I'm not here for you." Every time, as if we care. Who is she?"

And they all listed someone from their own era.

Queen Victoria. Belle Guiness. Lizzie Borden.

Queen Victoria almost made them expire with laughter.

"No one famous. My ancestor, Harriet. We thought she'd disappeared and she was here all along. You never told me. And you never told me that Burnett was a prisoner."

"You never asked," Grayson said, and they all thought that was very funny.

I wanted to know all she knew. More than she'd told me. I thought she could be a talisman, an aide, a good luck charm, a guide, that she would change my life.

"Kill me. Kill me."

What I felt was compassion. I'd felt nothing like it before. Even my stray animals I'd rescued more out of a sense of responsibility than anything else. And yet Harriet; I actually felt it almost physically, a tiny hand clutching my heart.

They'd chosen me for my lack of compassion. Because they were sure I'd feel nothing for the prisoners and not be tempted to help them.

Well, fuck that. Don't you judge me. Don't you decide I'm a particular kind of person then pigeonhole me there.

I carried her outside. We stopped at the door and she looked down. She said, "Sit? Can we sit? I used to sit the sun, before I got too sick. When they let me out for hours at a time."

I asked her. I said, "How do you want me to do it? Drowning? If I cut you, I have to do it a thousand times. If you starve, it's years. You could die of thirst in three months."

"Drowning. Hold me under."

Her skin sizzled in the sun. She felt like a bag of twigs.

"Live well," she said. "Pray to God and live well."

"I will," I told her. I told her all the things I would do. The charity work. The lives I would save.

She said, "Good girl. Be strong. Love. Learn to feel."

I did feel; it hurt. Physically, my legs were cut and bruised from the rocks. My eyes stung from the salt water.

And I didn't want her to die. I wanted secrets and truth, I wanted knowledge, wisdom and love.

"He will do this to you, too, if he can. He will not want to lose you."

Her throat constricted.

"Let them go," she said. "Let them all go."

Her last words.

It took a very long time. There is no easy way for it.

I felt changed by it, though.

I felt as if I could create the most amazing things, as if I were a true artist now, because I felt compassion.

I did.

After I'd done Harriet, I realized I couldn't leave them all. I felt pity, and I could see the gratitude in Harriet, the great relief. Blessed relief like that offered by Saint Peter. I knew what Renata would do. What she'd want me to do. She'd release every one of them and sleep well at night.

I cut out her Harriet's heartstone. No point wasting it. It was different than the other one. Harder. Less malleable.

I called out, *I'm ready for another night*, and that got them worked up. I bet Grayson had told them everything. What I looked like while I slept.

The masturbator went at it, as fast as he could. Not fast.

I picked up Grayson. His lips against my neck.

We went down, not up.

"No bath," he said.

"No. I'm going to let you go."

Poison wouldn't work on them. It'd be out of the body before it did any damage.

I carried him around to the dark side of the tower, where we'd be unseen by the town.

He clung to me. "Thank you. God bless you. Thank you."

"It's okay," I said. It didn't matter what he said to me. I settled him on the rocks, the dark shadow of the tower deep and chilling as I steadied myself.

"This is what you want still?"

"Yes." The word was so drawn out, it sounded like a slow wave.

"Bless you," he said. I tied a rock around his waist and set him afloat, face down.

I cut his heartstone out first.

"What's she doing? She hasn't brought him back up. What's she done?"

"I helped him," I said.

I helped all of them.

It's 2014, I told them all. November. Each one of them looked at me, so filled with horror at the year, at the passage of time.

I set markers in the rocks for all of them, like I did for the dead pets in my backyard.

At first, I kept the heartstones separate, but I ran out of jars and had to squeeze two or three together.

I set them all adrift.

They floated away like driftwood, the tide taking them like old friends

I was more powerful, more in control than at any other time in my life.

And then, the silence. The pure quietness of them gone. Of me alone. I heard the whirring of mechanisms, the gentle slap of water on the rocks, and the wind. But there were no voices. No grunts. No intake of breath of call for attention.

Weeks.
The Ball dropped.
The Ball dropped.
The Ball dropped.
The silence.

The creak of the front door barely registered.

Creak of door. I will see what the noise is. I could smell something; boat oil. And chicken feathers.

My sense of smell intensified by taking the heartstone of that man whose sense of smell was extreme. Were they all the same? Keepers taking on characteristics? I thought of Jerry Butler, 1990, and his fame as a masturbator. Checked the files.

He had taken The Greyhound's heartstone.

And Tyson Adler had taken the heartstone of the same prisoner as me.

Balldropped.

I thought I'd hidden what I'd done, that I could spend the rest of the year out there, quietly, quietly.

I did, for a ball drop, for ten ball drops.

I heard a noise downstairs. For a while, it didn't register. Then I thought; rocks against the wall. Clutter of driftwood.

Then I heard, "Pip? You there?"

It was Nolan.

My brother.

He shouldn't be here.

He wasn't a keeper.

"Of course I'm here," I called down. "Where else?"

He climbed the steps. He was wearing fishing gear, all over rubber. Gloves on. His hair in a knot at the top. He looked so weird, I laughed.

"What are you doing, Nolan?"

"I'm here to clean up your mess."

"I didn't make any! Jeez, did Mum send you? Well, I haven't cleaned the toilet for a few days. But seriously?"

"It's not just you, Phillipa. I always come in at the end."

"It's not the end, yet." I was hoping they didn't know. That I could see out the year, then go home.

"It is the end. You've finished it, haven't you? Done what no one else would do. Done the worst thing you could have done. You've unleashed shit you have no idea about."

But his eyes shifted as he said that, as if he was figuring out what shit I'd unleashed.

"Did you know about Harriet? Kept locked in the wall? You can't do that. That's not what we're about."

"Didn't Burnett ever tell you? I guess he doesn't care about you as much as you think he does. She's there as a sacrifice. For all of us. To keep vigil over the town and over the tower."

"She wasn't watching anything. She was locked in a wall."

"To keep vigil. To keep us safe. Now who'll do that?"

"Whoever the next keeper is, I guess. That's what we're supposed to do. I don't get what you're supposed to do, though."

"I'm just the next in line. We're the real thing. We watch over the keepers, make sure they're doing their job. I failed with you, though, didn't I? That will be on me. You've actually fucked me up. We clean up the messes. Most of you are too caught up in yourselves to even notice. We keep the sacrifice safe. We watched over her."

"That's not the idea."

"Of course it is. The prisoners are the reason we all exist, why this place does, why we haven't fallen into the pits of hell."

What?

How many of them came for me? Held me down? How many of my own people hated me so much?

They charged me with murder.

They charged me with the death of Harriet. The loss of our sacrifice. They dosed me up.

They left me. They wanted to wall me up, but I said, too soon. Let me dry out first or your clean-up will be awful. I've learned a lot from the prisoners about manipulation and I talked them into letting me be free for a bit.

Idiots.

The ball drops
And drops
And drops

I have lost track of how many times. At first I counted, but I lost track. There is no day and night but

The ball drops
The ball drops
The ball drops

They don't understand what I want.

I have been here a long time
I have been here forever.
I'm glad I killed the prisoners before this
If only
If only someone will come
And do the same for me

I feel my heartbeat shouting blood into my ear drums.
Fuck you
fuck you
fuck
you.

SUMMARY OF CONDITIONS: I found the prisoners.

Phillipa Muskett

Swimming. It's easier now. I need to take fewer breaths, can leave my face in the water for minutes at a time. I swam to shore one dark night, leaving from the blind side and going slow. Slow.

I made it to the old pier, and I rested there a long time. I was hungry, and glad of the vacuum-packed snacks I'd brought with me.

I rested.

The Ball dropped.

It took a long time to dry off. The sun was weak that day, muted. I craved heat, wanted to feel the burn.

There were no protestors. Their job was done, and I'd done it for them.

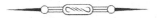

I found Renata at home. I had to wait for her mother to leave, because I didn't want to see anyone else. Her mother had put on weight and I could see why; she sat in front of her laptop reading gossip pages, the debris of crap around her. Fast food, sweet wrappers, soft drinks. I wondered if she was lost without her mission to save the prisoners, and she'd chosen this way to an early death.

Finally, she went out. I walked in the back gate; they always left it open. Renata sat on a sun chair, reading a fat book. She looked great. Alive.

"It's me! Don't freak!"

She looked at me, stunned. "They said you'd killed yourself."

"No. Just all of them." I jerked my thumb at the Time Ball Tower. "They preserved me. Bastards."

"You're amazing. You're incredible. I can't believe what you did."

"The rest of them hate me."

"Fuck those evil arseholes."

She was the one who got me out of there. She lent me a heap of money, knowing she'd get it back. My money was frozen for a year, but after that it could be distributed, and it would go to her. The protestors adored me, worshipped me, built a shrine to me for doing what they always wanted done. Renata gave me the funds they'd collected over the years. She didn't tell them why; she didn't give me up.

Over time, until she died, Renata sent me money. When she got sick, she deposited close to a million in an off-shore account for me. I didn't need it by then, but it was a nice gesture.

I wrote away for my birth certificate. I wanted it to be true. Real.

Would I take revenge on my brother? I would not. As Burnett says, there is no survival in revenge.

Burnett. Burnett. I didn't want to leave him to Renata to sort out. He didn't deserve that. I lied to her; told her I'd do it myself. She dragged him out for me. We shoved him in the trunk of the car I bought and there he stayed. He came to all the funerals with me, although he didn't know it. We traveled the country, but he didn't know that, either.

We went to the funerals of family. Of the keepers, of friends. We went to Renata's, and to Max's. He kept his looks right to the end, even after a decade in jail, but he never married.

I hated attending; I just wanted the photos. The memento mori. The reminder of death. You Will Die.

I tell that to Burnett sometimes.

I've seen them all buried.

I've seen a war that brought mass funerals and I've photographed that.

I've seen the death of grass and the birth of the new grain. I've seen the loss of more species than will ever live again. I've felt the cold and the heat and watched towns collapse around me.

I did make a call to the federal police, about all those missing women. The teacher, the others, all of them blamed for going to the city and not returning, every last one of them murdered out there, perhaps.

That's what the prisoners told me.

Would they lie about that?

I've been to Tempuston, fallen and lost. Little remains. The tower is empty. People moved away after the scandal of the murders and so many of the keepers in jail for it. The mission was gone, but so it should be. I regret nothing.

If I shift aside the rubble (and who has the strength for that?) perhaps I'll find the armchair that Harriet's cruel son died in, or my father's favorite beer glass, or perhaps a whisky bottle with only sludge left, one last swallow he never took.

I can't eat spicy food. I barely eat at all. It is a release, a freedom.

And now I sit.

The Ball drops. I don't think they even hear it any more.

In 2022CE, I paid a boy to sail me out there and I set up a time-lapse camera, triggered by the drop. Such a beautiful thing. It captures the changing nature of life. Captures the end of things. The loss of place.

I've seen grand changes and nothing changing at all.

My jars are all yellow liquid now. Some globules remain but these too are dissolving.

If I offer you a taste, you should take it. But no more than a taste.

2150 CE

Renata's granddaughter buried; it feels the strangest at times like these. The death from old age of a person born seventy years after me.

2200 CE

Now I can feel it. The bone ache, the gentle stench of my skin, the hardening of everything from eyeball to sole. It won't be long now until I am incapacitated and then what? I have to make the decision before it gets too late.

Toothless. They were loose a long time. I don't wake up from this dream.

Y ou just have to be patient. Wait long enough and you will be the oldest
and the wisest.

Famous for being first at something is too hard. Famous for being last
is just a matter of survival.

Now I'm the one. Any story I tell is the truth; I am the keeper of facts.

My memories now. My way of telling the story. I am the keeper of history.

Gentle.

Gentle.

Do not go gentle.

But we all do, in the end.